Mu
No Votive
Confidence

PALM BEACH COUNTY
LIBRARY SYSTEM
3650 Summit Boulevard
West Palm Beach, FL 33406-4198

Murder's No Votive Confidence

Christin Brecher

KENSINGTON BOOKS
www.kensingtonbooks.com

This book is a work of fiction. Names, characters, places, and incidents either are products of the author's imagination or are used fictitiously. Any resemblance to actual persons, living or dead, events, or locales is entirely coincidental.

KENSINGTON BOOKS are published by

Kensington Publishing Corp.
119 West 40th Street
New York, NY 10018

Copyright © 2019 by Christin Brecher

All rights reserved. No part of this book may be reproduced in any form or by any means without the prior written consent of the Publisher, excepting brief quotes used in reviews.

If you purchased this book without a cover, you should be aware that this book is stolen property. It was reported as "unsold and destroyed" to the Publisher, and neither the Author nor the Publisher has received any payment for this "stripped book."

All Kensington titles, imprints, and distributed lines are available at special quantity discounts for bulk purchases for sales promotion, premiums, fund-raising, educational, or institutional use. Special book excerpts or customized printings can also be created to fit specific needs. For details, write or phone the office of the Kensington Sales Manager: Kensington Publishing Corp., 119 West 40th Street, New York, NY 10018. Attn. Sales Department. Phone: 1-800-221-2647.

Kensington and the K logo Reg. U.S. Pat. & TM Off.

ISBN-13: 978-1-4967-2140-2 (ebook)
ISBN-10: 1-4967-2140-3 (ebook)
Kensington Electronic Edition: July 2019

ISBN-13: 978-1-4967-2139-6
ISBN-10: 1-4967-2139-X
First Kensington Mass Market Edition: July 2019

10 9 8 7 6 5 4 3 2 1

Printed in the United States of America

Dedicated to *Serenity*

Chapter 1

Friday morning, I woke up before the first ferry's horn sounded its arrival to Nantucket Island, my hometown. I greeted the day by feeling around my bedsheets until I found my phone. Its bright light kicked in to tell me it was five thirty a.m., and to display a message I'd anticipated for weeks: "Memorial Day Weekend!" Following the announcement was a to-do list that I'd already committed to memory. The exciting days ahead signified the start of the retail high season, and the weekend of Jessica Sterling's wedding. As owner of the Wick & Flame, a small store in town where I make and sell candles, I'd been working on the wedding for two months, since my oldest friend, Emily Gardner, Nantucket's top event coordinator, introduced me to her client. I fixate on every angle when I undertake a project and Jessica Sterling's wedding was no exception.

"I want something historic. Something that captures the spirit of Nantucket, but isn't too cheesy," the bride-to-be had said to me on our first meeting. "I've picked the Melville Inn for the venue, and now I'm thinking about a candle theme."

I nodded professionally, as if this type of proposal came my way every day, but I felt I'd won the lottery. To put it in perspective, the candy store in town has hundreds of orders for chocolate-covered cranberries when the party season hits, but no one has ever had a candle-themed event. I was dying to lead the design, and I was honored to be part of Jessica's fairy-tale wedding. So big was this opportunity, that in my memory I gave my pitch in a flashy conference room with cushy chairs and a PowerPoint presentation. In reality, we were at The Bean, my favorite coffee shop in town.

That day, I proposed something traditional, yet original: a unique wedding scent, inspired by the couple's love, and the wedding's seaside venue. My thought was to infuse the scent into two featured items.

First, a unity candle.

"What's a unity candle?" Jessica had said. I explained that it's a candle that symbolizes a couples' love, which is lit during a wedding ceremony. She liked it.

Second, I proposed to infuse the scent into votive candles to give as party favors to all of the guests. To my delight, Jessica loved both ideas, and gave me the job. We ended our first meeting feeling giddy about the weekend. So giddy that we clinked coffee cups to toast our success. I will never forget the moment that Jessica raised her chai latte.

"You have my votive confidence," she said.

We laughed at the pun, but I took her words seriously.

Following our meeting, I mapped out designs to ensconce the wedding in candlelight, from the simple Siasconset Chapel down the road whose perfect motto is "a lantern held by a friendly hand," to the party tent that would be erected on a picturesque field across from the Melville for the evening reception, to the guest rooms and facilities throughout the inn. Only the ivory-colored votives and unity candle would carry the personalized scent, while the other candles would be dyed pastel shades to match the wedding's color scheme of purple, blue, and pink. Heaven. Really. I'd recommend the idea to anyone, and not just because I'd like the business.

Now, I stretched my arms above my head and wiggled my toes, enjoying the memory of my biggest sales pitch, but moving on to the tasks at hand. In fact, now that Friday had come, I noticed that the morning air held a hint more of the sea than the scent Jessica had signed off on from the five samples I had created for her. I hated to admit it, but one scent in particular struck me as a better match to the weekend weather than the one she had chosen. It had a touch more sea salt and a dash more of white tea. It was late in the game for making changes, but I knew my customer. Only two days ago, Jessica had rescheduled the start of her rehearsal dinner so that she could hire a flock of doves to fly dramatically into the sunset. She was going for perfection. So was I.

I calculated how late I'd be up if I remade over two hundred gift candles and a unity candle, then I tossed off my blanket and sprinted across my squeaky floorboards to the kitchen of my one-bedroom apartment where I grabbed an iced coffee from my fridge. As I closed the door, a sign reading *Leftovers*, made out of macaroni, slid from its magnet. People like to name their houses on Nantucket. It's a thing. You'll see quarter boards, inspired by sailing ships of yore, hanging on one house after another with names like "Serenity" and

"Why Worry." My pasta quarter board was lovingly made by my cousin Chris's young son. Chris is a contractor, and the historic house outside of town that he and his wife bought and lovingly restored came with an old carriage house out back, which they turned into a garage with my apartment on top. It's a one-bedroom with a living room and small kitchen, and other than painting it a soft blue throughout, it's mostly decorated with the items it held the first day I dropped my bags there, seven years ago, after I graduated from college. Hence, the name of my home (and often, the contents of my fridge).

After throwing on my jeans and a thick sweater, I jumped into my red VW Beetle, still zipping up my boots. I cursed the back window that last weekend suddenly refused to close about the last three inches. The weather had been nicer during the week, and I'd forgotten to take the car to be fixed, but now it was c-o-l-d. So cold, it took a minute for my phone to register my fingers as I dialed Emily to let her know I was heading over to my store and then to the Melville. In addition to offering my services to bring anything to the inn this morning, I wanted to make sure that Emily and I stayed on the same page. There was no room for surprises in her meticulously planned event. The call went to voice mail, but it was only six in the morning. Pulling out of the driveway, I left a message.

When I reached town, the streets were quiet and the morning fog still hung low. The vibe would be very different in a matter of hours, when tourists arrived for Memorial Day weekend along with a mob of sailing enthusiasts who come each year for the island's one-of-a-kind annual sailing competition, called FIGAWI, which stands for "Where the #%$! are we?" (Correct pronunciation: *where the fug ah we?*) The race started decades ago as a dare between two friends, who at one point got lost en route to the island, hence the name. It is now an international sailing event that brings a great boon to local retail. Some folks go into shock over the onslaught of visitors, but the business girl in me looks forward to FIGAWI all year.

Rounding onto the bumpy cobblestone pavement of Main Street, which I like to describe as offering a full-body massage when experienced in my car, I saw my cousins Ted and Docker, who run a private trash removal business. They looked like they were loading nautical supplies into the back of their truck, which seemed a funny thing to do on Main Street, but they often have unusual jobs.

I waved. They waved. My family, the Wrights, have been a fixture on the island for as long as anyone can remember. Only my mother, Millie Wright, had the itch to leave. Like one of Nantucket's legendary whaling captains, my mother would disappear for months at a time while in her twenties, only to return with treasured oils and extracts to make perfumes, her passion. One day she returned home, opened a perfume store and settled, for a stretch, with a different kind of treasure.

"It was a treasure that trumped them all," she used to say. "My little Stella Wright."

I used to love to hear her say this to me. I always felt different from the Wrights with my unruly dark hair and olive complexion, which is at odds with their infamous red hair and fair skin. And whereas they're all willing to laugh things off, I can have, I admit, a bit of a temper when push comes to shove.

Nearing the Wick & Flame, I slowed my car, not that there was traffic, but because I passed Officer Andy Southerland and I knew the cops in town were on the lookout for traffic violations during the busy weekend. As I drove by him, he smiled. I smiled, too, then lifted a finger to my eye and pointed to him to let him know I was on my feet today. It got a laugh, and he returned the gesture.

Andy and I have had a lifetime of friendly antagonism that I've never quite shared with anyone else. We are twenty-nine now, but we've been at it since seventh grade, when I alone smelled a gas leak during a science lab, and Andy called me The Hound. Having spent many afternoons connecting a customer to their perfect scent at my mother's store, my sense of smell had become keen, to be sure, but that afternoon exemplified my talent's pros and cons. On the con side, a teenager does not aspire to the nickname Hound. It suggests a dog, not something you want to be thinking about when you're buying your first mascara. But my classmates howled like dogs to thank me that day in science, and that was that. I still stand by my comeback. I'd like to think I squared my shoulders when I turned to Andy and said, "That's *Miss* Hound, to you. And be careful. I bite."

They were fighting words. Later that week, he put a frog in my lunchbox. I retaliated by sticking gum in his hair. As they say in the movies, it was the start of a beautiful friendship. Who would ever guess that a guy who loved pranks and teasing seventh-grade girls would choose law enforcement as a career? When I opened Wick & Flame, he offered a conciliatory change of my nickname to The Candle Girl.

"That's Candle *Lady*," I had responded, shoulders definitely squared by then.

A moment later, I parked in a legal spot in front of the Wick & Flame. Unlike half the stores in town, I keep my place open year-round, but I'd put extra care into my current store window in anticipation of the weekend. As I retrieved the store keys from my back pocket to let myself in, I thought how my brightly colored display was at odds with the dreary morning sky, but I hoped my color palate would make people think of summer days ahead and indulge in a candle or two.

I entered my store where I was greeted by a cacophony of scents, from wild lilies to mango peach to basil and mint. I straightened a new display I'd added last week. It featured a unity candle similar to the Sterling's creation, and it had a small advertisement underneath for personalized wedding scents. Like the Sterling's candle, my display was about six inches in diameter and a full two feet tall. I'd recently found a stronger wax than the coconut bases I usually use, so I could build height while maintaining strength. Word had already spread about the Sterling's nuptials, and I was working on an unprecedented six weddings for June. I hoped by the end of the weekend, a few more people might consider my services. My rent had recently gone up and, quite frankly, I needed the business.

From a room behind the cash register where I also hold candle-making classes, I grabbed a small vial with a sample of the sea salt and white tea oils I had in mind for the alternative scent. In two hours, I'd be back at my shop to greet the Candleers, a self-named band of some of my favorite characters in town, for our last class of "Color Infusions 101." The clock ticking, I popped back into my car and headed out to the Melville.

I've always said that if I had the money for a big wedding, and a man I wanted to marry, I'd love a wedding at the Melville. The inn opened its doors two years ago as a sophisticated, but somehow still understated, inn at a quiet point of the island. Originally an old white elephant of a home, the inn had been renovated and expanded to almost one hundred rooms, which are beautifully appointed with New England décor and antiques. A row of French doors at the back of the inn opens to a swimming pool, followed by a rolling lawn where guests can play croquet while sipping cocktails from Adirondack chairs. The property ends at the harbor where the Melville's private launch takes guests across the sparkling waters in to town, thereby skipping the winding road that takes three times as long to drive. Oh, and the food! The inn has a restaurant, Ahab's, where the aroma of the dishes, and I am saying this as someone who's biased, is as irresistible as the scented candles I make at the Wick & Flame.

Had I known what I was driving toward, however, I might have decided the Sterling scent we had chosen was perfect as it was.

Chapter 2

Jessica Sterling was an early riser, too. Or maybe she had as long a to-do list as I had. Either way, I was glad to find her awake when I arrived at the Melville about thirty minutes later. She was having breakfast with her mother at Ahab's. Jessica is a couple of inches taller than I am, and I played JV basketball in high school. Her hair has that golden color that is so bright she looks like a light bulb going off. Her mother is equally tall and gray haired, but an elegant gray that tells you to mind your manners. I had been told by Emily that she was addressed as "mom" by Jessica and "Mrs. Sterling" by everyone else, including Jessica's fiancé, Joe Handler.

Some locals have it in for rich people who come to their island. They think they'll be snobs, or disrespectful. Funny thing about being a local on Nantucket is that you can be either a big fish in a small pond, or invisible to the seasonal visitors. Jessica, however, was not the type to see through anyone. She's a good egg. I was dying to meet her fiancé, Joe. He was certainly a lucky guy. I imagined he must be some sort of Disney-

looking prince with a British accent and maybe small
children, waifs, hanging off of him, whom he had
saved from peril while wearing a custom-made James
Bond–type suit. I don't know. It was a slow spring.

Something about the body language between Jessica and her mother made me pause at the entrance
to the restaurant rather than interrupt them. Both
mother and daughter had presumably rolled out of
bed for an early coffee, but what would have been
sweats and whatever T-shirt was on the floor for me,
they were in outfits that were perfectly pressed. Jessica
was wearing her now infamous engagement ring,
which shined ruby, emerald, sapphire, and diamond
reflections across the room. The ring did not fit Jessica's approachable personality, but it was a family
heirloom and Emily had told me it meant a lot to Mrs.
Sterling that she wear it. I like the idea of a huge
gaudy ring, but maybe that's because I don't have to
lug one around on my finger every day. Ah, who am I
kidding? I think I could manage that kind of problem.

"It's not that I think Joe's a bad man," Mrs. Sterling
was saying to her daughter. Her brow was furrowed
over her coffee cup. "I just hope he's strong enough
for you. And, I don't see why you two had to do so
much of the wedding yourselves. A mother should be
in on everything, even if the groom was a surprise
choice."

"I know you're disappointed, Mom," said Jessica. "It
breaks my heart. But we won't let you down."

On the one hand, I was suddenly aware that I was
walking in on a private conversation. On the other
hand, I couldn't walk away from the smell of freshly
baked goods and brewed coffee. I inhaled the welcoming aromas.

"Stella," Jessica said with a big smile, perhaps one of relief at my arrival.

It was too late to make a quiet exit. Jessica waved at me and I crossed the room to their table.

"Good morning," I said, shaking hands upon introduction to her mother. "I woke up thinking of you."

"Why doesn't that surprise me? Stella is stellar," said Jessica to her mother. I immediately liked the pun much better than Hound or Candle Lady.

"Hopefully still stellar when you hear me out," I said, as if I were used to the nickname. "I noticed the air is a bit crisper this weekend than we anticipated, and I'm wondering if you would prefer Option Three from the samples we tested for the scented candles. Since we're linking the island to the wedding and the couple, I'll gladly remake the gifts and unity candle, and have them to you this afternoon. No extra costs for you."

Jessica reached behind her and grabbed an unused china cup and saucer from an empty table.

"Sit," she said, and patted an empty chair at their square table.

I sat.

Jessica poured a steaming cup of coffee that looked delicious and pushed it toward me.

"I love that candle, Stella. I expect that it will remind me forever of this special weekend." Jessica suddenly got a little misty. "In fact, I'm planning to order more so I can light them every year on Joe and my anniversary and we can tell the kids all about our wedding."

"I already made you extras," I said, waving off my own set of waterworks. "You're sure you still like it?"

"She's sure," said her mother, pouring a pack of

sugar into her cup in a way that told us to cut out the sentiment before she lost it, too.

"Come on," Jessica said to her mother. "Let's take a last look at the unity candle. Tomorrow it will be up on the altar."

"No. You've made it clear. You've got everything covered," said Mrs. Sterling definitively. If Emily were here, she would understand the subtleties of this dynamic from years of experience, but I was winging it.

"It's no problem," I said, rising.

"Please?" Jessica said to her mother.

A deep love flickered across Mrs. Sterling's otherwise controlled face as she looked at her daughter. I concluded in that moment that whatever issues Mrs. Sterling was having about her daughter's wedding, she adored Jessica more than anything else in the world. She rose and adjusted her sweater.

"It is a beautiful scent, Stella," said Mrs. Sterling. "I like the seagrass note."

I beamed at the compliment, feeling that Mrs. Sterling did not hand them out lightly, and I led our small group to a room off the kitchen that had become the wedding's staging and storage area. Given its size, it was more like a glorified closet, but it had a window and a good-sized worktable in the middle, plus lots of shelves along the walls to keep track of things in an organized way. I opened the door to find all of my boxes of candles and ten times more of Emily's supplies. Yesterday, I'd placed the unity candle on a shelf in a shaded area of the room, but now, to my horror, I noticed that the shelf was empty.

"Jessica, did someone move the unity candle?" I asked. I wondered if perhaps it had been moved to the Siasconset Chapel about twenty minutes down the road, in anticipation of the evening's rehearsal.

"I took it to the Game Room to show Joe and the others last night. The bartender said he would return it safe and sound," said Jessica. "Why?"

"Is there a problem?" said Mrs. Sterling in full-on Mom mode that scared the socks off of me.

"No," I said lightly. I picked up the phone to call the inn's manager to find out if he had seen the candle, but Jessica motioned to me to hang up.

"I bet Joe has it," she said. "That's so damn sweet. All I've done is tell him how much I love it. He probably didn't trust the bartender to bring it back in here last night."

Jessica called Joe, and gushed a little. They were so cute. She hung up a moment later, however, looking confused.

"Joe says he doesn't have it."

"Call Tony," said her mother, folding her arms. She looked at me. "Have you met Tony Carlson?"

I shook my head, although I knew she was referring to the best man. I also knew there were a total of five members of the Sterling-Handler wedding who had arrived last night. They were Jessica, Mrs. Sterling, Joe Handler, Tony Carlson, and Jessica's uncle, Simon Sterling. As I understood it from Emily, Jessica's father had died just over a year ago.

"Tony probably had too much to drink last night and thought it would be funny to take it," said Mrs. Sterling.

Jessica dutifully called Tony. She apologized for waking him, then hung up looking more concerned.

"No, again," she said.

"Well, I can't imagine what Simon would want with it, so someone at the hotel must have it," said Mrs. Sterling. "Call the manager."

"Let me call Simon," said Jessica. She flipped through

her contacts, called, and waited. Then, she frowned, looked at her watch, and dialed again. "No answer. Maybe he has his phone on mute. I'll knock. Mom, you look for the manager. Stella, can you come with me? I don't know Simon Sterling very well. He's my dad's brother, but they were estranged so I'd never met him before last night. That probably sounds weird, but I need someone to walk me down the aisle. If for some reason he took the candle, though, I wouldn't mind if you, *um*—"

"I understand," I said. "I'll tell him we need it back so there's no tension between you two."

She squeezed my arm in thanks as we headed up the stairs to the second floor. Ten paces down the hall, however, we heard a strange scratching noise against Uncle Simon's door.

"What's that?" said Jessica. She lagged behind me, but I forged ahead in search of my candle.

I knocked on the door.

"Uncle Simon?" Jessica said from behind me.

The scratching stopped for a moment. We both put our ears against the door. I don't know why I did. I surely did not want to hear that noise again.

"Uncle Simon?" said Jessica, more loudly.

"*Eeeeow*," came an unmistakable sound from the other side of the door.

It was a cat. Not a quiet cat, but one with a screeching, horrible mew.

"Excuse me," said Jessica to a passing housekeeper. The woman was Maude Duffy, a dear family friend whose son I used to babysit when I was in high school. "Can you let me into this room? My uncle is staying in here, but we can't seem to rouse him."

Maude looked at me and I gave her an all-go nod, so

she fished out her passkey. No sooner had she opened
the door than a flash of black fur, darker than my own
wild mane, dashed out of the room and down the
stairs. We peeked inside, but the bed was still made.
No sign of Uncle Simon.

"Did you already clean the room?" I asked Maude.

"It's seven in the morning," she said without a trace
of defensiveness. "I just got here."

In the distance, the sound of scratching and mew-
ing resumed.

For a moment there was silence.

Then, came a scream I'll never forget.

They say that when people go into shock, they
sometimes do the opposite of what they should. Like
someone pulls out a gun, and the person just stands
there. Or an earthquake hits and instead of staying inside, everyone runs outside. Stuff like that. A scream
would suggest danger ahead. The scream I heard
would suggest that as creepy as Uncle Simon's empty
room was, the best idea would be to run into it, lock
the door, and dodge under his bed. Instead, we all did
the opposite. We ran down the stairs, past the reception desk, and toward two open doors to the Game
Room, in front of which that cursed cat sat, still and
erect, eyes on us like a sentry.

Inside, Mrs. Sterling stood shaking and looking as if
she were ready for another scream. The inn's manager, Frank, a tall, slim man, about my age, who was
impeccably dressed for work at this early hour, was beside her looking as if he were summoning every fiber
of strength not to join her.

"What's wrong?" I asked, but didn't get a chance to
hear the answer because Jessica, a step or two ahead of
me, let out her own scream.

Doors above us started opening.

Footsteps from other areas of the hotel began to stampede toward us.

Maude, who I once saw kill a snake with her own hands, fainted.

And then I saw the most horrible image I'd ever seen.

Lying on the floor, was my once mighty unity candle, broken in two.

The candle itself would be easy enough to fix, but the fact that Jessica's estranged uncle, Simon Sterling, was lying next to it with his head bashed in suggested a cause of death no one could dispute.

Chapter 3

"Shut the door," said Frank, his phone out and already dialing 9-1-1.

"Don't touch the doorknobs!" said Maude, regaining consciousness. "Fingerprints."

Maude's a woman of few words, but when she speaks, people listen. No one closed the door. Frank was too busy relaying the situation to the police to notice that no one followed his orders.

I tried desperately not to look at the dead body of Simon Sterling. Instead, I looked at the wood-paneled bookshelves, a billiards table, the fireplace, the portrait of a whaling captain over the mantel. I stared through the doors and into the lobby. There, the concierge was holding back an elderly couple and a busboy from Ahab's by making himself into a human yellow-tape barrier with his outstretched arms. Good man. The Melville is a seasonal resort that does not officially open until Memorial Day weekend. Even so, I suspected the concierge would have his work cut out for him. I knew from Emily that other than the Sterling party, there were three other rooms occupied last night, a sort of soft launch, and that those guests were leaving today.

While I did my best to avoid looking at the crime scene, others in the room had their own reactions. Mrs. Sterling sank to her knees over the dead body while Jessica retched over an empty vase I knew Emily was planning to fill with freesia at about eleven this morning when she and I were scheduled to arrive for setup. We'd planned to have the hotel transformed by two o'clock in the afternoon, before the wedding guests arrived for the long weekend. Looking at that vase, I suddenly registered the fact that the weekend's plans had profoundly changed.

"He looks so much like your father. How did I never notice?" said Mrs. Sterling. She sat over her brother-in-law's body and touched his arm.

Still lying on the floor, Maude turned her head toward the dead man and raised an eyebrow. I followed her gaze across the navy Persian carpet upon which Simon Sterling lay splayed on his back, and I knew what Maude was getting at. Although his tweed jacket was beautifully cut, and his thick hair combed in perfect lines, I could only assume that Jessica's father was an unusual-looking man if he looked anything like his brother did right now. Simon's eyes, for one, stared fiercely at us. I should say eye. One, which was punctuated by a solid black bruise, looked boldly ahead while the other was closed in a mocking wink that gave him an ironically taunting expression for someone in his position. I only gave myself five seconds to view the body, but I'll never be able to erase the image. Trust me, I've tried. I reached down and helped Maude to her feet. She brushed me off with a look that warned me never to tell a soul she'd fainted.

"God, I miss Henry," Mrs. Sterling said, choking a

tear. "If it wasn't for this good-for-nothing brother of his, he might still be alive."

So much for keeping unkind words about the dead to oneself.

Jessica sank beside her mother and put her arms around her. The two women held each other, crying for Henry Sterling while his dead brother kind of smirked at them. I started to have a feeling that Simon Sterling was not the greatest guy, in spite of the fact that he had offered to walk his niece down the aisle.

"Oh my God, Jessica," said a new arrival to the scene who dashed past the beleaguered concierge and into the room, tripping over his own two feet. "Get back. Everyone, get back."

The man had a thick mop of hair that stuck up in ways it should not. He was about my age, but his face was a deep, flushed red. It was a shade that suggested high blood pressure, and it got brighter around the rims of his ears. I found it fascinating that he wore socks with his pajamas, and, given the wedding's price tag, that the socks had holes in them. He ran toward Jessica, peeled her away from her mother, and pulled the ladies to the far end of the room.

"Oh, Joe," said Jessica, clinging to his neck, which was an inch or two below her shoulders.

I'm not proud of it, but all I was thinking at that moment was: Get. Out. Of. Town. Joe Handler must be insanely rich or funny or I don't know what, because he was the opposite of my James Bond–Disney Prince image. I know, I know. This was a ridiculous and trivial detail to notice in the middle of a violent tragedy, but I was freaked out about the dead body that I was *still* standing near. I think it was a coping mechanism.

"What's happened?" said a man, trailing behind Joe, who needed a good shave. He looked at the room, and then let out an expletive that fit the moment.

"Language, Tony," Mrs. Sterling said to the wedding's best man through her tears.

Another man entered a pace or two behind Tony. He let out the same expletive, then closed the doors. Fortunately for him, he did not touch the knobs or I suspect his wife, Maude, would have had a strong word or two of her own. Bill Duffy, the hotel's bartender and off-season caretaker, immediately crossed over to his wife and put his arm around her. Bill wouldn't be on duty until the lunch seating at Ahab's, but he walked Maude to work every day from an old cottage the inn provided for them down the road. I've known the Duffys since I was in high school. Bill ran a handyman business and was a regular visitor to my mother's store, which in those days had a leak that was always giving her problems. He even taught me how to dunk a basketball in high school when I was trying out for the team. In exchange for a hefty discount for his handy services, I babysat for their son. I wasn't really supposed to get paid, but Bill and Maude are a generous couple. They always slipped me what they could when I'd leave their house.

Bill gave me a reassuring smile, which I returned. I didn't see the Duffys as much as I used to, but I have a very soft spot for them. They're a good family, and a great couple. Bill and Maude remind me of a poem my grandma taught me as a kid about Jack Sprat who would eat no fat and his wife who eats no lean. Except the minute you see them together, you know they were meant for each other. That's what I'm going for.

"I'll tell you what happened," Jessica said to Tony in an angry outburst that brought me back to the moment. "Uncle Simon was murdered. This can't be happening. Oh my God, is that our unity candle?"

I started to feel nauseous. It seemed out of the question to leave the scene, but the room was beginning to feel claustrophobic. I found a seat at a card table by the window where I was as far from the body as possible. As the chaotic and panicky conversation in the room continued to swirl around me, I focused on the unity candle.

Yesterday morning, I had delivered the candle to the inn and had put it on a dark and cool shelf, away from everything else, to protect its delicate gold embellishments. The candle's ornamentation was an exact copy of the beaded flowers on Jessica's wedding dress. The design twisted around the entire circumference of the smooth wax. It looked deceivingly delicate, but I knew how heavy and strong the wax was. It would take a lot of force to break this candle in half as someone had done. Simon Sterling had not stood a chance.

I instinctively found the need to reclaim my candle before it became an official part of a crime scene. I stood, surprised at how steady my legs were, crossed the room, and leaned over to pick up both ends of the candle, which were still strung together by the wick. When I stood, I noticed that Tony was taking pictures of the room. He seemed to be the only one who was thinking about the crime scene. I was impressed until he leaned over the body to take a picture and dropped his phone on the dead man. He picked it up off the body, which elicited a communal groan.

"Don't touch the body, Tony. Or take pictures. And you. Put the candle down," said Mrs. Sterling. She grabbed the candle from me and put it back on the floor. "This is evidence."

Immediately, I saw the error of my ways. The Melville's shaken manager did, too. I didn't know Frank well, but he had been working at the Melville since it had opened two years ago. This was his worst nightmare come true. He covered the body with a cashmere throw that hung on the arm of a leather couch for the guests' comfort, while I tried to rearrange the candle ends in their original position. I was hoping Tony had gotten a photo of the candle before I had tampered with the evidence when I heard my name.

"Seriously, Stella?"

"Cut it out, Andy," I said without needing to look up. "I panicked."

Andy Southerland stood tall and looked at the mess. When this guy's off duty, he is all smiles. You'll find him in a T-shirt, jeans, and hiking boots with a baseball cap topping off his thick, dark hair. He shares a hello and a joke with everyone in town, and they reciprocate happily. When Andy is on duty, however, he is all business. His smile transforms into a strong and serious jawline, and his body language shifts to controlled and skilled action. Right now, he looked something like an animal on the hunt. I watched his quiet, dark eyes scan the room and take in the situation.

As I slunk back to my chair at the card table, the nausea returned and I realized it was from a smell in the room. Tobacco. I hate the smell of pipe tobacco. One summer, I tried to develop more musky scents, things that our social constructs would deem masculine. I spent one evening on a tobacco blend and got a migraine. Now, I remembered the same odor in Simon's room. I had been too busy dodging his cat to focus at the time, but there was no doubt that the scent was one and the same. Confirming my suspicions, I noticed the offending pipe about two feet away from

Simon, beneath the vase to which Jessica was once more clinging.

With Andy's entrance, the room calmed down. There were eight of us, and we all looked expectantly at Andy, but I knew he'd never had a murder case before. In Nantucket we have our fair share of stolen bikes, and definitely some drunk and disorderly conduct. Occasionally we have car accidents. But murder? No. We're a town where people feel comfortable leaving doors unlocked for the most part. You might come home to find someone has entered your house, but in that case it would be to leave a freshly caught lobster, or homemade clam chowder. We don't go around murdering each other.

"I need everyone to remain calm," said Andy.

"How?" said Joe. "There's a dead body."

Jessica and her mother began to cry again.

"Frank," said Andy to the manager without flinching, "can you open up this room over here?" He motioned to a set of window-paned French doors off the Game Room. "Folks, let's go onto this porch."

"Sun Room," said Frank.

"Sun Room," said Andy graciously. His nose flared a little, so I knew he wasn't feeling as kindly as he sounded. "We'll close the blinds on the doors to the Game Room, and sit and talk while my chief and our team come to dust for fingerprints, and collect evidence."

"Your chief isn't here?" said Joe with a little "you, local yokel" kind of insinuation that made me feel less guilty about my critical reaction to him.

"Luckily, I was handling a FIGAWI situation nearby, and was close to the inn. Others are on their way. In a case like this, however, we don't want to waste a minute, so let's talk while the facts are still fresh in your minds."

As he spoke, the group walked as if in a daze to the Sun Room off of the Game Room. I, however, felt my senses come alive as we found seats on the soft quilted cushions of wicker furniture. In contrast to the Game Room's rich colors and wood-paneled walls, we were now surrounded by potted ferns and blue checks that were more suited to the summer. It would have been a pleasant room except for the sirens blaring down the road in the background.

"Let me explain what is going to happen," Andy continued as if he did this every day. "While we're talking, the police, detectives, and a medical examiner will arrive. By the time we're finished talking, the body will have been examined and removed. You'll no longer have to see it."

"Thank you," said Joe, looking both relieved and concerned about the Sterling women. I noticed he'd at least flattened down his hair.

"Let's start simply," said Andy, joining us on a wicker sofa and pulling out a pad of paper and a pen from his jacket pocket. "Does anyone know the deceased? And if so, what can you tell me about him?"

Chapter 4

"The man is Uncle Simon," said Jessica, wiping her tears.

Andy pulled a packet of tissues out of his pocket.

"Thanks." Jessica blew shamelessly. "I'm supposed to be getting married this weekend. He, the deceased, was going to walk me down the aisle. Mom said not to invite him. When my father was sick, Uncle Simon refused to help him with a business matter."

"It was much worse than that," said Mrs. Sterling, her eyes ablaze. "My husband wanted to sell property in Italy that he and his brother had jointly inherited from their parents, years ago. At the last minute, Simon backed out. The stress of the deal, compounded by Simon's obstinance, well . . . Poor Henry." She sniffed and stopped speaking, but I thought her implication was pretty obvious. She believed that Simon had pushed his brother over the edge.

"Who was the first to find the body?" Andy continued. Whether or not he had come to the same conclusion I had, he spoke gently. Even though we were talking about a horrible and recent experience, his calm was contagious. We all looked at each other for a moment, collectively trying to remember the chain of events.

"Mrs. Sterling and I were in search of a candle, the unity candle for the wedding," said Frank.

Andy shot a look at me that implied he had not forgotten that I had already tampered with said candle. I was a little irritated that everyone got his warm bedside manner except for me. Little did he know it, but the police would soon realize how poorly we'd all handled finding Simon's body. In our panic and shock, we'd all been touching the candle, the body, things in the room. I think they called it contaminate evidence on one of the detective shows I watch. The only thing we'd probably left untouched were doorknobs, thanks to Maude.

"In the middle of our search," the manager continued, "we heard the cat screaming in front of the Game Room. We went to see what was bothering him. I opened the door and . . . we saw the body."

"I screamed," said Mrs. Sterling, her hand rising to her mouth.

"Is this a resident cat?" said Andy.

"No," said Frank.

At the mention of the cat, we all started to look around the room. The creature was not there. I hoped it was not sniffing around Simon. Andy probably had the same thought. He went to the door and opened it. Others had arrived in the next room and he took the opportunity to update them about the animal.

"There are no pets allowed in the hotel," said Frank when Andy rejoined us.

"It was Simon's cat," said Jessica. "I guess he snuck it in. Stella and I heard it when we were searching for my uncle, and when we opened the door to his room the cat sped out and I guess it ran right to the body."

"When did you all last see Simon?" said Andy, moving on from the illicit cat.

"Dinner last night," said Mrs. Sterling. "At least I did. I've been feeling a little under the weather, so I went upstairs after our meal."

"After dinner"—Joe cleared his throat—"Tony and I played cards with Simon in the Game Room, before heading to bed. Mr. Duffy was with us, too."

Maude stepped away from Bill and squinted her eyes at her husband. They were a good couple, but Maude was a tough cookie.

"I didn't gamble with them," said Bill indignantly. "I was working overtime. The guys wanted the drinks to keep coming."

Now it was Jessica's turn to cast a disparaging look at her man. Joe motioned indelicately with his eyes at Tony, to suggest that his friend had been behind the libations. Tony took the look in stride and nodded. He really was the best man. At least at the moment.

"So, Tony, Joe, and Simon Sterling were in the Game Room playing cards, while Bill served drinks," said Andy.

"In the drawing room, with the candlestick," said Tony with a chuckle that did not go over well.

"Did you turn in at the same time?"

The men nodded.

"We left Simon at about two," said Tony. "I don't know what time he went upstairs."

"Nine minutes later," said Bill, who had been on the clock. "I got home by three."

Maude nodded. "He was snoring by three fifteen, I can tell you that much."

"Frank," said Andy. "Did anyone leave or enter the inn after Bill left?"

"We don't have a security camera for the sake of our guests' privacy," said Frank. "But we have an alarm for the windows and doors. It automatically turns on at midnight, when the inn closes for the night. If anyone wants to get in after midnight, they use their room's key card. It's programmed to let guests in and out of the front door, without setting off the alarm. If someone who is not staying at the inn would like to get in, they ring the bell, I disable the alarm, and open the door for them. No one rang the bell last night."

"Did you hear anything in the Game Room?" said Andy.

"I'm sorry I didn't," said Frank. "I sleep like a log."

"Did anyone else see Simon Sterling after two o'clock this morning?" said Andy.

We all looked at each other. No one said anything. Maybe realizing he had been the last person to see Simon Sterling alive, Bill bit his thumbnail.

"How'd you get the bruise on your hand, Bill?" said Andy.

He was right. There was a bright red and blue mark on Bill's right knuckle.

Bill looked at his hand.

"This?" he said. "I was fixing the kitchen sink and dropped the wrench on it funny. I'm fine though, thanks."

"What about the murder weapon?" said Jessica. "Mr. Duffy, did you bring the candle back to the wedding's staging room as you promised?"

"I'm sorry," said Bill, looking at the floor. "I didn't."

"Why not?" said Andy.

"I wish you had," said Joe, tenderly holding his fiancée's hand and twirling her ring.

"It was late," said Bill. "I was tired. I'd already tidied up the room. I can't think how I forgot to return it, but I did."

I couldn't either. The Bill I knew was one of the most reliable people I'd ever met.

"Thanks for your honesty, Bill," said Andy. He closed his notebook. "Who won the card game?"

"Simon," said Joe glumly.

The others nodded their heads in agreement, Bill Duffy included. Something about their expressions seemed to say that they did not truly believe Simon had won fair and square, but that there was no way to prove it. The man's character kept getting worse and worse. Not only had Simon allegedly sped up his brother's demise, but perhaps he had swindled his niece's groom and best man the night before their wedding.

"How much did you play?" said Andy.

Tony shook his head.

"I'd say we both lost about, what? Eight hundred bucks?" said Joe.

"About that," said Tony. "But when we started the game, Simon pulled out a wad of hundred-dollar bills. Way more than we needed for the game. He kept them sitting beside us. It was like he wanted to break us, because we'd see he had unlimited funds."

"Or tempt us," said Joe.

"We'll need to have an officer search the victim's room," Andy said to Frank. Then he poked his head into the Game Room, which had become much noisier by this point. Looking satisfied, he turned to us. "I'm going to let you all go, for now. No one is allowed to leave the inn, however, until I've spoken with each of you separately."

"I'm going to be in my room resting," said Mrs. Sterling. "You can find me there."

Everyone else grumbled. No one wanted to be at the inn right now, especially me. I had a candle class to teach in less than an hour, and I had no intention of sticking around. Andy could take it up with me later if he wanted to. It's not like I could add anything to his investigation. I had never even met the man.

As promised, when we left the Sun Room, there was no longer a body in the Game Room. All signs of Simon, down to his pipe, had been removed. There were police taking pictures, dusting, and doing pretty much everything I see in the detective TV shows I love to watch. I looked for Nantucket's Chief of Police, but he was nowhere in sight.

"Move along," a stout man, about twenty years my senior, said to us. His most fascinating feature was a bald spot among his sparse brown hair that was off-center. It was the strangest sight.

"Who're you?" said Joe.

I was wondering the same thing.

"Who're you?" said the man.

"This is Joe Handler," said Andy, intervening. "He's the groom at this weekend's wedding here at the inn. Everyone, this is Chief Bellamy. He comes to us from the Cape. Chief Bellamy was on the island for a meeting this morning, since his department is supplying mutual assistance to help with FIGAWI this weekend. He was on his way back to the Cape when the news came. We're fortunate that Chief Bellamy has experience in handling this kind of crime, and that he's agreed to stay and help us."

"It's lovely to meet you, Chief," said Mrs. Sterling, her hand outstretched. "I'm Mrs. Sterling, the bride's mother. We're so grateful that you can help us with our family's shocking loss. This is all new to us, as I'm sure you can understand."

"Not to worry, madam," said Bellamy with a gracious bow. "We'll get this unsettling mess in order as quickly as we can. It's my goal to have the murderer under arrest immediately."

"Do you have any leads?" asked Jessica.

"I will soon," he said with a puffed chest. "I have a reputation for quick arrests. Given that Nantucket has a huge sailing event, and a beautiful wedding about to take place, it is imperative that we move quickly. You have my word."

"What about our own Chief of Police?" I said.

Bellamy looked me up and down. Rather than answer, he returned to the investigation. Andy also ignored my looks of protest at this stranger's arrival, and herded us into the lobby.

I could play that game, too. I opened a BuzzFeed quiz on my phone about picking a favorite pizza topping to learn who your perfect superhero boyfriend is. I've noticed that when a person stares hard at their phone people give them a pass at any other social interaction, which was just what I needed to dodge a long interview right now. It was a good plan, too. No one looked at me as I passed Jessica and Joe, who were huddled in the lobby, consoling each other, while Frank was attempting to explain the situation to the inn's other guests.

"We have to catch a ferry back to the mainland in an hour," I heard a harried-looking man say to Frank as I clicked "pepperoni" on my quiz.

I watched Andy intervene, and tell the man and the elderly couple, who had stuck around for the excitement, that they would be interviewed first so that they could make their journeys home. We're a service-oriented island, and even in the middle of a murder, I was happy to see one of our own still trying to be accommodating.

I tried to size up the guests from Andy's perspective as I skirted across the lobby. Both the elderly man and woman looked as if it would be impossible to pick up my unity candle, forget about using it as a murder weapon. They'd have probably killed themselves in the process. As for the younger man, he stood next to his wife, who held a coughing toddler. From their look of fatigue, I guessed they'd spent their vacation helping the baby through the croup. I helped my cousin Chris with his little one two years ago, when he was alone with the kids. I still haven't gotten over it. Emily, who is expecting her first in less than a month, read a book that says that the adrenaline kicks in and you can do anything as a parent. So, in fact, parents are *actually* superhuman. No need for Spider-Man, my perfect superhero match according to my quiz. At any rate, I knew enough to know that there was no way you could take a break from the croup to kill a guy.

I heard Frank tell Andy that there was only one other guest, but that he had broken his foot badly yesterday on a hike and was currently in a wheelchair. I guessed Andy would want to talk to him to see if he'd heard anything, but I didn't think a guy with a newly broken foot would have been able to wield my strong candle against someone's head with enough force to kill him.

With no one looking at me, I stepped outside the inn and breathed the fresh air. The bracing cold of early morning was better than a strong drink, which I also would have welcomed. I noticed Tony had slipped out with success, too. He stood at the end of the inn, smoking a cigarette. He was leaning against the building, looking up at the sky and I was surprised when I noticed him making smoke rings. I mean, who was I to judge how people handle their emotions, but smoke rings? They felt more like a victory lap than the sort of thing you do when your best friend finds a dead body at his wedding. I shuddered and realized I was thinking the worst. The truth of the matter, however, was that I might very well have been in a room with a murderer.

Now that I was outside, the second half of my plan was to pull out quietly in my car, then hit the road and be home for my candle class. I slipped into my Beetle, which I had thankfully parked along the side of the road rather than in Ahab's parking lot, where at least six police cars now congregated. The island has about a dozen cars, but as Andy had said, due to FIGAWI, we had extra police and volunteers from the mainland for the weekend, in addition to the less than charming Bellamy.

Once I was convinced no one was looking at me, I started up the car and pulled out onto the first of two roads that would lead me back to town. I was cruising along the curvy road, checking my rearview mirror to make sure no one was following me, and trying to make sense of what had just happened, when the blast of a horn brought my eyes back to the road. My car swerved as a small blue Ford pulled out in front of me and sped ahead. A shock of blond hair peeked over the driver's seat. As I yelled at the car, I realized my nerves were really shot.

"One, two, three." I breathed and chanted to myself. I wondered if Tony had been counting rings to calm his nerves after realizing a murderer was on the loose. If so, maybe Mrs. Sterling, Jessica, or Joe were guilty. The Sterling women were certainly unhappy with Simon Sterling, but it seemed unlikely that they would invite him to give away Jessica and then kill him instead, especially by means of the candle Jessica loved so much.

I thought of Emily. This would be a nightmare for her. I could not begin to imagine whether Jessica and Joe would want to move ahead with the weekend's plans. The reception tent was far enough away from the inn that Jessica and Joe could conceivably still host their reception as planned, but I wondered if the inn itself would be shut down. The Melville was now a crime scene. That would mean guests would need to find other accommodations, which would be just about impossible at this late date and on such a busy weekend.

With my heart resuming the heavy thud it had beat on my way to the inn this morning, I also realized that within the next hour or so, everyone on Nantucket would know the story of Simon Sterling's murder. Assuming Maude or the concierge or even someone from the police department had called at least one person, the chain had already begun.

I wished I was not driving. I really wanted to be the one to tell Emily. I checked my rearview mirror, and confirmed there was no one behind me. I pulled over to a small shoulder off the road and dialed Emily. *Call Failed* was the only answer I got. I love Nantucket, but for the life of me, I still can't understand why cell service here is sometimes so spotty.

I threw my phone onto the seat next to me, started up my car, and pressed my foot on the accelerator. I was willing to risk a speeding ticket.

"Four, five, six." I exhaled. I was almost to Milestone Road, which is the main road that would lead me back into town. I started to feel a lot better. Part of me was thinking, "Nah, that didn't just happen. Emily's biggest wedding of the season wasn't just ruined. I didn't see a dead guy. Andy didn't look really impressive when he was interviewing potential suspects."

But my thoughts were interrupted as a cold chill suddenly crept down my spine that was more terrifying than Simon Sterling's cracked skull.

A finger tapped my right shoulder from the back seat of my empty car.

Chapter 5

Istepped hard on the brakes in the middle of the road, and glimpsed movement in my back seat as someone ducked. I screamed and jumped out of the car. Not thinking about traffic behind me or coming at me, I ran toward the bike lane beside the road. On instinct, I ducked behind the only cover, a wildflower shrub. I crouched low, but my legs betrayed me and I fell flat on the ground. Grabbing the branches of the bush, I pulled myself up and peered back at my car.

No one got out of my Beetle, nor could I see movement inside, but I knew what I knew. I felt my pockets for my phone to call for help, then remembered it was in the car. I wondered if I should try to make a run for it, but my legs were frozen. I prayed someone would appear on the empty road from either direction. I have a small can of mace in my glove compartment that Emily gave me when I went to college in Boston. I've always known it was a dumb place to keep it, but since I'd never needed it in Boston, I'd certainly never expected to need it on Nantucket. Out of options, I rounded my hands into a fist, and readied myself for whatever was about to come at me.

Oh, and it came. A small, dark head rose from the back window that was still open a tad.

I screamed again, so loudly that birds flew from the trees. And then I stopped, and I cursed like a sailor, on the road, by myself.

Darn that cat.

Simon Sterling's cat looked at me with a sort of bored but accommodating stare, and climbed over my cup holder to the passenger seat where he settled down for a nap. I could swear he adjusted the heater with his tail as he swept by. I sighed, wondering if the cat was evidence. Climbing back into my car, I slammed the door to spite his peacefully curled up body, and then felt a little petty.

When I pulled up in front of the Wick & Flame about twenty minutes later, I was happy to see Emily, who was the image of cool, calm, and collected. Wearing a fur-trimmed jacket, she was seated on a bench on the sidewalk in front of my store. After her husband, Neal, had found her rearranging the attic one day last month, he and her obstetrician had staged an intervention. She now had to stay off of her feet as much as possible, which is akin to torture for Emily, so an occasional rest on a bench had become their compromise. She had not, however, given up her heels. At eight and a half months pregnant. On cobblestones.

I looked in my rearview mirror and realized the ride home had done a number on me, and that I was still wearing the clothes I'd thrown on this morning, which was not a good look for work. I pulled my long, dark hair into a ponytail and pinched my cheeks to regain some color. I was glad when I remembered the cute outfit I'd bought during my lunch break last week that was hanging in the back room at the store.

"I thought you hated cats," Emily said as I threw my car keys into my bag and grabbed the kitty. "I got your message. Six in the morning?"

She handed me a coffee, so I knew she wasn't really mad about the early call. Emily and I have been friends since we were tots at Wee Whalers when we discovered we both liked to pretend we were business owners during playtime. While others were building with blocks or playing dress-up, we were setting up stands with plastic fruits or stray pieces of Lego and trying to sell them to our classmates. I went through a brief but ultimately banned handcrafted greeting card phase, trading them for extra cookies at snack time. Emily's favorite job was cleanup monitor. Not that she cleaned up, mind you. The job entailed circling the room to remind people to clean up. She was good at getting people moving, even then.

"Did you pick up that red number from the dry cleaners?" she said to me as she followed me inside my store where I lit the featured candle of the day, a splashy summer scent I hoped would be a best seller in the coming months.

"It's in my car trunk," I said, hoping it wasn't getting wrinkled since I'd forgotten to take it out last night. I turned on the heater to low, because of the wax, and then I pulled out the stool from behind my register for her to sit on. "Listen, we need to talk."

"First," said Emily as the cat jumped onto a prime spot by the heater, "I need to hear from you that you're over the unity candle situation, that Jessica is happy with her candle's scent, and that you're going to wear that sexy red dress tomorrow night. There might be some cute guys at the wedding, and I'm not going to have you go through another winter where the Candleers are your best company. You're too young to live such a spinsterly life, and if you haven't noticed from my whale of a belly, who knows what kind of wreck I'm going to be."

Her reference to "spinsterly" was a little harsh and I could see she knew it because she dutifully sat on the stool. The fact of the matter was that I'd come close to marriage almost two years ago. A man-who-will-remain-nameless, AKA Voldemort to the two of us, had swept me off my feet when he moved to the island to open a real estate company. Once the isolation and cold of February hit, however, he bolted with some parting words that I was missing out on the "real world." Be that as it may, I thought he was really missing the point about me, so I said goodbye. Then, I ate ice cream for about two weeks. Instead of wagging my finger at Emily, however, I sat down next to the cat and recounted the last couple of hours.

Emily took it pretty well, all things considered.

"Did the bride and groom look like they were going to cancel?" she said.

I realized I was starting my second interrogation of the day.

"They were in shock," I said, and put a pot of water on a small burner behind my counter. "They looked like they had seen a dead body."

Emily nodded.

"Did Mrs. Sterling look like she wanted to call off the wedding?"

I thought about it for a second.

"No. Shock, too. Although she seems to have hated Simon Sterling."

"That doesn't surprise me," said Emily. "I gathered from Jessica that the choice was controversial. Brides confess a lot to their wedding planners. The job is half administrative, half therapist."

"So you've told me," I said. I knew we were both thinking of a wedding she'd organized three years ago where the bride had given Emily a love letter from the groom's brother to hold for safekeeping before the wedding.

"Jessica had never met her uncle until the wedding," said Emily, "but she told me that as far as Mrs. Sterling was concerned, this Simon fellow was a bad seed. I'd never have thought he'd be killed though. I just thought he'd be a poser."

"Why?" I took the opportunity of our gossipy digression to slip into my candle-making room to change as we spoke.

"Jessica told me a couple of stories," she said. "Her father and his brother came from money that their father made in agriculture. For a while, their father imported olive oil from Italy before shifting everything to the United States. As adults, Mr. Sterling ran the business and his brother, Simon, took his dividends and lived the good life. When Jessica's dad needed to sell the land in Italy to expand into organic fruits back in the States, he needed Simon's help, but Simon bailed. Jessica's mother is convinced the stress made her husband's already weak heart finally give out, but Jessica was at a loss on who would walk her down the aisle. She's very traditional. She even got separate rooms for her and Joe this weekend."

"Why couldn't Joe's father walk her down the aisle?" I called out from the workroom. "That would have been sweet."

"Joe's parents are deceased."

"Sad," I said, returning to the sales room in my new

gray wool dress with a cowl neck, gray ribbed tights, and my boots.

"Cute."

"On sale, too. Mascara?"

Emily fished into her bag of tricks and handed me a pink tube of Great Lash and a mirror.

"You should tell that story to the police," I said, taking a couple of swipes at each lash and handing the tube and mirror back to her.

"I guess," said Emily, who was clearly, first and foremost, focused on making her client happy.

"Stella?" said an elderly voice through the front door. I realized the time. My class was about to start and Cherry Waddle, my favorite pupil, had arrived.

"Come in Cherry," I said, and unlocked the door for her.

"I've got to go," said Emily. She checked her phone. "Still no messages from the Sterlings, but I'm going to head out to the inn and see what's going on. Meet me at eleven as planned?"

"You got it. Andy's out there," I said. "Maybe he can help."

"Is this about the murder?" said Cherry, bright eyed.

As I had suspected, news had already spread.

"Was he really hit on the head with your candle?" Cherry began to unwrap an endlessly long scarf she'd made in the knitting shop's class around the corner. "Poor dear."

"I wouldn't really say he was a dear," I said. I knew since I'd been at the crime scene that I'd be expected to share some dirt this morning. I'd decided to limit myself to the fact that Simon was an estranged uncle. Better that than relive the image of Simon's battered

head. And there was no way I would tell anyone that
the cat in my store was the dead man's pet. In fact, I
picked up my phone to text Andy that he should come
get the animal.

"Oh, no," said Cherry. "I meant you, poor dear. Will
anyone want to buy a candle from you after such a
tragedy? Brides are suspicious, you know."

She cast a disparaging look at my unity candle display, as if to question my judgment.

I had to hand it to Cherry. She was honest. It had
not even occurred to me that Simon Sterling's death
could affect my business. I looked at Emily for reassur-
ance. She looked back at me with a smile, but I knew
that smile. It was the kind she gave to customers who
wanted a million-dollar wedding on a five-thousand-
dollar budget. It said, this is going to be a problem,
but we'll do our best.

"I'll let you know what I hear," Emily said. With a
kiss to my cheek, she walked out the door as my other
three students arrived.

"Smile, Stella," said Cherry. She flashed her phone
at us and snapped a selfie. "I'm going to put this on
my Instagram. You look good for someone who just
saw a dead body. It will be helpful for your business if
people see you haven't fallen apart. I have five thousand followers, you know. Don't worry, sweetie, I've
got you covered."

I put my own phone away, and decided to drop off
the cat at the station rather than have a police officer
show up at the store. The first day of the retail season
was not the one for any untoward activities. By the
time I poured a cup of tea for Cherry, her three com-
rades in crafts had unwrapped their equally long
scarves. Cherry was their ring leader; her friend Flo
followed a close second.

At nine o'clock on the dot, we started our class. I usually begin with a short lecture about the history of candles before we jump into our work. When I was in high school, I had a summer job at the Whaling Museum on Broad Street in town, so I know a lot of fun facts about whale oil and its uses. During Nantucket's heyday, the whalers discovered that the waxy oil from a sperm whale's head cavity produced candles with a bright, odorless flame. These valuable candles, which accounted for at least a quarter of the island's wealth, were sold internationally. When I learned about the island's role in lighting the world, I knew I wanted to fuse the scents my mother had taught me with one of Nantucket's great traditions. The Whaling Museum itself was originally a candle factory, so I like to think I'm part of a long history on the island.

Today, I found it a little harder to focus on my talk as my mind kept wandering back to the murder scene at the Melville. Winding up my remarks with a bit more speed than usual, I gave a demonstration on mixing colors. Then, we got to work. It's during our crafting time that the ladies chat about everything in their lives, from grandkids to all the local gossip. I was prepared for the Sterling murder to take the top spot. I expected that I would be the one supplying the details, but these ladies always surprise me.

"Did you hear that Gina Ginelli is on the island?" said Cherry.

"Gina Ginelli?" I said and practically dropped the bottle of green dye I'd been preparing for Flo's candle.

They all nodded as if I was the last to know.

I'm not a starstruck kind of person. I don't follow celebrities, or that sort of thing, but Gina Ginelli is one of those old-fashioned, real-life movie stars that everyone loves, right? I even snuck in as a kid to see her in *Swan Song*, back when the Dreamland theater still had a crescent-shaped tear in the screen. I wondered why she was on island, and I wondered if her equally glamorous and famous husband, Kevin Bunch, was here, too.

"She's staying near the Melville," said Flo. "I wonder if she saw the murdered man. So sorry about the bad luck, Stella. I'm not superstitious, by the way."

"I doubt she saw anything. She's in one of the cottages by the beach," said Cherry. The ladies reminded me of seagulls squawking back and forth to each other.

I suddenly remembered the blue Ford and the shock of blond hair. I realized it might have been Gina Ginelli who had cut me off on the road. It was such an exciting thought that the horrific images still branded in my head from this morning faded just a bit.

"I wonder why she's here?" I said.

There was a knock on the door. I'd hired a high school senior, Lucy, to help me for the weekend, since I was going to be at the Melville a lot. Lucy showed up right on time. Contrary to traditional belief that teens are unreliable, I think this generation is the most dependable, hardworking group of people. Maybe they're afraid of getting stuck with the loafer reputation of the Millennials before them. Maybe they know that times are going to be tough for a while. Whatever it is, my money's on them.

Turning my door sign from closed to open, I remembered the cat and texted Andy.

Where are you? I hit send.

About to arrest you, he replied. *I told you not to leave the inn*

Seriously?

Seriously, I need to take your statement. Am in town and on my way to you.

Meet me at The Bean in five, I texted. *I have something for you.*

Five minutes later, I left my Candleers to enjoy the rest of their morning gossip with Lucy in charge and rounded the corner with the cat in my arms to my favorite coffee spot. The fur ball was squirming in my arms as if he knew he was about to be arrested. The streets were busy. Cars were filling up the narrow, two-way lanes. Many were filled with luggage since the ferry on the Steamboat Wharf had just dropped off a new group of arrivals. I sped up to beat the line for coffee that usually follows the ferry's arrival, but my phone pinged. I stopped, propped the cat on my hip, and read.

Wedding's on! read Emily's message. *Get here when you can.*

I couldn't wait to hear how she'd pulled off that one.

Andy was waiting outside The Bean. He, too, was on his phone. He looked at the cat and his expression shifted from one of deep concern at whatever was being said on the other end of the line to complete interest at the bundle in my arms.

"We've been looking for that thing all morning," he whispered.

Recovering the cat had been an accident, but I gave a cocky smile since he looked so impressed that I'd found it for him.

"OK," he said into his phone. "I'm as shocked as you are, sir. This is going to be big. Do you trust Bellamy?"

I was dying to know what was going to be big, but I stayed quiet. Also, I liked his last question because I, for one, did not trust Bellamy. He had rubbed me the wrong way with his quick arrest speech.

"Listen, sir," said Andy. "I've located the cat. . . . Thank you, sir. . . . Stella Wright has it. . . . not sure, but I'll let you know . . . OK, sir. That's two creams and a cruller, right?"

He hung up.

"You're such a cop," I said.

"How'd you get the cat?" he said.

"He jumped in my car, and scared the living daylights out of me," I said as we walked inside. Cats weren't normally allowed in food establishments, but being a cop has some perks. Aside from a curious look from the barista, no one bothered us.

"Hello, Tinker," said Andy. He took the cat and patted his head.

"Tinker?" I said. "We can come up with something better."

"We could, but his name is Tinker," said Andy, jiggling the cat's collar. I hadn't thought to look.

"Hi," I said across the counter. "Two iced almond lattes, one black coffee with two creams, and a cruller." I ordered for me and Andy. It was the least I could do for our finest. "Funny that Simon Sterling would have a cat named Tinker. He looked like he'd go for, I don't know, Tiger or Killer."

"The guy's a mystery, that's for sure," said Andy as we grabbed a spot by the window overlooking the street.

"Do you really need my statement?" I said.

"Yup," said Andy. "Did you see anything strange when you walked into Sterling's room?"

I thought.

"Yeah. A cat," I said. "The room was tidy though."

Andy made a note and proceeded with his questions, which I answered. Fortunately, the cat drew more attention than our conversation.

"What about Bellamy and his amazing arrests?" I asked when we were finished. I thought I might leave with some scoop for Emily.

Andy rubbed his hands across his head.

"Bellamy was good to his word," he said. "There's already been an arrest."

"You've been keeping this from me over an entire cup of coffee?" I said. "And a cat?"

I didn't like the look on Andy's face.

"Who is it?"

"Bill Duffy," he said.

I felt my very un-Wright-like temper begin to rise.

"That's ridiculous," I said. A couple of people next to us looked over. Tinker stopped crawling over Andy and sat at attention. "Bill Duffy wouldn't harm a fly."

"Maude said that she told him his ways would catch up to him as he was taken away. That didn't help his case, although I'm sure she didn't mean anything by it. But then she smashed a vase in the Game Room."

"That doesn't sound like her," I said.

"I think it was out of shock, but technically, the vase might have been evidence."

"But why would Bill kill the man? That's ridiculous. He has nothing to do with the Sterlings."

"Seems he did," said Andy. "After we left the Sun Room, Bellamy questioned him. He didn't like his answers, so they searched him. Lo and behold, they found twenty-five hundred dollars on him, which he confessed he'd taken from the dead man. I'll give Bellamy one thing, he knows how to break a guy. Before you know it, Bill started yelling that Simon Sterling had screwed him over and that the money and more was his. Then he bragged about punching his eye out."

I sat back, stunned. Other than Jessica, who would never sabotage her own wedding, let alone ruin the candle she loved so much, Bill was the last person on earth I would ever have expected to be Simon Sterling's murderer.

"I don't believe Bill did it," I said. "Do you?"

The man who had helped out my single mom, had slipped me some babysitting money, and had been such a kind and loving husband and father was not a murderer. No one was going to convince me otherwise.

"It's really hard to believe Bill would kill someone," said Andy, "but he was probably the last to see Simon Sterling. He was in charge of the candle yet somehow forgot to put it away, and he had a bone to pick with the man. Bellamy is convinced the murder was not premeditated, and that it had to do with the card game."

"It doesn't make sense. Bill, a murderer?" I said.

"Bellamy's confident he's got his guy," said Andy. "There are no motives to implicate anyone else. Bill as much as confessed."

"This is wrong," I said and rose to go.

"The good news is Bellamy gave the all clear. The Melville is back open for business. The Game Room is still cordoned off, as is Sterling's room, but otherwise things are resuming some sense of normalcy. Of course, everyone's shaken about the idea that Bill could do such a thing."

"Because he didn't," I said.

"Here," said Andy, handing the cat to me and picking up his extra coffee and crullers. "Someone has to look after Tinker and the station's a madhouse. I'm officially making you his caretaker. If we need him as evidence, I'll call you."

"Nope," I said.

"Yup," he said and dodged out the door.

I looked at the cat. He purred, which just made me angrier.

Leaving The Bean, I passed an expensive gift shop that had recently opened. Inside, I caught sight of Tony. I thought about saying hi, but for all I knew Tony could have killed Simon Sterling as easily as anyone else. I wasn't buying Bellamy's quick arrest procedurals. I decided to keep my distance, and headed toward my store.

Rather than stop inside, I jumped into my car with Tinker, and slammed the door. Then, I hit the road for my second drive to the Melville that morning. Andy and the police might be under Bellamy's orders to wrap up the case now that an arrest had been made, but there was no way I was going to let a murderer roam around my island while Bill Duffy rotted in jail for a murder he did not commit. Hell if I wasn't going to find the guy who really killed Simon Sterling.

Chapter 6

During my drive to the inn, with the wind singing through the crack in my back window, I was upset about Bill and heartbroken for Jessica, and even Joe. Then, Tinker bolted upright from a solid nap to claw at a leaf that flew by our window. I almost had a heart attack, but my furry charge reminded me that I was on the investigation team, more or less. I was an honorary member on the case, whether Andy had intended so or not. I would keep my antenna up for anything funky going on at the inn while setting up for the wedding. No one, not even the murderer, would be any wiser for it. The thought was terrifying. And irresistible.

I was early, but I wasn't surprised to see Emily had already arrived.

"This event is crazier than the Fortman wedding," she said when I pulled up beside her car in the Melville's parking lot.

"I don't know," I said as I got out of the car with Tinker in tow. "I'll never forget you chasing after that little ring bearer who decided to take off with the loot."

"OK, you're freaking me out with this cat. Where did it come from?"

"It was Simon Sterling's," I said, and remembered Frank's rule that Tinker was off-limits at the Melville.

Emily stood stock-still.

"Put it back in the car," she said, which I was already doing. "No bad omens. Jessica and Joe have had a tough enough morning. They don't need anything to remind them of Simon Sterling. What are you doing with a dead man's cat?"

"Andy made me its official minder," I said. I shoved an old beach towel I'd left on my back seat into the crack of the open window so Tinker couldn't get out. "I can now add police work to my resumé."

"Is Andy still dating that Florida woman he met last summer?" Emily said. She peered into her open trunk at a pile of boxes and picked out a couple.

"Georgianna," I said, closing the trunk and taking the boxes from her. He'd started dating her not long after Voldemort left me.

"Tan, flat stomach, always wears stripes, even the unflattering horizontal ones?" said Emily. "I'm not being unkind. She pulls them off."

"That's the one," I said. Georgianna was also obsessed with sailing, which is not Andy's thing. He's a surf caster, especially after a good storm when the blues are practically rolling in on the waves. They say opposites attract, so she was probably the one for him. I wondered if she was planning to sail in the weekend's regatta.

Emily and I walked along the crunchy dirt road toward the inn. I noticed there was only one police car parked out in front. I did not need to peer into the car to know that the officer was not from the island's police force. If he'd been one of ours, he'd be front and center, on the hunt for the real murderer, convinced of Bill's innocence. Instead, this guy was blowing on a hot coffee, and looking at his phone.

"Did you hear about Bill?" I said, as we reached the door to the inn.

Emily flared her eyes to warn me to keep any bad news outside the door. We had an event to plan.

I nodded, but I was not satisfied.

Emily looked me straight in the eyes, as if she could see something was up. I stared back with a look that said she was imagining things. I won. She opened the door.

Two steps inside, Jessica flung her arms around my friend and burst into a new flood of tears. Mrs. Sterling stood right behind her daughter. She had stopped crying. Her expression was stoic. Clearly, she was being strong for her daughter, but I noticed tight lines around her eyes.

I said hello in a casual sort of way, given that the last time we'd been together was over a dead body. I must not have been as slick as I thought because Emily whooshed her client over to a roaring fire in the hotel lobby that Frank had made sure was lit on the cold day, in spite of the madness. I could see Emily go straight to work on the psychology part of her job. I knew in a few minutes she would have Jessica filled with renewed joy at her upcoming nuptials. It was her gift.

"She's a stubborn girl," Mrs. Sterling said, watching her daughter.

I wasn't sure if she was talking to me, exactly, but I nodded along.

"The moment she set eyes on Joe, she decided he was the one," she said. "He has the charisma to sell ice to an Eskimo. Jessica thinks he's going to be a self-made man, and that they'll have a storybook life."

Mrs. Sterling looked at me. I was right. I could tell that she hadn't exactly been speaking to me. She bit her lip, then smiled.

"I guess you could say we're lucky, all things considered," she said. "The police were kind enough to let us move ahead, now that the bartender is under arrest."

"Hard to believe Bill would do that," I said.

"I trust the police know their job," said Mrs. Sterling. I assumed the pointed look she gave me was meant to telegraph the same message Emily had given me a moment before: No drama while on the wedding's turf.

I gave her a conciliatory nod. Message received.

"Let's make sure that when the guests arrive this afternoon, there's no trace of murder," she said.

"I'm not sure if I said it earlier, but I'm so sorry for your loss," I said.

"You probably think we're cold people, to have a wedding after having just lost a family member to a violent end. You should know, Simon was a stranger to Jessica."

"Did you know him well?" I asked.

Mrs. Sterling looked into my eyes but her expression cut right through me. I knew I'd have to be a little savvier to get someone like her to open up.

"Emily said that Jessica thought he would be a lovely addition to the wedding," I said. I had no idea if that was true, but I'd seen her get fired up about Simon once already, so I thought a compliment might set her off. I was right.

"Ha!" she said with excellent staccato to make her point. "She would have changed her mind in no time if she had had more time to get to know him. I know I should be playing the part of the grieving family, but what's the point? Everyone knows that I've been onto Simon's routine for years."

I took my chances and gave her a doubtful look to stir the pot. She raised an eyebrow.

"The poor man came to walk his niece down the aisle," I said. I glanced across the lobby to make sure that Emily could not see me aggravating her client's mother. Fortunately, she was still focused on Jessica, who had gone from the edge of her seat to a more comfortable position. "He must have had some redeeming qualities."

"All smoke and mirrors," Mrs. Sterling said. I seemed to have hit the jackpot, because Mrs. Sterling looked ready to hit me over the head with a candlestick if she had had one handy. "Trust me. I met Simon Sterling when I was as young as Jessica is now. We traveled in the same crowd. He had a lot of charm, loved to spend money, treat people to things, but ultimately, he was lacking in character. For one thing, he never understood the value of money. Henry, on the other hand, appreciated the value of a nickel even as a wealthy, wealthy man. We never spoiled Jessica. I fear now, however, that this is why she thinks she will be happy with Joe, but she really doesn't understand how the other half lives."

I thought we lived perfectly nicely, but I stayed focused on Simon.

"So, Simon was a big spender," I said, thinking about the card game.

"People loved him because he got others to come out of themselves, live it up, but there was always a price to pay. Once he got to know you, he'd play with you, your insecurities. One day, I was at one of Simon's parties and Henry walked into the room." Mrs. Sterling's eyes welled up. "Once Henry and I started to date, Simon was never happy unless he was toying with me. Finally, Henry and I cut ties with him. I can only imagine what he put over on the Melville's bartender to drive him to murder. Trust me, if the deceased had been anyone other than Simon, I'd have a lawsuit again the Melville in the works as we speak."

We both shuddered, but probably for different reasons.

"Jessica was hell-bent on having Simon walk her down the aisle though," she said. "Tradition and all that."

"Family, huh?" I nodded conspiratorially, but I was at a loss. There were a dozen Wrights to walk down an aisle, and we aren't big on bullying each other, as Simon seemed to have done to Mrs. Sterling.

I studied Mrs. Sterling, a woman who must have been in her late fifties, but who seemed fit for her age. I wondered if she could wield a candle with enough force to kill Simon. She probably could.

"What about the unity candle?" said Mrs. Sterling. "Can you make a new one?"

"Does Jessica want one?" I was surprised, excited, daunted.

"She doesn't want the one you designed, that's for sure," said Mrs. Sterling. "Can we come up with something a little different?"

"What are the readings at the ceremony?" The wheels were already beginning to turn away from murder and on to what I knew best.

"It's the 'to everything' one," she said and then hummed the "turn, turn, turn" chorus from the Byrds song from the '60s.

"Ecclesiastes 3," I said. I'd been to my fair share of weddings at this point, so I know this is the all-time standard. An idea began to form. "What if I make a unity wreath with four candles? One for every season? A play on the usual? And I can use the votive candles we've already made for the guests and which have the scent. As I said, I've already made extras."

"I like it," said Mrs. Sterling with genuine enthusiasm. I could tell she was happy to have a hand in an element of the wedding that her daughter had loved, in spite of her thoughts about Joe.

As we spoke, I noticed that the magic of Emily Gardner Events was already beginning to unfold. Quietly, three people from Emily's company had arrived and after a few words with Frank, they hauled in two potted fiddle leaf fig trees that they placed in front of the closed doors to the Game Room. The yellow tape that covered one end of the door to the other was promptly covered in a garland that I'd unknowingly carried in one of Emily's boxes. Next, they began to shift some of the furniture in the lobby to round out the room's new design. In no time, it was as if the Game Room did not exist. I looked over to Emily and Jessica, and I saw a flood of relief spread across Jessica's face. She sat back in her wing chair, looking as if the ugliness of the morning was some sort of nightmare she had dreamt. Emily was a genius.

"If you've got this covered, Stella, I've got some things to look into," Mrs. Sterling said, and she headed upstairs. I hoped I had not gone too far in questioning her.

I approached the fireplace and shared my candle idea delicately with Emily and Jessica.

"I like it," said Jessica immediately.

Emily smiled, and I hoped I had redeemed myself from showing up with Simon's cat.

"I'm sure my mom thinks I should reschedule the wedding after what's happened this weekend, but she doesn't realize how much time, effort, and money our friends have put into getting here," said Jessica.

I could not help think that Mrs. Sterling had done a better job than she realized about teaching Jessica how the "other half" lived.

"I was afraid Joe would be scared off, too," said Jessica, "but he's all for moving ahead. He said he's hell-bent on getting that ring on my finger so he can call me his own. There's no way we're going to let anything curse our nuptials. If we can have a new unity candle, I'll feel like it's a sign that we're unstoppable. We'll show them all we're meant to be together."

"Yes, you are," Emily said.

"Will you be able to re-create the beautiful floral design from my wedding dress on the new candles?" asked Jessica. She looked so hopeful.

"Of course," I said. The one candle had taken me five hours to decorate. I had an all-nighter ahead of me, but I smiled as if they were already done.

Jessica rose. My phone pinged and I glanced down at my texts to find a message from one of my wedding clients.

Sorry we decided not to have a unity candle after all. I'll stop by next week to pick up my refund. Sorry!!

Unbelievable. Cherry was right. Brides were superstitious. I realized that although Jessica and Joe decided it was bad luck not to move forward with the wedding, they could just as easily have decided the opposite.

"I'm going to check on my mom," said Jessica. "Emily, please call me on my cell if you need anything."

Jessica gave me her best smile, and excused herself. Emily and I headed to Ahab's where Emily's staff was at work on the rehearsal dinner and the florists were arriving. We made our way through the kitchen to our staging room.

We looked around our room, which was in complete disarray.

"Ugh," said Emily. "I guess this was the trade-off." The police had done a very thorough once-over to dust, look for clues, whatever they do. The result, however, was that our perfectly ordered setup was now a project in and of itself.

"Don't worry about my end of things," I said. I noticed that my candles were still somewhat grouped together, but I was still worried about their condition. I had a few extra candles on hand to be on the safe side, but not enough to replace the whole lot. If I hadn't been so angry when I'd left town, I'd have probably brought more.

I found my candles, and after resorting all of them into groups for the hotel décor, the rehearsal dinner centerpieces, and the boxes of scented gifts, I was relieved to see that only a couple of tapers had broken. I was lucky. Emily and I can sometimes go overboard with our organization, but today the efforts were paying off.

First things first, I placed the candles meant to decorate the hotel in a flat-bottomed basket and put candleholders in another. From there, I headed back to the public guest areas, staging my creations throughout the lobby and surrounding rooms. The work was easy. I had a diagram of where each candle would go, so it was only a matter of checking off boxes. As I graced the rooms, I tried to look for something suspicious or out of place, but I wasn't really sure what I was looking for. Everything was very tidy, immaculate, and ready for business. Like the police, I concluded the action had taken place in the Game Room, but I had no excuse at the moment to go back into the room of the crime scene.

Next, I returned to the storage room, which was becoming emptier and emptier as our decorations filled the hotel. Bits of tissue paper and scattered beads and unused vases were sprinkled about. I collected the candles that would be used for tonight's rehearsal dinner at Ahab's. The Sterlings had plans to seat about four dozen evening arrivals at round tables of ten. Emily had chosen varying shades of purple for the table clothes, punctuated with simple white flowers in tall glass vases around which I would arrange my candles.

Inside the restaurant, the tables were already set for the evening and florists were arriving. I went right to work, placing an array of tapers in purple shades with a dash of deep blues around the vases. These candles were unscented, of course. Rule number one in candles is to never have a competing scent at a dinner table. Instead, I relied on colors and heights to seduce the Sterlings' guests. Then, I laced the edges of the room with tea lights. The idea was that there would be no need for electric lighting once the evening began. We'd had a trial run about a week ago, and the effect was stunning. The room was both romantic and had the touch of history that Jessica aspired to. Plus, everyone looks great in candlelight, which always puts people in a good mood.

About an hour later, I was done with the hotel and restaurant décor, but I had not found any evidence to convict or acquit Bill. My last duty was to put the party gifts in each guest's room. Emily had already put my candles in the five rooms occupied by the Sterling-Handler party last night, but there was one room I wanted to see. I wanted a better look at Simon Sterling's room.

Chapter 7

I had originally expected to have Maude's help in delivering the votive candles to each guest's room, but we were all pitching in today with the Duffys' absence. Frank had kindly found a cart for me that would allow me to load up my candles and deliver them to all one hundred rooms in one trip. As I rolled the cart to a service elevator off the kitchen, however, I realized that without Maude I had no keys to enter the rooms. I headed out to the lobby to see if Frank could help me out.

In one motion, he handed me a master passkey from a cubby under the reception desk as he picked up a ringing phone. Frank was doing a good job keeping things together. Down two staff members this morning, the concierge looked a little haggard, but I had faith that the Melville would be good to go.

The passkey was attached to a ring that included a couple of larger, old-fashioned keys as well. I knew at least one of them was for our storage room, which was part of the original house that had not been fully upgraded. It took all of one second, but holding the batch of keys in my hand, I decided to visit all of the Sterling-Handler rooms while I had the opportunity to enter them. My cart was waiting for me when I returned, and I took the elevator up to the third floor. Arriving at the inn's top floor, I headed down the hallway, stopping in each room, one by one. At the end of the hallway, I paused in front of the suite in which Jessica was staying. Her door was right next to that of her mother's.

I pushed the cart down the hallway, then knocked on Jessica's door, to be safe. When there was no answer, I unlocked the door and crept inside.

Poor Maude. She must have left before she had tidied the room this morning. It was a mess. Clothes on a chair, bed unmade. Thinking of Maude and Bill upset me, and I looked out of the bedroom window to calm myself. I walked closer and opened the window a smidge to let in a sea breeze from the harbor. The wind, however, caught some papers on an old desk and blew them to the floor. Quickly, I closed the window and gathered the papers.

As I put them back on the desk, something caught my eye. It was a black-and-white photo of a field. On closer inspection, I realized that the trees in the image were in perfect lines, too perfect to be natural, and I decided it was of some sort of farm. I opened a folder that was also on the desk.

I'm no real estate expert, but I could see that Jessica Sterling had brought a mountain of paperwork that looked a lot like the papers I'd heard described of her father's last deal, his failed attempt to sell his olive groves in Italy. I wondered if perhaps Jessica's invitation to Simon to walk her down the aisle had been motivated by her desire to finish the deal. I did have to wonder who would get Simon's share in the land now that he was dead.

My mind was racing in all directions when I heard footsteps in the hallway and a key in the room's lock. I closed the folder, and ran to the closet so Jessica would at least find me studying her wedding dress rather than snooping through her private papers. I actually did want a look at Jessica's dress. I had pictures of it that I used to decorate the original unity candle, but I really wanted to make the new unity candles stand out. If there was a certain kind of bead or applique I had missed in the photos, I wanted the opportunity to copy it.

Two steps away from the closet, I realized that finding me admiring her dress was just as odd. Worse, Jessica might decide it was a bad omen, and Emily would be furious. I was wondering if I could fit under the bed in the time that it took to open a door when the key stopped.

"I need my sweater," Jessica said to someone.

I made a desperate dash toward the curtains, as if the old movie gimmick stood a chance.

"Take my blue one," said her mother, her voice coming from the threshold of her door. "It's better for the weather."

With that, I heard Jessica walk to her mother's room. I realized, too, that the living quarters connected through interior doors. I hoped that the women had not unlocked these doors in order to enter in and out of each other's rooms.

Creeping back across the room, I tidied the papers.

"I'm not going to lie to you, Mom," I heard Jessica say through the closed door. "Your lack of faith in me is hurtful. I've got everything covered."

"You can never be too careful," said her mother.

"We went over this yesterday," said Jessica. "We don't need to again."

I was dying to know what "this" was, but a floorboard under me squeaked as I took a step back. The women stopped talking. I could not be sure if it was because they had heard me, but I didn't wait. I tiptoed across the room and out of Jessica's front door as quickly as Tinker had fled Simon's room this morning.

Out in the hall, I ran back to my cart. Relieved that Jessica and her mom had not caught me, I resumed my walk back down the hallway to the elevator, disappointed by the fact that I had not been able to enter Mrs. Sterling's room. Overall, however, I was impressed with myself as I headed downstairs. My first bit of sleuthing had yielded a couple of results. For one, Jessica had been actively thinking about the land deal. Number two, Jessica and her mother were stressed. Given the morning that had passed and the wedding ahead their emotions were understandable, but I wondered what I should make of their words.

I realized that there were secrets in the Melville. Figuring out which ones were important might lead me to Simon's killer.

When the service elevator opened on the second floor, the first thing I saw was yellow tape over Simon Sterling's room. I made a mental note to tell Emily. There was no way we were going to have guests focusing on the fact that they were sleeping near a murdered man's room. Next to Simon's room was Joe's. I had not remembered that the two men's rooms were side by side. I slipped the passkey into Joe's lock and entered.

Similar to Jessica's room, the groom's bed was unmade. His suitcase lay half open. I peeked into Joe's trash bin. There was a tag for a new pair of socks from H&M, which I thought was a good call on his part after having seen his holey attire this morning. I also spied a note that said: *Let's meet after dinner in the Game Room?* I wondered who had written it—Simon or Tony?—and if it mattered to the murder.

On the desk, I noticed the usual stuff one would expect to see from a groom. There was a passport, cufflinks, a lightly scented pink scarf that Jessica had probably given him to think of her before bed. There was a note from a jeweler with a valuation of the ring that was so expensive I can't even repeat it . . . but there were five zeros after the number two. In my life, I never knew a piece of jewelry could be worth so much. There was no yellow tape in front of the interior door connecting Joe's room to Simon's. It was like an open invitation to enter Simon's room. I slipped the key into the connecting door.

Nothing had changed much since I'd been in Simon's room earlier. The bed was still made, Simon's suitcase was meticulously unpacked. There was only one can of cat food that I could see. I made a note of the brand so I could pick some up for Tinker. The only thing out of place was an open desk drawer.

Inside, I saw a passport. I really wanted to open it, but I was afraid of fingerprints. Beside the passport was a bag of tobacco, next to which was a set of cufflinks, a comb, some red ribbon neatly rolled, and a small bottle of hair gel in one of those 2.5ml travel bottles. I knew it was hair gel because of a handwritten sticker across it that advertised it as such. I quickly returned to Joe's room to look at the handwritten invitation to poker. The handwriting was one and the same. Simon had evidently been the one to think of playing cards last night. I thought about Mrs. Sterling's comments about Simon and his penchant for messing with people. Her description fit with Joe's, Tony's, and Bill's feeling that the game had not been played fairly. I could see how Tony or Joe might have ended up in an altercation with Simon, but not Bill. Bill had had no skin in the game. He had just been pouring drinks. Yet for some reason, Bill had taken twenty-five hundred dollars from Simon, and had punched him, while mysteriously abandoning his responsibility to take care of the candle.

I noticed that the gift box with my votive candle was shut, but I could tell from the aroma that Simon had at least peeked inside. Silly, but I hoped he'd liked my work.

Deciding that there was nothing else to see, I left his room through Joe's door and delivered the rest of my candles to the other rooms. Tony Carlson's room was the last door at the end of the hallway. I had just reached it when I got a text from Emily to meet her.

Big news, her text said.

I wavered at Tony's door. If something related to the case had been uncovered, I wanted to find out right away. The more information I had, the easier it would be for me to know what I was looking for. I headed downstairs with my empty cart, and parked it in front of our staging room. Inside, I saw Emily's feet propped against a table.

"Hello!" I said, leaving the cart outside the room. "All done. What's up?"

"I've got good stuff," said Emily from a chair. "Oh, look at my swollen feet. I've barely been working three hours. I don't know how I'm going to do the Litskys' wedding next month."

"I'll help. What's your good stuff?"

"Gina Ginelli," said Emily with full-on jazz hands.

I sat on the edge of the table, wishing I had poked around Tony's room.

"I saw her," said Emily. "In the lobby."

"Why was she here?" I said.

"I don't know," she said. "She poked her head in, smiled when I started to wave, and then left. I didn't get to take a picture. I want a picture!"

I looked at Emily's tired feet.

"I heard she's staying down the beach path," I said. "Are you up for it?"

"Are you kidding?" she said and looked at me like I was a fool to think otherwise.

"That's why I love you," I said. "Guess what?"

"What?"

"I broke into a lot of rooms." I shared my discoveries to Emily, room by room.

"I hope no one saw you," she said after I'd ended with my visit to Simon's room. "What if there really is a murderer hanging around the Melville, and he saw you? I mean, you could be in danger."

"I seriously doubt that," I said. "I was just putting my candles in the rooms, as directed."

Emily opened her mouth to disagree, but she didn't have to. Proving her point, the door to our room slammed shut, followed by the sound of the lock turning.

Chapter 8

Instinctively, I picked up an empty glass vase next to me, and held it like a baseball bat. Emily looked at me like I had seen one too many dead bodies this morning.

"Hello?" she said calmly to the whitewashed door. "Frank, we're in here."

There was no answer.

"Hello?" she said again, still polite but with a little less humor.

We heard movement on the other side of the door, but no one answered. Emily and I looked at each other, saw nothing helpful in either of each other's eyes, then looked back at the door. Emily was no longer feeling friendly. Without shifting her gaze from the door, she grabbed a bag of rice that the guests were meant to toss tomorrow night.

"Who's out there?" I said in the bravest voice I could muster. The fact that I could speak gave me some confidence. "Open the door."

No one opened the door. Instead, we heard footsteps leaving.

"What the—" Emily said to me in a whisper even though we were alone. "He left! Did he leave? He did. Unlock the door." She hugged her rice. "No, don't unlock the door. Should we unlock the door?"

"How am I going to unlock the door? The keys are on the cart outside."

"Someone took the keys and locked us in." Her eyes popped out more than her belly.

I nodded in agreement with her summary.

"The murderer?" she said.

"No," I said, worried. She needed to calm down. I feared she might go into labor.

"I'll text Frank." She looked at her phone, then at me. "What if Frank's the murderer? I'll text Andy."

"I'll get us out of here," I said.

"Don't!" said Emily, hugging her bag of rice more tightly. "OK, do. I have to finish the place cards for dinner. I am not getting paid enough."

Emily continued to speak to herself as she typed on her phone. I crossed the room, took a deep breath, and reached my hand slowly toward the doorknob like it might be covered in hot lava. My heart sank when I confirmed that the door was locked tightly from the outside and that there was no way of unlocking it from the inside.

I was about to bang on the door in hopes that someone was back from lunch to help us, when there was a thud from behind me. I spun around, afraid something had happened to Emily, but she was fine. She was sitting on her chair and pointing to the small window in the room that looked out over the back of the restaurant, to the parking lot. I held up my vase, but I saw nothing.

I walked toward the window.

"What are you doing?" said Emily. "Maybe he's trying to get in through the window to kill us."

"He locks the door and then breaks in through the window?" I said. "That's the stupidest killer alive." I lifted my vase higher. "Come on," I said to the window. Emily crouched behind me.

There was another pounce on the window. A black ball hit the pane with force, then dropped. I ran to the window and opened it.

"It's the cat," I said.

Sure enough, Tinker was below me. I made a mental note that shoving a towel into the back window was not enough to stop this mad cat. He was circling the bottom of the window, looking for another way to attack, but looked up and mewed when he saw my face.

"This is not the time," I said to him, but I now worried about my charge escaping, on top of being locked in a room.

Emily budged in next to me.

"Hey," she cried out to the police car in the parking lot. She waved her arms, but the officer in the car was still looking at his phone.

Tinker hissed. He was not pleased, and I wondered what his issue was this time. Having gotten my attention, however, he jumped onto the top of the white picket fence that separated the parking lot from the building and began to walk across its thin edge.

"I've got to go after the cat," I said to Emily.

"Don't you dare leave me here," she said with the fury of ten thousand wedding planners on a bad day.

"I'll grab the cat, then get Frank to open the door," I said, my body half out the window. Fortunately, the screens hadn't yet been installed for the summer season, but it was a bit more of a drop than I'd expected. Regaining my balance, I looked up at Emily.

"Just go," she said. "I have to go to the bathroom for the sixth time today."

"OK," I said, but I was already off and running after Tinker before she could say another word.

When I reached the end of the fence, I stopped in my tracks. Tinker was seated on the top of the fence, looking into the mid-distance in a very Gina Ginelli sort of way. I followed his gaze.

I had to give it to this cat. He had a good nose for juicy stuff. Across the parking lot, I saw Mrs. Sterling get into a rental car. I wondered if she'd heard me speaking to Emily and had locked me in. But why?

I decided to find out. Grabbing Tinker, I waited until Mrs. Sterling's car pulled out, then ran to the police car and rapped on the window. The officer looked at me with a blank stare, then opened his window. I thought about asking him to follow Mrs. Sterling while I helped Emily, it was his job after all, but what would I say? The bride's mother had left the inn? That didn't seem suspicious.

"The party planner for this weekend's wedding is locked in the storage room and I need to get going," I said. "No cats at the inn." I lifted Tinker for emphasis. "Can you let Frank know while I get this little guy out of here? Thanks."

I didn't wait for him to answer. I jumped into my car and hit the road. Watching my rearview mirror for the second time today, I was relieved to see the officer get out of his car.

Fortunately, there was only one main drag for a few miles, so I pressed hard on the accelerator and sped ahead to catch up to Mrs. Sterling. As I did, I wondered what I would do once I found her. I also realized that I was basically following the instructions of a cat, which made me feel sort of silly. No, very silly. I replayed the last few minutes and tried to put things into some sort of narrative. First, I'd been chatting rather openly, I now had to admit, to Emily about sneaking into people's rooms and snooping about. I'd spoken freely about the real estate papers I'd seen in Jessica's room, the conversation between mother and daughter, the note in Joe's trash bin, and also the contents of Simon's drawer. Then, someone had locked me and Emily in the storage room. Why? To spook us?

My phone rang. I noticed Emily's name on the screen and hit reply.

"Where are you?" she said. "We're such idiots."

"What do you mean?" I said.

"Frank opened the door," she said. "Your keys were right where you left them, but he said the door has a knack for locking on its own when it slams shut. It's one of the old locks. One of the florists was probably leaving and a draft pulled the door closed. Oh, Stella, I swear we're starting to become those paranoid kinds of people."

Ahead of me, I watched Mrs. Sterling's car.

"Are you driving?" said Emily. I knew it was a rhetorical question, and I could tell she was not happy.

"I'm dropping the cat back at the store," I said. "I'll call you from there and you can let me know if you need anything else. I should get to work on the new unity candles."

"Fine," said Emily. "I sent a text to Andy that we had a false alarm. Call me later and let me know you're OK. I don't like any of this, even if it was the wind. No more snooping around. Promise?"

"Lesson learned," I said.

"Stay cool," said Emily.

"You too," I said and hung up as Tinker sunk into the passenger seat for his nap. I was impressed by his ability to sleep after having found his master dead this morning and his new mistress locked in a room this afternoon. Very Zen.

As we headed down the road, I watched the car in front of me. Aside from driving faster than the speed limit, there was nothing unusual about the car. Mrs. Sterling's speed was understandable. She was likely behind schedule after the unexpected events this morning.

I still could not accept that Bill was the murderer, but to prove to myself that I was not being unreasonable, I considered the facts from Bellamy's perspective. After Joe and Tony had left, Simon could have made a final wager with Bill. Whatever it was, Bill had felt conned in the end. It followed that an altercation could have ensued and, accidentally, Bill could have struck and killed Simon. It was all feasible, but then I remembered the day that Maude had killed that snake. It was because Bill had been terrified it might hurt someone. Bill was not a violent man.

Mrs. Sterling's car reached the end of the road and took a right toward town. I followed her to a roundabout, but I was surprised when she passed the exit for town and circled toward one leading to the airport. I knew that Emily had an entire spreadsheet dedicated to making sure vans from the Melville would pick up all of the guests. The earliest pick up was three o'clock, but it was now only two.

I followed.

After a couple of miles, Mrs. Sterling turned right onto Airport Road. She had the lead, but when I reached the road, I took the same right turn as well. In addition to ending at the airport, the road includes a gas station on the left and a motel, The Nantucket Inn, on the right. I followed the road to the airport's entrance and swung into the parking lot, where I trolled for Mrs. Sterling's car. I saw no sign of it. I circled around to the front of the terminal, where there was space for cars to drop off or pick up passengers. Still, no sign of the Sterling's car. The Nantucket Memorial Airport has grown about ten times since I was born, but it's still a pin dot compared to most airports. If you want to find a car, you can. And I could not find this one.

At a loss, I pulled out of the airport and took a right to head back to town. I decided to get back to my store and start the candles, as I'd promised Emily. I passed the motel, and peeked into the parking lot as I was picking up speed.

Bingo.

Chapter 9

Mrs. Sterling was opening her car door by the side entrance to the Nantucket Inn. Both the Melville and the Nantucket call themselves inns, but there's no comparison. Although tidy and inviting, the airport's lodgings were nothing compared to the luxurious spread at the Melville.

I slowed down and made a U-turn, crawling to the inn's parking lot where I drove around back. When I turned off the car, however, I didn't move. I strummed the top of the steering wheel, bit my lip. Then, I took the mace out of my glove compartment, opened the car door, and headed to the lobby.

Fortunately for me, the doors to the Nantucket Inn are four wide and all paned glass, so there's a good view inside. Added to that is a nice oversized shrub by the entry, which now offered more than enough coverage so that I could lay low, rather than barge in behind the woman and scare her away from me for life. I pressed myself behind the foliage and peeked inside.

Mrs. Sterling was speaking to the concierge. I tried to make out what she was saying, but Emily is the only one whose lips I can read. The concierge was typing on his computer, looking serious. Mrs. Sterling opened her purse. She slipped the concierge what looked like money, along with a card of some sort.

At that moment, a hand slipped around my waist and I was pulled from the bushes by the arm of Andy. Before I could say a word, he put a finger over my lips.

"I'll do the talking. What are you doing hiding in a hedge?" he said.

"What are you doing finding me in a hedge?"

"It's my job to make sure people don't lurk in places they're not supposed to. Plus, I got a text from Emily and then a call on my radio that a car with your plate number was speeding away from the Melville. Listen," he said. I noticed he was still holding me. "I know it's been a rough morning, but you need to chill."

"Mrs. Sterling is inside," I said. "Why?"

"Why not?" he said. "She's hosting a wedding this weekend. Perhaps everyone is not staying at the uber-expensive Melville."

"No," I said. "I would've had instructions to drop off candles here if they had rented rooms."

"I'll pass the info to Bellamy," said Andy. "Meantime, let's get out of the hedges. I've got a major headache going on at FIGAWI. Someone had the bright idea of leaving creations made of old lobster-trap buoys around town."

"From the Lifesaving Museum?" I said. There was always a spirit of mischief that went along with our sailing event's revelry, but this was new.

The Lifesaving Museum, which was not far at all from the Melville, had started a drive during the off-season to collect old lobster-trap buoys, some wooden, some foam, in order to provide projects and activities during the summer. Lobster-trap buoys are brightly colored and small and lend themselves to creative inspiration. I'd heard a couple of towns on the Cape even made Christmas trees out of them. The museum's plan was to clean and refinish them for reuse, but right now, the project had gotten no further than an impressive pile of items people had donated that was lying on the lawn behind the museum.

"Exactly," said Andy. "People are already calling him the Buoy Bandit. The museum's supply is depleted. Meanwhile, they are popping up around town as art installations, if you can call them that. I've been combing through buoys all morning, looking for anything that might tell me who this guy is. There was one in the shape of a life preserver at Jetties Beach. Kids were climbing all over it. The parents were steaming because their kids stank."

"Then this shrubbery here is a step up for you today," I said. Maybe it was just the idea of it, but I thought Andy might be smelling a little bit like low tide. I stepped back from his arm. "I'm telling you," I said. "Something's up with these two."

Andy sighed, then looked through the lobby's window.

"Well," he said. "Whatever it was, she's gone now, probably through the back door. I know it's upsetting, what we saw this morning, and Bill being under arrest, but the police know their stuff and Bellamy is highly respected. Meanwhile, we have a thousand sailing enthusiasts on the island this weekend who deserve our care. I don't want someone to get hurt over something silly because I don't have my head in the game."

"I understand," I said.

"Promise?" Andy said.

"I've got work to do," I said. "I have to redesign the unity candle."

"You're kidding," he said. "They really want another candle? The idea seems a little cursed."

"You're not the only one with that thought," I said. "I've already had a cancellation from another wedding."

"Sorry," he said.

"By the way," I said. "If you talk to Bellamy, let him know that Jessica Sterling brought loads of papers about the failed deal between her father and Simon Sterling."

"How'd you learn this?" said Andy.

"No laws were broken," I said, and decided to leave it at that. "But given the story Mrs. Sterling told us this morning about the land, just makes me wonder if Jessica didn't feel that bygones were bygones after all."

"Let's leave the puzzling to Bellamy, OK?" Andy crossed his arms. "It's an interesting idea, but I have strict orders for the weekend and they do not include this murder. I'd get fired if anyone knew I was even poking around."

"I get it. By the way," I added. "Gina Ginelli was at the Melville this morning. I was thinking of stopping by to see how she's doing, all alone and so close to a murder scene. Who knows? She might have seen something last night."

Andy did this thing where he shifts his jaw the slightest bit so that it sort of winks at you.

"You might want to warn her about the FIGAWI crowd's fondness for going to the beach at night. In case she has visitors," I said. "I think that falls within your orders this weekend."

"You aren't going to let this go, are you?" he said.

"Give me five minutes," I said. "I just need to use the ladies' room."

I headed toward the hotel lobby as Andy climbed back into his car. When I entered the motel, I went right to the concierge desk.

"Hi," I said. "Stella Wright. I own the Wick & Flame in town."

"Oh?" said the man. He barely bothered to look up from his computer screen.

"Listen," I said. "The woman who was just in here. Can you tell me if she rented rooms here for the weekend? I'm working on the daughter's wedding and I need to know if I should drop off some gifts for their guests. I don't want to bother them though. They've had a busy morning."

The concierge shook his head.

"No," he said. "But she was looking for someone."

I wrinkled my brow.

"Who?" I said.

"A woman, but she just missed her. She checked out about an hour ago," he said. He glanced into the trash bin beside him. I peeked as well. The card I had seen Mrs. Sterling pass the concierge was a photo of a woman with henna-dyed hair and big gold hoop ear-rings. She was clearly not of the same ilk as the Ster-lings, but she had a friendly look about her. I gathered that Mrs. Sterling had given the man both the picture and some money to keep an eye out for her.

"Weddings, right?" I said.

"I guess," he said and returned to his computer screen.

I figured I'd taken enough of his time, and I didn't want Andy to pull around and see me talking to the concierge. I said thanks and headed outside where I popped back in my car and pulled up behind Andy's patrol car. Following his lead, we headed back toward the Melville.

When we reached the inn, instead of pulling ahead to the parking lot, Andy took a right down a dirt road toward the harbor. There were a few cottages scattered here and there, and Andy's car slowed. I pulled up beside one with a light blue car parked in the small driveway. Tinker had no interest in this part of the day, so I left my motor running with the heat on so he could nap in peace. I hoped the warmth would be a better incentive to stay in the car than my towel had been.

"I've only got five minutes," said Andy when I got out. "I need to head over to Bartlett's Farm. The line outside of Cisco Brewery is getting too long."

He knocked on the door. I thought how Emily was going to kill me for coming here without her.

There was no answer.

Andy knocked again.

"Looks like you're out of luck," he said. "You'll have to find an excuse to meet her some other way. Just make sure I don't have to arrest you in the process."

"That's ridiculous," I said. "Other than the time Emily and I broke into that hot tub, when have you ever had to arrest us?"

I hated to leave without some story to tell Emily, so I reached over the bush beside the door and peered into the window. It's not like I thought I'd see Gina Ginelli's Academy Award on the kitchen counter, but I thought there might be something colorful to share.

I grabbed Andy's arm, and didn't let go. Without saying a word, I pointed through the window. Without needing to say a word back, he began looking for an open door or window.

Lying on the sofa was Gina Ginelli, her eyes closed. Like a tableau from one of her films, her body languished across the furniture. One arm was raised above her head. The other was draped to the floor. And in the hand of that arm, she held a gun.

Chapter 10

"Miss Ginelli?" Andy banged on the door. "Police." He turned to me. "Get in the car, Stella."

"As if," I said.

He didn't have a chance to lecture me further, because the door opened.

Gina Ginelli greeted us in a chiffon kaftan. It was covered in a matching flowy robe, but it was still too flimsy for the day. Her hair blew on cue, and I swear there was a tear in her eye. Well past fifty, she had full and dewy skin, high cheekbones that still held up her face, yet she didn't look like she'd had plastic surgery. I was distracted from her beauty, however, because she was still holding her gun. Andy's hand was on his hip and ready to draw.

"May I help you?" she asked, sounding brave and noble.

She lifted the gun. I ducked, but I was surprised to feel Andy's shoulders relax.

"No need for the police," she said with a small laugh. "I was just practicing lines for a new movie."

She waved the prop gun. "Looks pretty convincing, doesn't it?"

"Can we come in?" I said.

"I'm sorry," she said. "I'm working right now. Maybe another time?"

"Sorry to bother you, ma'am," said Andy. He took a step backward, as if to leave, but I wasn't going to let this opportunity pass me by.

"Given that your role includes a gun," I said, "I bet you could benefit from some insights from the police."

Andy said nothing, but the look he gave me was less than subtle. He had other things to do today than train a movie star.

Gina rubbed her chin with her gun.

"All right," she said. "Come in."

Before Andy could object, she turned and walked into the cottage. I let out a giggle that would make a teenaged girl die of embarrassment.

"I thought it was real," I said.

Gina fell onto the sofa and patted the cushion next to her. I wasn't sure if the overture was for me or Andy, but I sat. Gina's cottage was small but charming. The first floor was an open loft with a kitchen and seating area. Stairs led up to a bedroom, whose door was visible from an open landing. It could have been a set for a stage.

"And you are?" she said to me, laying her gun down.

"Oh, I'm Stella Wright," I said, dying. "I make candles in town."

"I love candles," she said with so much warmth that I felt right at home.

The first thing I noticed now that I was up close and personal with Gina Ginelli was a faint but distinct fragrance. Bergamot with a touch of vanilla and something else. When we became better friends, I would ask her. It would make a good scent. The Ginelli. I'd sell out in seconds.

"I suppose you're wondering what I'm doing alone in this cottage in the middle of nowhere," said Gina. "I'm preparing for a new film. It takes place in a remote part of Scotland, so I wanted someplace isolated, cold, and foggy to get into the part."

"What's the movie about?" I asked. I was not too pleased at her description of my island, but I couldn't resist asking.

"It's a mystery," she said with such mystery that I was already hooked. "A murder mystery."

"Really?" Andy said. He had been quiet until now, but suddenly he looked interested.

She countered his interest with an almost mocking smile.

"Indeed," she said. "Looks like my choice to come here was fortuitous, wouldn't you say?" She winked at him and I felt my eyes widen in surprise.

"Why do you say that?" said Andy. He seemed unflustered by the wink. I wondered if police officers were often winked at.

"Because now I have a wonderful story to tell when I'm on the film's junket. That's when the lead actors of a film do a series of interviews before the film opens."

"And what will that story be?" said Andy. "I heard you stopped at the Melville this morning. Was it to inquire about the murder?"

I knew Andy wouldn't be able to resist a few questions once I got him here.

"Officer, I can see you know what goes on in this town," said Gina. "I heard about your murder down the road this morning, and I wanted to check it out. Here I am, studying for the role of an investigator on an isolated island, who needs to discover who killed a man in his study. And I wake up this morning to find out there was a dead body at the inn. I know I sound crude, but the timing was fantastic. Can I get either of you something to drink?"

"No, thank you." said Andy. He gave me the slightest glance, but it was enough that I could tell he didn't want me to take a drink either.

I shook my head to decline the offer. It was hard though. I really would have loved to accept a drink from Gina Ginelli.

"Stella was correct," said Gina. "I could use a little help from someone on the local police force. You know, for some tips about how small-town police work, on an island and all. Maybe some information about the murder last night?"

"I'm not at liberty to discuss the crime at the Melville," said Andy. "Stella and I came by to let you know that there's an event on the island this weekend." He described FIGAWI to her. "You should be aware that the revelers can sometimes spill onto the beach at night."

"Wonderful," she said. "I might join them for a skinny dip. There's nothing better than ice-cold water on the skin, under the moonlight. Am I right?"

She had the tact to turn to me for an answer, but I was torn about Gina Ginelli at that moment.

"Were you practicing a sad scene?" I asked.

Gina looked confused.

"You looked like you were crying when we . . ." I stopped. I didn't want to tell her I was peeking through her window. "When you opened the door."

"You are a very perceptive reader of human emotion," she said. I thought she was right. "I was practicing a moment from my script where my character finds out she has been betrayed by the man she loves."

"So sad," I said.

"It is," said Gina. She patted my hand.

"I hope we didn't bother you," said Andy. He shifted to indicate that our visit was over.

"You didn't at all," said Gina, rising.

I took her cue, no film pun intended, and rose as well.

Andy opened the door. Tinker stood outside as if he'd knocked and was expecting us to open it. I didn't even bother, at this point, to pick him up or even worry.

"Well, look at this little creature," Gina said to Tinker. Even the cat seemed to know a celebrity when he saw one. He purred and rubbed himself in circles around her feet.

"Sorry about that," said Andy. He scooped up Tinker, and handed him to me.

"No worries," she said. "I love animals."

After a little more gushing from me, Gina closed the door, and we headed back to our cars.

"OK," said Andy. "I hope you got Mrs. Sterling and Gina Ginelli out of your system. From now on, no more nosing about Simon Sterling's death. Deal?"

"I think you have a new friend," I said. "Hope your girlfriend doesn't mind."

"I'm sure Georgianna could take on Gina Ginelli," said Andy. "And, I can't help it if I'm irresistible."

"You are so lame," I said and opened my car door. "See you."

"See you," he said.

I knew if I did not see Emily right now, to tell her about my encounter with Gina Ginelli, she would never forgive me. As Andy pulled past me, I motioned for him to stop. He lowered his window. I lowered mine.

"Hang on a sec," I said, and fussed around the front seat as if something important was happening in my car.

"What's wrong?" he said.

"Hold him for a moment?" I said and passed Tinker to him. "I need"—I feigned a look at the passenger floor—"um, hold on." I then looked up and smiled. "Thanks," I said and sped away before Andy could hand Tinker back to me. No offense to the cat, but he was off-limits at the Melville.

It only took a minute rattling down the dirt road to get to the Melville. Frank was outside when I pulled up. He was delivering hot coffee to the police officer designated to watch the inn. I figured that when a police car is parked beside a group of new guests arriving at your inn, you make sure the officer at least has a smile on his face. I was both impressed with Frank and, once again, disappointed in our visiting police.

Frank tapped the roof of the car and said goodbye as I headed to the inn's entrance. He and I reached the front door at the same time.

"Hi! Do you know where Emily is?" I asked him.

"She left for the airport about five minutes ago," said Frank. "Everything looks great and some of the guests have arrived. She wanted to put up a welcome sign with balloons at the airport though. Apparently, a group of arrivals didn't see the van and they're en route in a taxi. Emily felt bad. Ah, here they are."

"Let me get the door for you," said a voice behind me as Frank dashed toward a taxi pulling up.

I turned around to find a man about my own age with messy blond hair that fell over his shockingly blue eyes. I noticed that unlike the new arrivals who were unloading several bags from the trunk of their taxi, he was traveling light. He only had a backpack slung over his shoulder. He must have noticed me trying to figure him out because he extended his hand.

"I'm Peter Bailey. I moved here about two weeks ago to work at the Inky Mirror." The Inky Mirror is the affectionate name for the island's weekly newspaper, the *Inquirer & Mirror*.

"Stella Wright," I said, taking his hand.

"The Wick & Flame," he said. "I've heard about your store."

My phone buzzed a text, but I let it go without a glance.

"You've walked into quite a scoop, haven't you?" I said.

"I think I did," he said. Perhaps it was the drama of Gina Ginelli still surrounding me, but I had a flash of surfing the waves and biking the island with this man during the summer months ahead.

"I'll have your bags brought to your room," said Frank as he pushed through us to open the door for the new arrivals. When the door closed, he turned to Peter. "Listen, I'm sure you want to work on your story for next week's edition, but I can't let you in here right now, poking around, asking questions. We have a wedding tomorrow, guests arriving, and we're down a couple of hands."

"I get it and I'm sorry about Bill Duffy," said Peter. "Were you close?"

Frank flashed his eyes, opened the door, and went inside. Through the open door, I noticed an older couple, likely friends of Mrs. Sterling's, who were demanding a room with a view. They clearly did not understand that every room had a view at the Melville.

"Timing is everything," I said when the door closed.

"Was I too pushy?" said Peter, folding his arms. "When I'm on a case, I'm like a hound on the trail."

"You're on a case?" I said, trying not to let his hound metaphor throw me.

"A good reporter looks at any story like a case," he said. "I'm like a policeman, but with a pen instead of a gun."

I liked the imagery. I agreed, except I replaced "good reporter" with "whip-smart candlemaker."

"Do you have a lot of experience reporting on crimes?" I said.

A broad smile spread across Peter's face.

"This is my second," he said. "The first one was practice."

I knew we'd probably overstayed our welcome on the Melville's stoop, but I found that Peter Bailey interested me on many different levels.

"It didn't go too well?" I said.

He shrugged and put his hands in his pockets in a way that suggested he hadn't lost much sleep over his setback. I liked his spunk.

"My specialty is obituaries, weddings, and community interest," he said. "Unfortunately, the Sterling-Handlers gave me their wedding announcement last week. I have no excuse to interview them today. That's why I thought I'd try Frank."

"It's a good idea, but maybe focus on other angles until someone at the Melville is ready to talk," I said.

"I've been looking into Simon Sterling," he said.

"Obituary?" I asked.

He nodded.

"Did you find out anything interesting about him?"

"Sounds like you're on your own case," said Peter.

"I don't think Bill Duffy killed that man."

Peter smiled approvingly.

"I haven't got much on Simon Sterling. Although I heard he'd applied for Italian citizenship."

"He owned land there," I said, wondering how Peter had gotten his scoop. "Olive groves. Maybe he was trying to rebuild the business."

"Maybe," he said. "If I hear anything interesting, I'll let you know."

"Thanks," I said. "And don't worry about Frank. This is a small town. Bellamy might move at the speed of light, but a lot of people here don't. You'll come to love or hate it, probably by about February."

"Point taken," he said. "By the way, do you give interviews? How about something on the Wick & Flame? Look at it as a community interest story."

He pulled from his pocket a business card and handed it to me. I wondered if he was really interested in the store, or if he thought it might be a way to get me to talk about the murder weapon. Then I thought about the canceled order for one of my unity candles.

I decided to take the risk. If brides were as superstitious as Cherry said they were, I wouldn't mind an interview. I could use some good press after this morning.

"OK," I said. I checked my watch. "I have to get back to my store, but can you meet me there? I can give you the grand tour."

"Great," he said.

A moment later, I was looking through my rearview window once again, this time to make sure Peter was following me. I'd just met Gina Ginelli, and now a newcomer to town was going to interview me about my candles. Hopefully I could show Peter Bailey that my candles were newsworthy for more than being a murder weapon.

Chapter 11

Town was now packed. Great for business, but bad for parking. When I finally found a spot at the bottom of Main Street, I made my way up the brick sidewalks, looking for Peter. As I reached the corner of my street, I noticed two guys seated on one of the sidewalk benches. A tree slightly blocked them, but I knew their large feet anywhere.

"Stell*aaaa*," said my cousin Docker as I approached. Docker had been on the crew for a middle school play once, *A Streetcar Named Desire*, and now he loved to greet me like Stanley Kowalski. He and his brother now run a rubbish removal business. They bought their second truck last year.

"We heard you were at the Melville when they found the body this morning. Are you OK?" said his brother, Ted.

At that moment, my cousins Liz and Kate came dashing out of the real estate office on the corner.

"Why didn't you answer my text?" Liz said to me.

Liz is a real estate broker at the office she'd just left, and Kate, her sister, is a nurse in the Emergency Room at the Cottage Hospital. Liz looked ready for business, lipstick applied, her keys hanging from a ring on her pants, but Kate looked a little worse for wear. I had a feeling she'd had a long shift at the hospital and would be heading home to bed after a coffee with her sister.

"There was a lot to do at the Melville," I said. "There's no way Bill killed that man." I could not share my feelings about Bill's innocence while at the inn, and I had to be careful with Andy, who'd made his feelings clear about my interest in the case, but with my family I felt free to speak my mind.

"Are we sure?" said Docker. "He's a skinny guy, but have you ever arm wrestled with him? He's stronger than he looks."

"He didn't do it," said Ted. "He's married to Maude. She's no dope. No way she'd marry a murderer."

"Kate, did you hear or see anything at the hospital when they brought in Simon's body?" I said.

Kate adjusted her eyeglasses.

"The body was heliported off-island almost immediately after arriving at the hospital," she said. "But everyone got a little distracted, because Gina Ginelli came in shortly after and asked if she could see a nurse about a splinter. Everyone wanted to help her. I don't know why. She's just a celebrity."

"She's Gina Ginelli," I said. "That's why." I was bursting to tell everyone about how I had just met her, but I used tremendous willpower to stay focused. "So, you saw nothing?"

"No, I saw stuff. While everyone was gawking over Ginelli, I peeked at his body and his chart."

"You're awesome," Docker said to Kate. "She's got those serious round glasses, and then she's like, cool, a dead guy."

"Actually, there isn't really anything to tell," Kate said. "He's in his midfifties. He had been dead for about five to seven hours when he arrived. He had a tattoo of a bell on his shoulder that looked new. Chart said death due to blunt force trauma. That was about it."

"Well," I said. "That's something." I realized he died sometime between two and four. Maude had said Bill wasn't in bed until three fifteen a.m. Ugh. That was enough time for him to have been the murderer.

"But the wedding's still on, so that's good," said my cousin Liz, always one to find a bright side to things.

"Have you guys heard anything about the murder?" I said to Docker and Ted.

"Nah," they said.

"We've been hauling off buoys," said Ted. "The Buoy Bandit."

"I saw the cluster of red ones on the very top of Main Street," said Liz. "That's bizarre, by the way."

"It's a pain in the you-know-what," said Docker, nodding proudly at his discretion since Kate forbade all cursing.

"My friends down at the dock swear they saw a motorboat loaded with buoys yesterday," said Ted. "It was funny because they were piled so high they couldn't make out the driver. At the time, they assumed he might be heading out to the Lifesaving Museum for a drop-off. Now they wish they'd paid more attention."

Behind Ted and Docker, a horn beeped.

"Hey," said Chris. His wife, Suzie, sat beside him. In their back seat were several bags that I knew were filled with supplies for their annual Memorial Day cookout. The party was planned for tomorrow afternoon in their backyard.

"We've been worried about you," Suzie said to me.

At that moment, Peter crossed the street. There's

nothing like a family reunion when you're on your way to meet a guy. And they wonder why I'm not married.

He joined the crowd. I hate to say I blushed, but I did. Almost thirty and I'm blushing. It had been a long time since that had happened.

"This is Peter Bailey," I said, introducing him to each of my cousins. Liz, always in search of potential real estate customers, gave him her card when she realized he was the new guy at the Inky Mirror.

"Nice to meet you all," Peter said. "Nothing like meeting the family."

He winked at me. The gang took a moment to nod in approval, as if he couldn't see.

"Stella's granted me an interview about her store," he said.

"Thank God. She could use the good press," said Liz.

Kate flashed her a look.

"OK then," I said, hoping to avoid any discussion about my candles and bad luck. "See you all later."

Peter and I started to turn the corner to my store, but I had the feeling that something was following me. I turned to find Chris and Suzie in their car behind me.

"Stella," said Suzie from her window. She waved me over. "I'll put him on the list for our cookout tomorrow." Suzie is almost as bad as Emily when it comes to finding me the perfect man.

I smiled as graciously as I could and entered my store. The first thing I noticed was that my unity candle display was missing. I raised my eyebrows to Lucy.

"Cherry and I thought it was bad karma," she said. "But I can put it back if you want."

The empty spot where my candle had been proudly on display gave me yet another reason to want this murderer behind bars. I wondered if Peter could give me some information that could put me on the right path to solving Simon's murder.

"Let's help each other," I said to Peter as I headed to the counter and poured two cups of tea.

"What do you mean?" said Peter. He walked behind the counter and took a sugar from my tea stand as if he'd been there a million times before.

"You tell me what you know about the Sterling murder," I said. "I'll tell you anything you want to know about my candles."

Peter smiled, and took out a notebook from his shirt pocket.

"OK. Me first. When did you first decide you wanted to be a successful businesswoman?"

I liked the sound of that. I told Peter about my store, and a little about my life. A couple of customers came and went. Peter waited while I helped them find a candle. It was easy to talk to him about myself, but I still had a murderer I wanted to catch.

"Enough about me," I said. "I'm sure Frank wasn't your first attempt at gathering information about the murder. What can you tell me?"

"First things first," he said. "Have you seen the view from Tupancy Links?"

"Like, when I was in eighth grade," I said. "That's where the little kids fly kites and people walk their dogs." I didn't want to tell him that the area was also the middle school version of Lover's Lane. In reality, we would kick the sandy dune, whisper to each other about who liked whom, that sort of thing. Once, we had a game of spin the bottle there, too, but we all scattered when someone arrived, walking their dog.

Peter looked out the window.

"Want to go fly a kite?" he said with a ridiculous grin.

"No, I don't have time," I said. "I have a store to run and a new unity candle to make for a wedding tomorrow."

"Jessica Sterling still wants a unity candle from you?" said Peter.

"Yes, she wants a unity candle from me!" I said. "Why is that so hard for everyone to imagine?"

"Well, you did create a murder weapon," said Lucy.

"Maybe you should be advertising to a new clientele," said Peter.

I took a breath and tried not to laugh. My crumbling new line of business was not a laughing matter, but I did have a vision of the lowlifes in our community coming in to smell my scents and pick out creepy, weapon-inspired candle designs.

"I guess it's a better idea to talk about murder victims outside of my store," I said.

"The Sunken Ship is having a sale," said Lucy. The Sunken Ship is down the road from my store. They sell baseball caps and T-shirts and toys. And kites.

"That they are," said Peter. "I'll get one of the shark kites I saw in the window this morning, and I'll meet you at my car in ten. Oh," he said, looking at the day's featured candle that was still burning brightly from this morning. "And I'd like to buy this candle."

"You drive a hard bargain," I said. "But take this one." I handed him a different candle. "You're more of a musk and sandalwood guy, I think."

"All right then," he said, looking slightly lost but flattered. "Musk it is."

I had a good parking spot and I was tired of my back window not working, so I joined Peter in his car ten minutes later.

When we pulled up to Tupancy Links, I had to wonder why we'd stopped going as kids. The land, which used to be a private nine-hole golf course, had been donated to the island decades ago. Now, it was a rolling grassland favored by dog walkers. There were four chocolate Labs running about the field. Their two owners were throwing sticks and the dogs were chasing them. I guessed they had been cooped up this morning when the weather had been so cold, and now, they were lapping up the fresh air.

Peter had his shark kite up and running in no time. He had also bought one for me. A bomber plane. I hadn't flown a kite since my mom and I had raced each other up and down the beach one September weekend after school had started when I was about seven or eight. Since I'd left for college, my mom had taken off to resume her worldly travels, and I sometimes missed those impulsive outings she'd plan.

"Race you," I said.

"From where to where?" said Peter.

I looked across the empty field that ended on a high cliff over the harbor.

"From here to that tree," I said and pointed across the field. "And be careful of the dog poo."

We placed our kites on the ground in front of us.

"One, two, three," I said and started to run.

The wind was still hearty and my kite took off immediately. I was off and running across the field in no time. The wind whipped through my hair. I knew it would look like a hornet's nest when I reached the finish line, but the exercise felt great after the day I'd had and something about a kite in my hand gave me a feeling I could do anything. I let out a cheer, and relished the fact that everything about it was the opposite of Mrs. Sterling's scream this morning. My cry was one that said, "watch out world."

Behind me, the four dogs barked wildly. I turned around to see if they were joyfully following my lead.

They were not.

"Crap," I said, out of breath. I stopped running and watched the scene behind me as my kite smacked into the tree that was our finish line.

Peter had not had the same joyful run as I'd had. Rather than follow me, the dogs had tackled him to the ground as they'd tried to catch his kite. The animals were now wildly entangled in his kite strings. Their owners were running toward him with unhappy faces.

I watched as Peter frantically untangled the dogs as their barks turned to growls. The moment Peter freed them, he dashed across the field toward me with the dogs, once more hot on his trail. Peter waved his hands for me to run. Where, I could not say, but he surprised me by leaping onto the tree and shimmying up its trunk. Not easy. These are pitch pine trees. Not the kind you decorate for Christmas, but not your typical climbing tree either.

"Come on," he said. He reached a hand down to me from a tree limb.

I knew that two of the dogs were over ten years old and wouldn't make it across the field, but Peter's fear was comically overkill. I reached up to grab his hand, and with a good initial pull, I was able to get my footing to join him.

"I hate dogs," he said. He peeked through the branches to confirm he had escaped. The dogs' owners were busy putting leashes on them and looking at us like we were crazy. Peter's kite was picked up by the wind and disappeared over the horizon.

There was one main branch at climber's height and we were both standing on it. Unfortunately, our combined weight was a lot for the branch and I noticed it was beginning to crack. Peter noticed it, too, and jumped to a branch above us that looked much stronger. As he did, our tree limb cracked. In a moment, I felt my perch disappear. I was sure I was about to plummet to the ground. It was a sort of slo-mo experience, where I was thinking about what part of me was about to break as I was processing what was happening.

Slapping me back into the moment, however, was Peter's tight grip on my hand, which I guess I'd waved above my head in fear as I'd started to fall. The next thing I knew, I was dangling from his hand as he sat on the limb above.

"Pull up your feet," he said.

"Are you crazy?" I said. "Drop me."

"You'll hurt yourself." He had a point. "Come on. You can do it. Pull your feet up."

I took a breath. My hand was getting sweaty, so I didn't have a lot of time to debate the pros and cons. I looked up to Peter, and decided I could reach the branch.

Part of my amazing feat most definitely had to do with the fact that I didn't want to look any more ridiculous than I already did. I miraculously pulled my feet above my head. Next thing I knew, they were looped around the limb. With a little more help from Peter, I was upright on a thicker, stronger branch.

"So," I said, wiping a leaf from my hair and pulling it back into what I hoped was some semblance of order.

"So," said Peter, looking proud of me. "I've never given an interview in a tree before."

"How are we going to get back down?" I asked. Now

that the branch below us had broken, we were high up with little way of lowering ourselves.

"We'll figure something out," he said. Peter looked down to assess the situation, but he didn't look particularly concerned.

At that moment, my phone pinged a message from Andy.

Thanks for caring about the murder, by the way. I just don't want to have to come save you, too, he said.

I responded:

Please bring a rope and meet me at the large tree at Tupancy Links.

I hit send and hoped Andy was nearby.

"Here," said Peter, clearing some branches by the tree trunk, where one of the curvy limbs was widest. "This should be a comfy seat."

It was. With the branches fanning around us and the midafternoon sun peeking through a cloud, I wasn't too cold either. As I settled into my nest, I noticed Peter reach into his pocket and pull out, of all things, his notebook.

"My turn. Where did you work before this?" I asked.

"Alaska," he said. "Small paper, small town. I like small towns."

"Why'd you leave?" I asked, wondering if he, too, got the small-town February blues.

"I'm not sure the story would impress you," said Peter.

"I'm up a tree with you. I'm fairly sure nothing will shock me."

"Fair enough," he said. "I got caught breaking in to the mayor's house looking into a story my paper had not sanctioned. I thought the mayor was up to some no-good business, and I wanted to check it out before pitching the idea. The police found me. They asked the paper to corroborate my story, which they could not. The rest is history."

"Your first investigative report," I said.

Peter smiled proudly.

"Were you right?" I said. "About the mayor?"

"As a matter of fact," he said. "They asked the guy who replaced me to look into the story and sure enough, I was right. That's how I got the job here. Otherwise, I'd have had to find a new profession. Close call."

"Why doesn't that surprise me?" I said, looking to the ground far below me.

"If you don't mind my asking, what was it like to see Simon Sterling on the ground?"

I thought a moment.

"It was ugly. I watched everything as if it were a movie."

"What did your candle look like?"

"The break was pretty clean. The wick held the two pieces together," I said. Immediately, I regretted the detail and decided to change the angle of my story. "My candles were hand designed with a signature scent for the couple. They are one-of-a-kind and highly sought after by people getting married. In fact, I have orders for seven candles this summer." So, I fudged. Peter did not need to know that my orders were dropping.

"What was everyone doing after they saw the body?" Peter said.

I knew it was my turn to ask the questions, but I described the scene to him. Jessica and Mrs. Sterling on the floor, talking about her father. Joe running in to comfort Jessica. Tony and Bill behind him. I left out the fact that Maude fainted.

"What did Bill do?"

"Nothing at all suspicious," I said. "He comforted Maude."

"Yet he's a killer," said Peter.

"That's ridiculous," I said. "Have you met Bill? He's salt of the earth."

"I hear he gambles."

"Bill does not gamble," I said.

"You wanted me to tell you what I know," said Peter. He flipped the pages of his notebook. "He gambles. The police told me he went to Gambler's Anonymous."

"How do they know that?" I said, still incredulous.

Peter shrugged. "Someone on the police force gave him a ride one day, I think."

I leaned my head against the tree. I wondered if having a gambling problem and serving drinks during the poker match might have been too much for Bill to handle. I could see how Bill might have made a wager, lost unfairly to a con man, and then lost his temper. I still could not believe he'd intended to murder Simon, but the evidence against him was growing. I decided right then that I needed to speak with Bill before I took another step forward.

Chapter 12

"Stella?" I heard my name echo across the field. I pulled the branches in front of me aside and saw Andy walking across the field, holding a rope and looking confused.

"We're rescued!" I said to Peter.

"Yay," he said, not looking entirely pleased.

"Over here," I said. I shook the branches so Andy could see some sign of life.

Andy stopped as if he were not sure what he was seeing. I rattled the branch and shouted again.

He shook his head and headed our way.

"What are you doing?" Andy started, but stopped when he saw I was not alone.

"Peter Bailey," said Peter with a wave. "I've just started at the Inky Mirror. First story I'm going to write is about the rabid dogs who chased us up this tree."

Peter might have expected a laugh, but he didn't get one. Andy folded his arms.

"Just throw me the rope," I said.

"Don't forget the kite," Andy said.

I looked above me and noticed my bomber kite lodged above.

"I can't reach it," I said.

Andy threw the rope to me, which I caught. Peter pulled at the kite strings.

"She's right," he said. "It's pretty well tangled."

"Figure it out," said Andy. "Can't let kite strings fly into the harbor. They get wrapped around the seagull's legs."

I felt really bad for the seagulls when I thought about Peter's kite that had flown away. Peter must have, too, because he reached above him and pulled hard to release mine. I secured the rope Andy had thrown us around the tree limb and tied it tightly.

"Go," I told Peter.

"After you," he said and gallantly handed the rope back to me.

"I'm busy with actual work down here," said Andy. "Hurry up, please."

I shimmied to the ground and Peter followed right behind me.

"This makes sense," said Andy when we'd landed. "I got a call from Mrs. Hendricks that two drunken FI-GAWI partiers had attacked her dog. She's down at the station right now. Stella, perhaps you'd like to explain the situation to her. I guess she didn't recognize you with the kite and all. She's pretty upset. You know Bitters has a bad hip."

"I know," I said and pulled another leaf from my hair.

"I didn't see your car in the lot," said Andy. "I'll give you a lift."

"Thanks," I said, and I meant it. I was really happy

that Andy had offered me the chance to calm down Mrs. Hendricks. I didn't need another bad story attached to my name today and he knew it.

"You two know each other?" said Peter.

"Everyone knows each other," I said. With both men on either side of me, I wished, for once, I did not live on a small island. That made no sense and I knew it. Andy was a friend. A friend with a girlfriend. Nonetheless, the moment was odd.

"I'll call you later," said Peter before I got into Andy's car.

"Stella has a boyfriend," said Andy when he closed his own door.

I smiled a silly grin, and looked out the window. The weird moment had passed. And he was right. I was definitely on my way to something with Peter Bailey. I also realized I was on my way to Bill Duffy's new lodgings.

A few minutes later, I was in the police headquarters on mid-island, face-to-face with Mrs. Hendricks. She gave me a hard time for a little while, because she likes to be that way, but in the end, we left as friends and she was even laughing a little at my expense. I did not mind. I'd rather have a comical story about me than one in which I'm a vandal.

Our interview took place in a small conference room. Once Mrs. Hendricks had assured me she would not press any charges against me or Peter, she asked Andy for an escort to her car. She used to be his piano teacher and apparently, he did her favorite rendition of Ode to Joy. He flashed me a look that told me to stay put because he wasn't done with me. I nodded.

The moment they left, however, I opened the conference door and looked down the corridor to the jail cells. Usually they are empty. Once in a while, they have a visitor. When they do, the prisoners are usually left alone in their cells. Today, however, a policeman stood guard in front of the hall. The man was big; he was missing a front tooth. He wasn't the kind of guy you would ever want to meet in a dark alley.

"Psst," I said in his direction.

The guy smiled a big gappy smile at me.

"Hiya, Stella," he said.

"Hi, Ace. How's Bill?"

He shook his head, sadly.

"Not good," he said. "I think he was crying."

"Let me see him," I said. I still had one foot in the conference room in case Andy returned. Unless I was able to get in, I wasn't going to risk getting in trouble again today.

"I can't," Ace said.

"Yes, you can," I said. "Come on."

"Bellamy's orders," said Ace. "He said only Bill's lawyer can see him."

"Who's his lawyer?" I was no lawyer, but I'd taken a freshman Intro to Law class in college. I wondered if that counted for something.

Ace shrugged.

"He hasn't called anyone yet."

I walked down the hall.

"If Bellamy asks," I said, "tell him I was pitching for the job. Let me in."

"You're a hoot, Stella," said Ace, smiling. Ace is always so easily amused. He opened the cell and let me in, but Bill did not move. He lay in a fetal position on his cot, his back toward me.

"Bill," I whispered. "It's Stella Wright. You OK?"

He turned and squinted at me.

"Stella?"

"How're you doing?" I said, and sat beside him.

The jail cell was probably pretty nice compared to most, but its steel bench, cold bars, and bare, windowless walls gave me the creeps.

Bill sat up and rubbed his head.

"How's Maude?" he said.

"She'll be better once we get your name cleared and get you out of here," I said.

Bill stared at his feet and didn't say a word.

"Bill," I said with a pit in my stomach. "You didn't kill that guy, right?"

He took a deep breath, and looked at me with the most uncomfortable expression.

"I'm not without sin," said Bill as my blood froze, "but I didn't kill that guy."

"Of course you didn't," I said, feeling a little light-headed. "But why'd you have his money on you?"

"Just because the bastard had a bad ending, I shouldn't stand up for what's mine?" he said.

"What's yours?" I asked.

"I can't say," he said. He dropped his head in his hands.

"Tell me what happened, Bill," I said.

"What happened is that I made a deal with the devil," said Bill through some tears, "and now I'm paying for it."

I lent him my sleeve, which he took to dry his eyes.

"Stella," he said. "I'm going to tell you something, and you need to promise me you won't tell a soul."

"That's asking a lot," I said.

"I'm in a tough spot," he said.

I felt like that was the understatement of the century, but I held my tongue and waited for him to continue.

"Last night," he said. He exhaled deeply. "Last night."

He looked at me desperately. "I love my wife more than I love my own life."

"I know."

"She's a better woman than I've ever been a man. And all I've ever wanted to do is make her happy and proud of me. But, Stella, I'm a flawed guy."

I wasn't sure where he was going with this.

"Last night, I broke every promise I've ever made to Maude."

"Oh jeez, Bill," I said. "There's another woman involved?"

"No!" Bill shouted at me with the first sign of fight in him I'd seen yet. "Jesus, Stella. Aren't you listening to what I'm saying?"

"Who knows what you're saying, Bill? You're making no sense. What happened last night? Just spit it out."

"Fine," he said. "Last night, before that jerk Sterling and the other two—who seem like perfectly nice guys—started to play cards, Sterling approached me. He made me a deal."

"Go on." I felt like we were about to make some headway and I didn't want him to stop.

"He suggested I, you know." Bill clenched his fists and banged them on the bench. They echoed.

"I don't know. What was the deal, Bill?" I was afraid I was about to lose him.

"The table the guys were at was round, you know? And from where I was pouring, I could see the hands of Joe and Tony."

He gave me a meaningful look and sat back. I could tell he was relieved to have shared the information with another human being.

"Not that easy," I said. "I need the whole story."

Bill closed his eyes.

"He told me he'd give me half of his winnings if I'd give him a nod when one of the guys was bluffing."

"You helped Simon cheat at cards?" I said.

"Yes, I did."

Now I really was confused. Bill the Cheater. Was this the same guy who had answered an emergency call during Thanksgiving one year to fix our oven?

"The guy was persuasive. He was so good with words," said Bill in his defense. "It wasn't gambling, but I felt I was somehow in on the game. Before I really thought it through, I'd agreed. See, Maude and I are about to celebrate our twenty-fifth wedding anniversary. She's had her eye on one of those gold lightship basket brooches with a diamond in it. The one they sell at the jewelry store down by Aunt Leah's Fudge."

"Jewel in the Sea."

"That's the one," said Bill. "I realized that if I helped him, I'd be able to buy it for her. She's been such a saint, stood by me through some trouble, and I wanted, for once, to spoil her."

"Bill, that's both incredibly sweet and really, really horrible," I said.

"It gets worse," he said. "After the game ended, Joe got really mad at Simon. I think he knew something was up, but he couldn't figure out what it was. And you know what Simon did? He laughed. Right then and there, I decided to fess up to Joe and Tony, but the two of them stomped out before I could say anything. I realized it would be my word against his and, Stella, I'm not going to lie, it was a confusing predicament. I think that's why I forgot to put the candle away."

"I can imagine," I said, as I remembered Simon Sterling's gnarled expression this morning. I'd hate to have had that flashed at me.

"I decided that I'd get my winnings from Simon Sterling," he said. "Then, I'd give the money to Joe and Tony to split."

"Good call," I said. "Then you'd have proof."

"Right," said Bill with some enthusiasm. "I asked Simon for my share as he was counting his winnings, and the goddamn bastard, you know what he did?"

"What?"

"He laughed at me, too," said Bill. "So, I punched him. He fell like a sail with the wind knocked out of it, and then he ran out the door. I took my money, the half that was due to me, and left."

"The black eye," I said.

For all his troubles, Bill looked as if he had no remorse for that punch. I couldn't blame him.

"A nice shiner," he said, looking at the bruise on his hand. "I felt bad for the bride, having such a mess walk her down the aisle, but he was asking for it. I went home and passed out on the sofa, already ashamed to face Maude. I felt even worse in the morning. Maude never wakes up at night, but I opened my eyes before sunrise to find she'd put a blanket over me. That woman is a saint."

"Who lost the most money last night?" I asked.

"Tony. Every hand he lost, he was complaining that his wife was mad at him because this trip had cost him a fortune and she was home alone with their new twin babies."

"It seems a little extreme to kill someone over a couple thousand dollars," I said.

"Wealth is relative, Stella," said Bill.

We both nodded and sat on that thought for a moment.

"Bill," I finally said. "You need a lawyer."

"I don't trust lawyers."

"But Bellamy has to know about the cheating."

"I wouldn't tell that man the time of day," said Bill.

"Then tell Andy Southerland. He'll listen to you."

"Do you believe I killed that man?" said Bill.

"Of course I don't think you killed him," I said. "But you need to prove your innocence. What's holding you back?"

"I told you," he said. "I betrayed Maude."

"She'll understand," I said.

"No, she won't," he said. "The worst thing I did last night was help a gambler. Maude and I, we prefer not to talk about it, but a few years back, before you moved home, I had a gambling problem. Maude told me if I ever went near anything close to gambling again, she'd leave me. I'd rather rot in a prison than have her know I betrayed her."

"You're a stubborn man."

"That's a good summary of the situation," said Bill without any irony. "But nothing I've told you will clear my name. And in the meantime, I'll lose Maude. Can you help me?"

"You're a betting man," I said, taking full advantage of the situation. "If I help you, you'll have to make me a promise."

"What's that?" he said.

"You will go to Gamblers Anonymous."

Bill rolled his eyes.

"Look at where you are," I said. "You go back to Gamblers Anonymous, I won't tell Maude."

Bill's eyes brimmed with tears.

"Deal," he said.

I rose.

"Stella," he said. "Thanks."

I hugged Bill. Then I knocked on the bars for Ace.

"Finished?" said Ace, opening the cell door.

"What the hell?" Andy marched toward the cell. "I thought you were in the ladies' room. I've been waiting for you."

"Who goes to the ladies' for twenty minutes?" I said. "Can you give me a lift back to town?"

"No," said Andy, ushering me to the station's exit. I noticed he made sure to stand in front of me as we passed Bellamy's office, but I heard the captain inside, bragging to a couple of officers about Bill's arrest. "You're on your own. Maybe Peter can pick you up."

"Maybe he can," I said and dialed the Inky Mirror.

I was transferred. The phone rang, then went to voice mail. I smiled at Andy as if I were on hold and all was good and left the station for my phantom ride from Peter. Outside, I dialed a cab to take me to town. While I waited for someone to pick up, I got another call from Emily.

"I have so much to tell you," I said.

"Before you unload," she said. "I have a huge favor."

"Anything," I said.

"I'm at the doctor's," she said. "I thought I was going into labor, but it's something called Braxton-Hicks. Basically, fake labor pains. The problem, though, is that my doctor says I need to stay off my feet tonight."

"Then stay off your feet," I said.

"But I need to be at the Melville for the rehearsal dinner," she said. "The Dove Guy is coming to release his birds before the dinner, and I wanted to check in with the bride, and also make sure the restaurant is still good to go."

"I've got you covered," I said.

"Thank you," said Emily. "I've got you covered, too. Tomorrow, my team will set up your candles for the reception and ceremony. That way you can recover from the all-nighter I know you're about to have making the new unity candles. And I'm going to have Gary, the Dove Guy, bring you your red dress for tonight."

She hung up before I could answer.

Chapter 13

It took forever to get a cab, but I finally made it to the Melville. When I entered the inn, I respected Emily's request to leave the drama outside the door, and resisted a glance at the floral distractions in front of the Game Room. It was not hard, actually. I was blown away by how beautiful the lobby looked with the party now in full motion. My broken candle, the dead body, Jessica and her mother's cryptic activities, all seemed a distant memory. Instead, I appreciated the romantic glow of my candles, the crackling warmth of flames dancing in the lobby's fireplace, and the lively chatter of the Sterlings' guests who had managed to make it to the island, in spite of the morning's spotty weather.

I was also impressed, overall, by the women's hair. It was miraculously coiffed in spite of the usually ravaging effects of sea air. They made it look so easy, but as a native with a lot of hair, I know what it takes to keep it looking good. A LOT of time. Their outfits, too, were coordinated with pastel-colored cashmere sweaters or dresses from places like Lily Pulitzer that honored Nantucket's preppy reputation. Even the scents of their perfumes joined together as little notes in beautiful harmony. Many of the men had fished out their nautical-themed ties to wear, and all the guys were in nearly identical navy blazers and khaki pants. All in all, I felt like I was in a catalogue of beautiful people. My gray ensemble did not match their Ivy image, but at least I had on a dress. I hoped the Dove Guy arrived soon with my red number for tonight. I was now looking forward to having it. Not because any of the men caught my eye, which I knew would make Emily sad, but because I had a feeling this group would be heading upstairs to further gussy up in an hour or so.

In all the excitement, I suddenly realized I hadn't eaten since my meeting with Andy at The Bean. I headed to the kitchen to see if there were some left-over scones or whatnot on which to nibble. As I crossed the lobby, I noticed many of the guests were reviewing a list of the weekend's activities, which Emily had left throughout the inn as light reading. There would be golf and shopping tomorrow afternoon, in addition to tours of the island for some of their more sedentary friends. Some people were still checking in, while others were already settled for the weekend's fun. Most of the younger guests seemed to know each other. There were many warm hellos and hugs. I noticed a few whispers here and there, which I chalked up to the guests acknowledging the morning's gruesome murder, but the positive energy and excitement of the large party overtook the mood and became contagious.

The usual cast of characters was present. Jessica and her mother were holding court, bopping around the lobby with comfort and ease. I thought how they really knew how to compartmentalize their feelings. Jessica gave me a smile as she hugged a woman with bright pink lips, who looked about Mrs. Sterling's age. A new arrival, a woman Jessica's age, had also taken a starring role, and was standing next to the bride. She was blond, but the bottle kind, not the Jessica kind. And whereas Jessica wore small but clearly expensive jewels, her friend wore large and colorful baubles. I knew Jessica did not have a sister, but from the way they were holding hands, I could see they were close. The woman looked familiar, but I could not put my finger on where I'd seen her before.

Circling the room, I noticed Mrs. Sterling was making a fuss over a friend's phone. Presumably she was admiring their pictures of family members. In another corner of the lobby, Tony was grinning and high-fiving friends, but I thought the stress was getting to him. He kept pulling at his tie as if it were a noose. Not far from him, a group of older men, at least as old as Uncle Simon had been, were sitting around the fire and lighting up cigars. They chatted merrily and joked with one another, but they lacked the suave attire of Uncle Simon and I wondered how the dead man would have fared with this group. I suspected Simon Sterling would have been bored in ten minutes and in search of some other amusements. Finishing my tour of the room, I noticed Joe was missing from the crowd. I'd have thought he would be front and center.

I stopped thinking about Joe, however, and suddenly remembered where I'd seen Jessica's friend before. She was the woman I'd seen in the photograph at the Nantucket Inn.

"You helped check in everyone," I said to Frank as he passed me with one of Emily's activity lists in hand. "Who's that woman?"

"Maid of honor. I can't remember her name," said Frank. "I heard about Emily. Everything OK with the baby?"

"Everything's fine," I said, mostly to reassure myself.

Suddenly, there was a noticeable hush in the room. Then, I thought I heard one or two women squeal. I definitely heard another man sigh with the heartfelt appreciation of a young boy who has gotten a kiss from a beautiful girl. I looked to the center of the room to check out the cause of this communal flutter, then followed many eyes to the front door.

There stood Gina Ginelli. She smiled graciously, and I felt that the slight lift of her lips as they graced the room was the equivalent of a bow from the grandest stage on Broadway. I was almost tempted to clap. Nodding her head to the side in a way that put the room at ease, she made her way toward Frank and me. Frank, however, did not show any sign of star craze. He returned Gina's gaze with an equally charming one, and as she reached us, he offered his hand to meet hers.

"May I help you?" said Frank with a professional discretion that really impressed me.

"Stella," Gina said, to my amazement. Then, no joke, she kissed me on not one but both cheeks. Gina Ginelli kissed me. I almost pulled out my phone right then and there to call Emily and let her know. It was ridiculously embarrassing that as a grown woman I was so silly around this star, but honestly, if you'd ever seen her in person, you'd know why. She really had a magnetic quality about her that your usual guy on the street doesn't have.

"Frank," I said, before I could stop myself. "This is Gina Ginelli. She's staying in one of the cottages down the road."

"I'm sorry to bother you," said Gina. "I see you have a big affair underway. But I have a bit of a problem at the cottage and I didn't know where else to turn, as my realtor is not answering."

"No trouble," said Frank.

"It seems my electricity is out," she said. "No worries now, but in a couple of hours, the sun will be setting. I suspect the lights will go back on, but just to be on the safe side, I wondered if you have any extra flashlights or candles. I'd drive to town, but I'm trying to keep a low profile."

"I have some extra candles," I said, knowing I sounded like an overly enthusiastic fan but unable to stop myself. "Let me give you some."

"I'm sure your lights will be back on in no time," said Frank.

It occurred to me that the electricity at Gina's had been fine this afternoon. Usually the weather was behind an outage, but if anything, the skies had cleared not worsened.

"At this corner of the island," Frank continued, "we can get temporary blackouts, but they usually don't last long. We have generators so they don't disrupt our service, but I suppose a little cottage like yours does not."

"I guess it doesn't," said Gina, looking genuinely nervous. "Good to know they don't last long, but if you have some candles, Stella, I'd be grateful for them. With the news of the dead body this morning, it's got me a little rattled."

Frank and I exchanged glances at her mention of the unmentionable. The guests were still eyeing her, of course, and her interest in the murder was not good for the overall mood of the party.

"Why don't you come back here with us, and I'll get you those candles?" I said.

"Good idea," said Frank as he deftly maneuvered us across the room.

A few people said hello and a couple of people popped in front of us for selfies with Gina, for which she graciously smiled. We managed to make the journey, however, with no further conversation about the murder.

Once in the kitchen, the staff had their turn to say hello and take selfies while I entered the staging room and found a few candles I knew I would not need. As I packaged them up in tissue paper, I decided to tuck my card for the Wick & Flame into the bow.

". . . Yes. I'm preparing for a murder mystery film," said Gina from the other room as I looked through some baskets and drawers for matches.

"How exciting," said Frank.

"Can you tell me about the morning's murder?" she said. I noticed her voice shake a little at the word murder. I suspected this was going to be a terrifying night for her if the lights didn't go on. I wondered if Andy would really stop by and check on her.

"I can't say much," Frank said, diplomatically.

"Here you go," I said, returning to them with my package. "Don't worry about the murder. The police did a great job sweeping the hotel, securing the crime scene, and catching the criminal." Of course, I did not believe that Bill had murdered Simon, but I figured the idea would put her at ease. I also thought that making a public announcement that I thought Bill was the bad guy might ensure that I wasn't on any murderer's radar.

"Well, that's good news," said Gina.

My phone pinged and I looked at a text from Emily. "Oh darn," I said.

"What?" both Frank and Gina said in alarm. I realized my voice had been loud. And not too kind.

"Something about the murder?" said Gina.

"No," I said. "My dress. The Dove Guy was supposed to bring my red dress. He forgot it."

I really wanted that dress. I felt tired and shlumpy. I had unity candles to make tonight and a rehearsal dinner to oversee in a way that would reflect well on Emily. I just wanted to look nice doing it. I sat on one of the kitchen stools and slumped.

"Sometimes a girl really needs a nice red dress to get through the night. You know?" I said.

"Yes," said both Frank and Gina in unison.

"Oh well," I said, and tried to laugh.

"Oh well, nothing," said Gina. "You were very kind to stop everything in the middle of this party to get me some candles. Let me repay the favor. You can borrow something from me. I'm a diva. I travel with loads of evening wear. Even when I'm holed up practicing for a part." She laughed with self-deprecating comradery, which was in stark contrast to the ingenue she had played in front of Andy earlier. I noticed, but I was too grateful to be critical.

"Thanks so much," I said, checking my watch. "I only have about twenty minutes before I need to be back for final touches to the dinner."

"Easy," said Gina. "I once changed from swim clothes to a gown for the red carpet in Cannes from the time it took to take the launch from my boat to the shore. You're with a pro. Is this the back door?"

Before I could answer, she had already unlatched the back door and was heading out of the inn by way of the parking lot. As I followed, I noticed Gina was good at avoiding the crowds when she wanted to. She dodged around one car as she spied a couple kissing by the hotel's corner, and in no time, we were walking back down the dirt road toward her cottage.

"I'll drive you back," she said as if she were reading my mind. I did not want to get dressed only to soil an outfit or break a heel heading back to the inn on a dirt road. "Are your feet a seven?"

"How'd you know?" I said.

"Years of working in repertory with limited costumes shared by many. I can size up anyone. I met my husband back in those days."

"Is he planning to meet you here?" I blurted out. I was a little out of breath and considered I should go back to the gym. Here was Gina Ginelli, a good twenty years older than I and it felt like she wasn't even touching the ground as she sped us down the path.

Gina did not answer, but smiled at me and shrugged in a way that suggested she had no idea where he was. I suddenly felt sorry for this beautiful woman, alone in a beach cottage with no idea where her husband might be. I considered that being glamourous was more complicated than the pretty picture most people were allowed to see.

"The landscape here is so very different from LA," Gina said. "The fog last night was, I don't know. I can see why our setting in Scotland will be so perfect for a mystery."

"I guess you're used to warm weather," I said.

"It's the secret to love and romance," she said.

I thought about my afternoon in a tree with Peter, and decided Nantucket was pretty romantic, too.

"Were you at the hotel this morning?" said Gina.

"I was," I said. I was happy to help Gina with any information about the murder if it would help her prepare for her new role. For a moment, I even imagined her thanking me in her Academy Awards speech. *Thanks to Stella Wright, of the Wick & Flame candle store in Nantucket, Center Street, open Monday–Sundays, 10–5, for helping me to prepare for my role.*

"How did he look?" said Gina.

"He looked surprised," I said. "And a little cruel."

"Cruel?" said Gina.

"No, not cruel," I said. "But definitely not friendly."

"I heard the bartender assaulted him, but why would he?"

"It's hard to imagine," I said. I had no intention of spreading gossip about Bill.

"Do you think he felt any pain?" She squeezed my elbow as she spoke.

"I couldn't say."

"So sad, really. To live a sacred life, and then to die a dismal death."

"That sounds familiar," I said about her last comment.

We were heading up the path to her cottage by now, and Gina pulled a key from her pocket and let us inside. She flicked on the light switch, and breathed a sigh of relief. The lights went on.

"False alarm," she said. "I'm so sorry to have bothered you. I guess the murder really got to me."

"From *Swan Song*," I said. " 'To live a sacred life, and then to die a dismal death.' Isn't that your husband's famous line?"

Gina laughed.

"You," she said, "are a fan of Kevin's! He'll be so touched."

"Honestly," I said. "I'm your fan. I've seen every one of your movies except your first. I was too young and my parents wouldn't let me because they said it was risqué."

We both laughed, and she ushered me up the stairs and into her room.

"*The Feeling Season*," she said. "That was the first movie I made with my husband. God, he seemed so handsome back then. And smart. Can't believe I ever thought he was smart."

I was surprised to hear Gina speak this way about the famous Kevin Bunch.

"Here," she said. From a walk-in closet she handed me a floor-length, satin pencil skirt with a bottom ruffle that was the most beautiful shade of teal. She added to it a beaded top in a pale aqua that made my red number look like I'd made it myself. "Try this."

"I can't," I said, overwhelmed by the sheer luxury of the outfit.

"You can," she said. "Go for it. Who knows? Maybe you'll meet your prince charming tonight." She looked at it and ran her hand down the skirt. "One of us should get lucky tonight, right?"

I swear she had a tear in her eye when she handed the dress to me.

"Take these shoes and purse, too," she said, handing me the most beautiful accessories I'd ever laid eyes on. "And don't worry. I won't make you have them home by midnight," she said, with so much charm I found a tear in my eye, too. "Now, hurry up. You only have a few minutes, so let's not spend it arguing."

She closed the door, and I stood for a moment, soaking in the fact that I was in Gina Ginelli's bedroom. She had joked about Cinderella and being home by midnight, but as I dressed, I really did feel like she was my fairy godmother. I entered her bathroom to make sure my face looked OK, and caught my breath at my own reflection. It fit perfectly.

I eyed the vanity station Gina had set up. It was covered with makeup and I noticed a small bottle of perfume. No brand. I lifted it and sniffed. It was the lovely mix of vanilla, bergamot, and the mystery scent I had noticed this afternoon. This was the second time I could not identify her blend. That doesn't happen often. I knew it would be perfect, however, for my Ginelli-scented candle, if Gina was open to the idea.

It occurred to me that Gina wasn't really kidding when she said she was a diva. To be holed up alone for a week to work, she had an awful lot of niceties around her. I'd think a pair of sweatpants and a couple of warm sweaters, plus a good pair of flannel PJs would do the trick for such an endeavor. Gina's bathroom, however, included a pink silk negligee thrown over the bathroom door and some equally sexy underwear scattered about. The fun side of a life of glamour, I thought, as I considered how different the mess of clothes currently strewn about my room was. Well, at least she was human enough to be messy.

I dabbed a bit of Gina's perfume on my wrist, reapplied some lipstick from my purse, and pulled my hair up into a high chignon, which is a handy trick I've developed over the years to keep the crazy curls in my hair looking good after a long day. I picked up the purse Gina had lent me and my own bag. I was running out of time, so I decided to organize my bag on the car ride over. The Dove Guy would be arriving at any moment.

"Don't you look lovely," said Gina when I opened the bedroom door and smiled down at her from the open landing that overlooked the living room.

She had opened a bottle of wine and poured two glasses. As I descended her staircase, I was aware of how tightly her pencil skirt hugged my calves. As I reached her, she handed me a glass of wine, and for a moment I wondered if Jessica would mind a last-minute guest in the form of a world-famous celebrity. Then, I decided Emily would kill me for any more changes. I still hadn't eaten, but I took the glass she offered to me and clinked.

"Thank you so much," I said. "You're too kind."

She waved her hand and drank. "We girls have to stick together, right?" she said.

"Right." I smiled back.

"Shall we?" said Gina.

She grabbed the keys to her car and led me out the door.

I wasn't too comfortable with the fact that Gina drove like a race car driver, with a glass of wine in hand, but I was admittedly impressed she could pull it off. To distract myself, however, I opened my purse to decide what I would need to transfer into her small clutch. Lipstick. Phone. Driver's license. The mace I had taken from my car. I thought of Emily and the little extras she always carries around as an event planner. Since I'd be helping the Sterling women dress, I wished I had bobby pins. I felt like there was always a hair problem and Emily always had a bobby pin. Or double-sided tape for bra malfunctions. I considered that Emily would be a great mom. Her kid would want for nothing on the playground, from juice boxes to Band-Aids. I almost burst out laughing when I opened Gina's purse. Not only did she have bra tape and bobby pins, but a nail file stuck out of a small side pocket. Fantastic.

As I put my humble treasures into the purse, something behind the nail file caught my eye. A small piece of paper. I peeked. I couldn't help it, but I glanced at the paper, which was a little note.

Love You, My Tinkerbell

I smiled as I remembered that Tinkerbell was the name of her character in her first movie, the one my parents had never let me see. I imagined her now estranged husband had put the note in her purse on happier days. Then I realized this diva probably had loads of men who loved her. Perhaps one of them had slipped it in her purse.

"Here you go," said Gina, pulling up to the inn.

I opened the door to get out. Roll out, I should say. Once again, I noticed how restricting a lovely pencil skirt with a ruffle on the bottom can be. It was the opposite of the long and flowy outfits that Emily wore. I now understood my dear friend's fashion choice.

"Will you be OK?" I asked.

Gina took a healthy swig of her wine.

"Nothing a good sleep can't remedy," she said. "As we say in the theater, 'break a leg.' "

"Thanks," I said. "You've been a lifesaver."

"See you when I see you," said Gina and she pulled away, leaving a cloud of dust behind her.

"Wait," I cried, but it was too late. My purse and bag of clothes disappeared into the distance with her.

As the car drove away, I still couldn't believe my luck. I felt like a princess. I lifted my wrist to smell the lovely perfume I had borrowed.

As I stood in front of the Melville, sniffing my wrist and thinking of the little note in my bag and the gorgeous evening clothes my diva friend traveled with, my blood suddenly turned cold. One thing I know about scents is that most people like them because they remind them of something in their life. A good perfumer has more than a good nose. You need a little psychology, too. A scent can trigger a flood of memories. At that moment, the perfume on my wrist did just that. Suddenly, I was back in the Game Room, feeling nauseous this morning from Simon's cigar scent, the one I had also picked up in his room. At the time, I knew there were other competing aromas, but I had not paused to think of them. This time, however, I realized that one of the scents was now on my wrist.

My hand started to shake. I opened Gina's purse once more and read the note.

Tinkerbell.

The cat. Tinker.

The new tattoo on Simon's shoulder. A bell.

I tried to remember his handwriting from the note I'd seen in Joe's wastebasket, but I couldn't. Either way, some things clicked together. Jessica had said that the Sterling brothers' land was in Italy. Now Gina, the Italian diva, had made an unlikely trip to Nantucket.

I knew that I had to look for motives to solve Simon Sterling's murder. I had no idea what Gina's motive would be for killing Simon, but he did tend to upset those around him. And I'd put my money on the fact that Gina and Simon had been together in that Game Room last night.

I called Andy. I had so much to tell him, starting with my discovery of the woman from the photo I'd seen at the Nantucket Inn by the airport, and ending with my theories about Gina Ginelli.

I got no answer.

I left a message for Andy to call me as I watched the Dove Guy's truck amble up the road.

Chapter 14

"Gary?" I said to a man in jeans and a hoodie, his hair pulled back in a ponytail, as he got out of a van that read *The Dove Guy* along its side. "Stella Wright. I'm assisting Emily Gardner tonight. Let me show you where we'd like to release the birds."

I brought Gary back around to a patio outside of Ahab's. Since we were beside the harbor, the wind was a little crisp, so we were not going to use the outdoor space for cocktails. Everything would be inside. Fortunately, the restaurant had a fine view, and I indicated the perfect spot for the birds to be released. Gary circled the space like Andy might if he were searching for a clue. He kicked the ground, looking for the best place to position his bird pen, filled with a dozen beautiful birds that would fly a couple of miles back to their base once released.

I left Gary to it and entered Ahab's to make a final inspection of the space. Inside, I saw Tony at the mahogany bar nestled into a corner nook of the restaurant. He was the only guest in Ahab's and he was on his phone. Everyone else was either getting dressed or having a pre-dinner cocktail in the lobby before we opened the doors for dinner. I adjusted a flower or two, wondering what Emily would do. I wasn't sure if I should ask him to join the others or let him finish his conversation. I decided that if Tony was going to hang around on my turf, he could answer a few questions for me.

"Yes, honey," I heard him say as I scooted behind the bar in search for peanuts. "Well, that's a little unfair."

I noticed that with Bill's arrest, a substitute bartender had been called in, and he was now getting his head around the stock. I didn't want to interrupt him, so I opened my own can of peanuts and poured them into a bowl. Tony took a healthy swig of what looked like a whiskey, neat. He glanced in my direction, but my presence didn't faze him.

"He's my best friend," he said into the phone.

His shoulders sagged as he listened to the other end of the line. Something about his tone suggested that his wife was speaking to him.

"I know the twins are a handful," he said. "I wish you could be here with me, but as you said, we just can't afford babysitting and travel for the both of us . . . I'm not going wild here. . . . I haven't spent a penny since I've been here. The Sterlings are covering everything."

I wondered if he'd be more tactful about what he was saying if his friends were in here, instead of me.

"Listen, you can check every charge I've made once the credit card bill comes," he said.

Whatever his wife had said, it seemed like she decided to back off. Tony touched his hand to his temple in some relief and smiled into the phone.

"OK," he said. "Scout's honor. Except for a little bag of candy from the sweet store in town for you and the kids, not a penny. And I miss you. Joe's got his hands full here. I've never been to a wedding where a family member actually dies. I mean, I know everyone wants to kill each other at weddings, but this was off the charts."

He shared a laugh with his wife.

"Don't worry," he said. "They caught the guy. Otherwise, I'd be on the first ferry out of here."

I snagged a stool at the bar. I smiled at him, and popped a few peanuts into my mouth.

"Got to go," said Tony to his wife. "Love you."

"Hey," said Tony, putting his phone into his pocket. "You look nice."

"Thanks," I said at his understatement of the century. I mean, I was wearing couture. That qualifies for more than nice. On the other hand, I respected that his interest in his wife was stronger than the dazzle of a knock-'em-dead outfit.

"Ready for the weekend?" I said.

"Crazy wedding."

I had to agree.

"How are you friends with Joe, anyway?" I asked.

"We went to school together," he said. "We grew up on one side of the tracks. Jessica grew up on the other side. Maria is from our side, too. Jess and Maria became friends during their senior year in high school. They were both pitches or whatever it's called of their schools' singing groups. She introduced Joe to Jessica. Then Jessica joined the gym Joe was working at. He was her trainer, you know."

"So, he's marrying a girl from the other side of the tracks?" I said. "That's romantic."

"I guess," said Tony.

"You kind of sound like you disagree with me."

"Nah," he said. "Although Joe's gone soft around

the midsection since he's hit the high life. Not good for a trainer."

Tony reached over to my bowl of peanuts and began to munch on them. I was having a hard time cutting a break in the food department.

"Whatever," said Tony. "Weddings are just a fortune."

Normally, I would understand his gripe, but I remembered Tony, not a moment ago, telling his wife that the Sterlings were covering everything.

"What did you get them for a gift?" I said, thinking of his trip to the expensive gift shop.

"Nothing yet," said Tony. "They're registered everywhere though."

"I'm sure your wife can help you pick something out," I said.

"No way," said Tony. "I told my wife it was a no-gift wedding. She's already so mad I had to come here. We just had twins."

I was going to do the usual thing and ask to see a picture of the babies, but my phone pinged a text from Emily.

How's it going? Sterlings OK?

The Sterlings! I'd checked on the Dove Guy, done a tour of the restaurant to make sure the room was set up. Unfortunately, I'd not touched base with the Sterlings.

Everything good! I responded.

"Tony," I said. "I've got to go."

"Cheers!" he said.

Rather than kick him out, I decided to let Tony have a few moments of peace and quiet. Slipping out of the restaurant, I raced to the service elevator. Race is an exaggeration since the tight skirt only allowed me to take delicate steps. Anyway, I raced there in spirit, and pressed the call button. Frank approached and joined me. He was holding a small jug of flowers.

"Guest in Room 10 is allergic to lilies, so I'm replacing them," he said.

I nodded. "I'm checking on the Sterlings, but otherwise everything looks great for tonight."

"We've got you covered," Frank said with an earnest look that put me at ease. "Are you OK?"

"I guess," I said and focused on the descending floor dial over the elevator. "I still keep thinking about the murder. Out of curiosity, what did everyone do before dinner last night?"

"I don't think they did anything," said Frank. "People are usually pretty tired when they get here. Simon Sterling got antsy, and went for a walk. Mrs. Sterling forgot to go hit the ATM, so she had a van run her into town before dinner to get some money. Otherwise, I think that was it. Usual stuff."

"And none of those guests who checked out this morning knew anyone connected to the Sterlings?"

"No," said Frank.

The elevator door opened.

"I'm heading by Room 10," I said. "Let me drop these for you."

"You're a lifesaver," he said. "And that outfit is a knockout."

I smiled as the elevator door closed on me. A moment later, it opened to the third floor. I tapped on the door of Room 10. The occupants gratefully swapped vases with me. Then I continued to Jessica's room with lilies in hand.

"Those are beautiful," said Jessica when she opened the door. "Can you put them on the desk? I'm just getting my earrings on."

"Of course," I said. I headed to the desk by the win-

dow. "I'm just checking to see if you guys need anything. Emily is resting so she can be your superhero tomorrow, but I've got you covered tonight."

"Everything is perfect," she said. "Did the doves arrive?"

"They did," I said. As I placed the vase of lilies on
the desk, I noticed that all of the files about the land
transfer that I had seen this morning were now gone. I
glanced around the room. The rest of it was still a
mess. Only the papers had been put away. I wished I
had had more time to inspect them.

"I assume Joe is back and ready to go?" I asked.

"Joe was gone?" said Jessica, looking confused.
"Where did he go?"

"Oh," I said. "I don't know. I didn't see him earlier
during tea."

"No, no," said Jessica. "He was around. He had a
headache is all. He's feeling fine now. Nothing an Ex-
cedrin migraine couldn't cure. This morning took its
toll."

"I think it has on everyone," I said. It took every
ounce of self-control for me not to share my opinion
on Bill's unjust arrest. "Should I check on your mom?"

"Thanks," said Jessica. "She's feeling very emotional. She's been resting since tea ended. With me
getting married, and Uncle Simon's death stirring up
so many feelings about my father, this has been a hard
weekend. I, at least, am joyful about marrying Joe tomorrow. I think she feels she's losing a lot."

"I understand," I said. I wasn't sure if I did, but it
seemed like the sort of thing Emily would say. "Your
ring is beautiful."

"Really?" said Jessica with a laugh. "It's super sparkly
tonight. We had it polished at the jeweler's in town

yesterday. I haven't taken it off since. I woke up with dents in my fingers."

She flashed it to the room. It looked so silly on her, and we couldn't help it. We both laughed.

"I'll stop by your mom's room, and then I'll see you all downstairs in a few."

"Thanks," said Jessica.

She turned around for me to zip her blouse. I zipped and left.

One door down, I knocked on Mrs. Sterling's door.

"Come in," I heard her say.

I opened the door to find Mrs. Sterling. Her hair and makeup were perfect. Her jewelry was beautiful. But she was not dressed. Rather, she sat in a chair at a desk similar to the one in Jessica's room with a plush bathrobe wrapped around her. She was looking out of the window and across the rolling lawn to the harbor waters.

"Everything OK?" I said in a light but friendly voice. God help me, I had no idea what to do if the bride's mother lost it. This was Emily's department.

Fortunately, Mrs. Sterling flashed a warm and reassuring smile upon me, one that Gina Ginelli would be impressed by, I thought. He whole demeanor changed from melancholy to cheerful in a beat.

"Everything is good," said Mrs. Sterling. "I'm so glad they found the murderer. I don't know what Jessica would have done if we'd had to cancel the wedding. She's a remarkable girl, you know."

As she spoke, she rose and took a smart-looking, navy-blue suit from her closet. Before my eyes, she started to change. I took her place by the desk and tactfully looked out the window.

"Do you have children?" said Mrs. Sterling.

"Me?" I laughed. "No. I don't even have a boyfriend."

"You look gorgeous tonight," she said. "Who knows?"

I didn't want to tell her that no one in the crowd downstairs had done it for me, so I smiled and, as I had with her daughter, zipped up her cream-colored silk blouse.

"Children are a blessing," said Mrs. Sterling. "But, then they leave. You spend your whole life trying to make sure they're OK, and then one day someone walks in and says they'll take over that job, thank you very much. I mean, don't get me wrong. I like Joe well enough."

"Joe's a great guy," I said.

"He thinks I'm cheap," said Mrs. Sterling. "I don't give Jessica gobs of cash for entrepreneurial opportunities, and she's wealthy but not wealthy enough to bankroll him. They need to learn the value of money. When I die, it'll be a different story. They'll inherit loads of money and they can do whatever they want with it. But I intend to hang around for a long time."

I tried not to shudder, but money always seemed to be a huge motive for murder. Mrs. Sterling was probably a bigger target than Simon Sterling on that front. I was so glad that I hadn't found Mrs. Sterling on the floor this morning. I wondered, again, what the motive might be for his murder.

"I'd do anything for that girl," said Mrs. Sterling. "One day, you'll see."

"I feel that way already for Emily's baby," I said.

"I just need a moment alone," said Mrs. Sterling. "I'll meet you downstairs, OK?"

"Sounds good," I said. I looked out the window one more time. I knew Mrs. Sterling was waiting for me to leave, but I couldn't move for a moment. Through the window, I thought I saw Gina Ginelli on the widow's walk of her cottage. A widow's walk is the traditional roof deck on old Nantucket houses. They were used in the whaling days so that the ship captain's wife could look out to sea when a ship returned from years away in hopes of spying her husband's ship. Gina, however, was not looking at the sea. She was looking at the inn, and I swear she was crying.

Chapter 15

"Are you OK, Stella?" said Mrs. Sterling.

"Yes," I said. "I'm going. See you."

I unwisely took the stairs, which took a bit of skill given my attire. I thought that Gina walking the red carpet must be a lot easier than me hobbling down stairs, but I made it back to Ahab's as the crowd was heading in.

According to Emily's plans, dinner would begin with my greatest responsibility for the night. The doves. With a nod to Jessica when her mother joined the gathering a minute later, I headed outside to the patio beside Ahab's.

As I reached the back door, I collided with the maid of honor. She was wearing a flowing dress in bright blue with an even brighter green shawl to match her green feather earrings. It was a unique style compared to the perfectly coiffed ladies inside.

"Oh, hi!" she said. "Sorry."

"Can I help you?" I said. "I'm Stella Wright. I'm helping with the party tonight."

"Maria Blane, maid of honor. I love your outfit," she

said. "I'm just looking for the groom. Jessica thought he might be having a moment by the water."

With that, she dashed out the door past me, and I headed toward Gary, the Dove Guy, who looked very much like he wanted me to give him the all-go sign. I understood why. The sun would soon begin to set and the birds had to get home while there was still light in the sky. Without Joe in attendance, however, I assumed we should wait. I also made a note that for at least the second time today, Joe was absent from the wedding party. First, when the guests were arriving, and now at his own dinner. Right now, however, I needed to focus on the party or the doves would be flying who knows where in the dark.

"Breathe, breathe, breathe," I said.

The guests were, by now, all gathered in the restaurant. I held up my index finger to an unhappy-looking Gary, and shuffled back toward the restaurant's door. I reached for the handle, but the door opened right into me.

Joe stood in the frame. Halleluiah.

"Great. You're here," I said.

"I am," he said, smiling politely. "The guests are, too. Jessica was wondering about the birds?"

"Right," I said, backing up. "Get ready! We're about to start off your weekend with a bang!"

Turning around, I slid back to Gary's eyeline and gave him the thumbs-up. He nodded, and opened the coop in which his dozen feathered friends had been waiting for their big moment.

Rather than fly, however, one of the pigeons seemed to have been elected by his mates to check out the hotel first. He took a step onto the pavement, and looked around. Another one followed. Gary made a few whistling noises and a few more birds followed, but none flew. I looked desperately at the birds, then at Gary, who continued to make his bird calls.

All I could think was that if these birds didn't take off right now, Jessica and Joe might worry that their wedding's bad luck was destined to continue for the weekend. I sidestepped around the perimeter of the patio, smiling as if nothing bad was happening. My goal was to reach Gary and ask if I could help him. I didn't have to, however, because halfway around the patio, the birds gave a start, then took to the air.

"How beautiful!" I heard Maria say in a breathy voice from behind me.

I turned to see her running toward us, and remembered we had not waited for her to return from her search for Joe. The birds seemed to notice her, too, and as they began their journey home, they flew right toward her. Maria's delight at the doves turned to fear as they zoomed over her. She gave a huge yelp and fell into a puddle of mud behind her.

Maria froze for a moment, aware of what had happened. She looked at the faces in the window as they all stared back in shock. She looked at her dress, covered in mud. Then she looked back up and burst out laughing. The guests followed suit and applauded inside. Maria stood with as much grace as she could and bowed to the crowd. It was at that moment that I knew I liked Maria. I also noticed one sweet-looking guy's smile linger on her.

"This means you will always have good luck," she shouted and danced a jig on a dry patch of grass.

"Stella," she said, continuing to laugh. "Do you think you could give me a hand?"

"Of course," I said. If I wasn't so worried about ruining Gina's dress, I would have hugged her right there.

One covered in mud, the other taking delicate steps, Maria and I slipped into the service elevator off of the kitchen and somehow made it upstairs. In the privacy of her room, she took off her dress, which had seen the most damage, and rinsed off. Without the long sleeve of her dress covering her, I noticed she had a bandage around her wrist. I thought back to this afternoon and realized she had been wearing long sleeves then, too.

I knew Maria had been on the island yesterday, and that no one else in the wedding party seemed to know it. Now, I wondered what she had been doing.

"Did you know Jessica's uncle Simon?" I asked as we pieced together another outfit of a black skirt and sweater.

"No," she said. "But we're not supposed to talk about him. Bad luck."

She looked in the mirror. I liked her new, sleek look, even with the oversized neon pink earrings she added. After a minute or two more of last-minute touch-ups, we were ready to head back to the party.

"Why were you looking for Joe anyway?" I said as we walked to the elevator. "He was inside."

"Jessica said she was looking for him," she said. "I wanted to help."

"You're a good friend," I said.

"Thanks," she said. "I hope Jessica feels the same way. We've been besties since senior year in high school, but she's been edgy since she and Joe got engaged."

"How so?" I said, buzzing the elevator button.

"I don't know," she said. "Little things. Like when I made a fuss about her engagement ring, she got all defensive and said she didn't really love it or need it.

We've never had any tension over our financial disparities, but she made me feel like I was crossing a line."

The elevator arrived, and I gathered my courage as we stepped inside.

"What happened to your wrist?" I said as the door closed.

"Carpal tunnel syndrome," she said, rearranging her blouse and avoiding my eyes. "I type too much."

She was a terrible liar. I could not believe such a bad liar could pull off a murder, but I pushed onward.

"Maria, I know you were at the Nantucket Inn last night," I said. The elevator cab suddenly felt very small.

Maria looked at me like one of the startled birds that had flown the coop.

"You do?" she said.

I nodded.

"Please don't tell Jessica," she said. "I got a really cheap deal on travel, but it was for yesterday, not today. I didn't want to tell Jessica or Joe because they would have offered to put me up here. Tony took advantage of their hospitality, but that's so Tony."

"Given the circumstances, you should probably tell the police," I said. "They'll want an alibi from anyone connected to the wedding who was here yesterday. Do you have one?"

Maria nodded.

"It's so embarrassing though. I went to the Chicken Box," she said. The Chicken Box is one of the island's best music spots. If I had a night alone on the island, I'd have probably done the same. "They had a karaoke hour early on. I love karaoke." She raised her swollen wrist to me. "I had a few drinks though. And I fell off the stage. I ended up spending most of the night in the emergency room. Jessica would feel terrible if she knew."

"I'm the wedding help," I said, amazed we still had one more floor to go in this old thing. "We take an oath to keep secrets."

"I have one more secret," she said. "Mrs. Sterling terrifies me. Jessica told her I had a crush on Joe when we were in high school. Now, she keeps flashing me these unkind looks."

"Are you here with anyone?" I ventured, thinking of the sweet-smiling man who could not take his eyes off of her.

"Ha!" she said. "My luck with men is terrible."

The elevator doors opened, and we headed off the elevator and back to the dinner. Maria received a round of applause, which she good-naturedly accepted with a gracious bow. The party was well underway and with the sun now set, the candlelight was stunning. I listened to the warm toasts shared by the couple's friends. Everyone was doing a great job of keeping the murder at bay for the sake of Jessica and Joe.

Toward the end of dinner, I sent a text to my cousin Kate at the hospital, to see if she could confirm that Maria had been there. As much as I loved the maid of honor, I wanted to make sure her alibi lined up. Then I sent a photo of the party to Emily, who sent many thumbs-up emojis back to me. I was glad. The candlelit ambience of the party was as gorgeous as we'd hoped it would be.

How are you feeling? I asked her.

I'll be good to go tomorrow, she replied. *But I think this kid's going to be a tap dancer.*

I sent her a winky-smiley face.

Joe stood and tapped his spoon against his glass. Jessica rose beside him.

"Hey everyone," he said. Many of their friends hooted and cheered. "I want to thank you for coming this weekend, and to extend a special and heartfelt thanks to my soon-to-be mother-in-law for all the work she has put into this wedding and the support she has extended to me and Jess."

The room applauded.

"As you could all tell from Mrs. Sterling's toast," he said about a toast I'd clearly missed, "she is very attached to her daughter."

There was some laughter, but Mrs. Sterling held her head high.

"You all may laugh," said Joe, "but since my parents have both passed, I feel so lucky to be part of this kind of loyalty and love. I feel blessed to be around it."

Awws gushed from the crowd.

"I'd also like Mrs. Sterling to know how deeply committed I am to building a life that will keep Jessica in the comforts she knows." At this, Jessica playfully punched him in the arm. "And toward that goal, I'd like to let you all know that when we get back from our honeymoon we hope to break ground on the first of three gyms slated to open. We're going to work as a team on these enterprises, which will be called Sterling Bodies."

A murmur of support and some celebratory whistles ensued. Joe and Jessica enjoyed them for a moment before Joe continued. I thought Mrs. Sterling looked surprised by the idea of the Sterling name attached to bodies and gyms. Jessica glanced toward her mother for approval, but she stood confidently by her fiancé.

"And now," he said. "Let's continue the party into

town. The inn has a launch outside to take us on a trip across the harbor. Grab a sweater or whatever and meet us in ten minutes. Stella will help us follow the tea lights from the patio to the water where we can all board."

The crowd applauded, young and old, as the dinner convened. The group was truly committed to being joyful this weekend, in spite of all that had happened this morning. I took it as a sign of how solid and loved Jessica and Joe were. I was relieved all had gone as smoothly as it had, and that, most importantly, the couple of honor was happy. They stood by the big window and gave each other a huge kiss. I understood Joe's decision to announce their business news. Anything to bury the sadness of this morning was fair game.

My phone pinged. It was a text from my cousin Kate. She confirmed Maria's story, and added that her friend had been the attending nurse and had seen Maria. She had been alone and crying. As far as I was concerned, Maria Blane was off the hook for any connection to the murder of Simon Sterling.

Ten minutes later, I was directing everyone to the launch. I kept my eye open for the man who had seemed so interested in Maria.

"Fun night," I said when I found him. I noticed Maria was making her way to the dock as well. "Mind if I lean on your shoulder a moment? My shoe is killing me."

"Sure," said the man. As I suspected, kind.

I fumbled around, pretending my shoe was having some sort of strap malfunction, until Maria reached us.

"You were the star of the evening," I said to her.

"Yes, you were," said the man, looking quite happy to have the chance to speak to her. "David Simmons." He extended his hand toward Maria.

"Are you cold?" I said to Maria, who was not wearing a sweater or jacket.

"No," she said, but then stopped as David whipped off his jacket and put it around her shoulders. "Oh, thank you," she said as they continued down to the dock together, deep in conversation, as if they'd known each other forever. Warmed my heart.

Once everyone had piled into the launch, the boat took off and I waved goodbye. My thoughts immediately turned to my next job for the night—my four new unity candles. The wind blew and I shivered a little, but I enjoyed the sea breeze and the moon, which was reflecting across the water. It occurred to me that even though I was the help, I should have joined the launch. In all of the excitement, I had forgotten that I didn't have my car. I was thinking about how slowly the cab services were running during FIGAWI, when I heard the sound of a boat's engine coming toward me through the darkness.

Chapter 16

"Get out of town," I said as a small dinghy made its way to the water's edge.

"Surprise," said Peter. He was wearing a tuxedo, of all things, in a dinghy. "You're a vision. Last time I saw you, I remember leaves in your hair and a little dirt on your cheek."

"You don't look too bad yourself," I said. I was happy to see that Peter had not compromised his afternoon's fly-by-the-seat-of-his pants look. His tuxedo pants were shoved into rubber boots, and his bow tie was a red bandana.

"I heard you were working the Melville tonight," he said, shutting off his motor. "I called your cousin Liz. My luck I should find you standing here when I pulled up."

He smiled like he had been very, very clever and I smiled back. It was so awesome that this outfit would not go to waste after all. I'd have to thank Liz for giving Peter her card.

"Champagne?" he said, raising a bottle and jumping out of his boat. He tied the dinghy to a rock, flipped off his jacket, and laid it on my shoulders without my having to ask.

"Ha," I said about the champagne. "I haven't eaten since Andy and I were at The Bean at about ten this morning. One glass of champagne and I'll faint."

"No worries," said Peter. He jumped back into his boat and pulled out a picnic basket.

"My hero," I said.

"Really? Even after this afternoon's kerfuffle?"

"Did you just say kerfuffle?"

"I did," he said and laid a blanket on the ground.

I pulled his jacket around me as Peter laid out a platter of cheese and bread and meats that made my stomach leap for joy. I tried to join him on the ground as elegantly as possible. In the end, I did no justice to my couture. I had to hike my skirt to my thighs before I could bend my knees.

"So much for being a movie star," I said, settling down next him. "My outfit, by the way, is compliments of Gina Ginelli."

"Come on," said Peter, handing me a cracker with a glob of brie on it that was to die for. I swallowed it whole.

"She's pretty nice, actually," I said. "My dress didn't show up tonight. She'd stopped by the inn and heard me complaining. Then she offered me something to wear."

"Pretty fancy dress for someone holed up here to work," said Peter. "I wonder if there's a big party going down this weekend that she's planning to attend."

"Better than the Sterling wedding or a FIGAWI bash? I doubt it," I said. "She blamed her fancy packing job on the fact that she's a diva."

"She doesn't sound like one," he said. "That's a nice outfit to loan out."

"True," I said, admiring the appliquéd flowers across the bodice of my top as I shoved a piece of prosciutto into my mouth. I reached for a piece of Morbier cheese, starting to feel like myself again. Peter noticed I was going for it with his basket of goodies. He handed me his cracker and cheese. "Thanks." I popped it in my mouth and then lay back on the ground.

Peter leaned back beside me, his hands behind his head as he looked at the starry sky.

"What do you think about this murder?" he said. "I'm a good investigator, you know. Not, maybe, like your friend Andy. But I get on to something and follow it. Give me a lead that seems like nothing. You'll be amazed with what I can do with it."

"A lead, huh?" I said.

I thought of Gina crying on the roof. Of Joe disappearing during the day. Of Mrs. Sterling's interest in Maria Blane. I even thought about the fact that someone like Simon Sterling had a cat. I toyed with telling Peter about the note I'd found in Gina's purse, but then decided not to. I didn't want him to write about her, especially since it would connect her to the murdered man.

"Yup. Something totally random. I'll follow it and see where it takes us."

I tried to think of the most arbitrary angle of all that I'd seen today.

"OK," I finally said. "There was an elderly couple and a young family staying at the inn when we found the body this morning. Maybe they saw something. Maybe with Bill's quick arrest, they weren't questioned as well as they could have been."

"Sounds like a wild goose chase," he said, "but I'll take the challenge."

"And who benefits from Simon's will?"

"Now you're thinking," he said.

"Thank you, Watson," I said.

"Wait, you get to be Sherlock?" he said. He leaned his head on his elbow and looked at me. "How does a pipe and a deerstalker hat go with your look?"

"Perfectly," I said.

My phone pinged. It was Emily.

How are the new unity candles going?

I looked at the time. Ten o'clock.

"Being a power babe is not easy," I said. "I have to make four new unity candles tonight."

"Foiled again," said Peter. "I was planning to lure you out on my yacht."

I looked at his dinghy, which was bobbing with gusto in the night's waters, and I was tempted to join him on a trip across the harbor, back to town. Then, I rubbed my cheese-filled stomach and wondered how I'd feel after the ten-minute voyage. As lovely as the invitation was, I realized I had another option.

"Thanks," I said, "but I have enough supplies up at the inn to get my job done. I'll get more sleep if I knock things out here, then take the launch back in the morning."

I reached my hand up to straighten Peter's bow tie. He took my hand and kissed it. If I wasn't so worried about the candles, I suspected we could have had a lot of fun under the moonlight in our fancy attire.

"You do what you have to do," said Peter. "We have all summer to enjoy my yacht."

"I like the way you think," I said as he helped me to my feet.

I handed his jacket back to him.

"Thanks for this," I said. "Nantucket is lucky to have you here."

"I'm feeling pretty lucky to have found this little is-land."

Before I could say another word, he jumped in his dinghy, gave me a salute, and pulled back out into the darkness. I wondered if he'd head home or into town. He didn't strike me as the kind of guy who went to bed by ten on a Friday night.

I watched him travel across the harbor. I was beginning to notice I was cold when the quiet was broken by the sound of a speeding motorboat that suddenly flew by Peter without any lights on. In the moonlight, I tried to make out the driver, but all I caught was the silhouette of a woman's ponytail. Peter's boat began to rock in the wake. He made a few salty comments into the dark, but kept his course.

I, on the other hand, headed back to the inn, already beginning to imagine my new creations. Just the thought of sitting down with my candles gave me a sense of comfort I had missed all day. Entering the back of Ahab's as the restaurant staff was putting the last of the party's mess away, I entered the staging room, which would now be my workshop. The crew had returned some of the candles we used tonight. Most were still tall with a lot of wick left in them. I made a note to drop them at the food pantry. I was no chef, but I liked to make their Friday night dinners more festive when I could.

Before the last of the kitchen staff left, I borrowed a lazy Susan so that I could turn the candles as I decorated them without handling them. Then, I searched through my supplies for the four unity candles I would need. I was relieved I had brought extras. I had also brought extra gold and silver decorative wax that was the equivalent of piping icing on a cake. It was soft and malleable when warmed so that I could apply designs to the candles.

I hadn't bargained on one thing, however. Looking over my supplies again, I realized I only had three extra candles, not the four I needed for the new unity candle. I looked again, sure I'd brought enough extras, but no. There were only three. It occurred to me that someone from the kitchen could have easily taken an extra, having no idea I'd need it. Or perhaps Jessica gave a friend another one. Normally, I'd be flattered, but right now, I felt downright horrified. It was getting to be close to eleven at night and I was stuck on the other end of the island, minus a candle.

Desperately, I called a couple of taxi companies to see if I could get a lift home. All gave me a pickup time of at least forty minutes. With this time frame, I'd be working until dawn. I was about to agree to a ride when I had a thought. I had put a candle in Uncle Simon's room. Technically, the room was cordoned off, still a crime scene, but Simon wouldn't be needing that candle.

I couldn't. Could I?

Chapter 17

I decided I could.

I told myself that staying at the inn to work would be the best use of my time. I truly appreciated that Emily Gardner Events would be setting up my candles for the reception and ceremony tomorrow morning, but I knew I'd want to check in on both, which would be easier to do if I was already here. Plus, I argued, I wouldn't be rushing into the rest of my day. I also had my last Candleer class in the morning, and I was going to Chris and Suzie's Memorial Day cookout. They'd been planning it for weeks and both Emily and I promised them we'd attend for a short while, before heading out to the chapel for the Sterlings' wedding ceremony. Let's be honest, though. I also wanted to take another look at Simon's room.

In spite of my decision, however, I wasn't ready to dash upstairs to steal something from a dead man's room.

Instead, I brought the three candles I had to the worktable, and placed one on the lazy Susan. I was still wearing my skirt, however, and I needed much better mobility. Luckily, I found a pair of chef's pants in a closet and swapped them for Gina's skirt, which I folded carefully and put into an empty bag Emily had left behind. Feeling better already, I also threw on an apron over my beautiful chiffon blouse. The light in the room came from one overhead bulb, so I lit a couple of candles to add some light.

Finally, ready to begin my work, I took out my phone and looked at the photos I had of Jessica's wedding dress. Between the photos and the visit I'd made to her room earlier, I could not find anything new to add, so I turned my thoughts to the reading. After a few minutes, I decided to incorporate illustrations of the four seasons onto each candle. I love the fall, so I started there. An acorn came to mind. I drew a circle in which I sketched the acorn with my decorative wax. Once finished, I began to cover the rest of the candle with the delicate designs from Jessica's dress. Before I knew it, I was in the zone and every ounce of tension I had accumulated during the day began to melt away as the soft wax in my decorating pen oozed onto the candle. Fortunately, I had enough experience from the original unity candle that I was able to fall right into my routine. I lost track of time as I enjoyed the creation that was slowly forming in my hands. At some point, I heard the guests return from town. I heard the engines of their cabs, but at this point there was no way I could stop working to grab one back to town. I'm like that. Once I get into a project, I just can't stop.

When I finished the third candle, I stretched for a moment to admire my work. I had to admit, I liked what I saw even better than the original candle. The new design lacked the large, vertical statement of the original, but the four candles suggested a circle of love that would continue.

It was three in the morning, however, which was a problem. I don't scare easily, but I have a three-in-the-morning phobia, which had not been helped by Sterling's murder at the same hour last night. Every thought that I ever have at this hour takes on a frightening overtone. I could be thinking about kittens and somehow I'd shiver. Usually, I can pull the covers over my head and will myself back to sleep. If that fails, my phone keeps me company while I play a few games to get sleepy. I considered that Tinker would be the kind of roommate who'd be a good ally on those nights. He'd offer a reassuring purr and a snuggle, but right now I felt a pit in my stomach as I remembered that a murderer might be under the same roof I was. Added to that thought was that I still had to steal a candle from a crime scene.

I took off my apron and went to the door of my staging room.

"No," I said.

The door was once again locked.

Fool me once.

I was scared enough when the door had locked yesterday, but now I was alone, and fighting my wildest fears. I sank to my knees and crouched at the bottom of the door. As if on cue, the single bulb that lit the room flickered. I wondered if I should turn it off, in case someone could see me through the small window. I knew Frank had said that the room's door locked on its own, but right now, I wasn't buying it. I knew I had closed it carefully behind me, and I could swear I had not heard it lock.

I can't say how long I stayed crouched by that door.

Actually, I can. It was five minutes, but in that short time, I imagined every way I might die before sunrise. When I found myself dwelling on an image of myself attacked by my new unity candles, I knew I had to get a grip. I glanced around the room in hopes of seeing a key, which I already knew would not be here. Once confirmed, I debated what I should do next.

The purse I had borrowed from Gina was on my worktable. I crawled across the floor, reached a hand to it, and slid it down. From inside, I took out my phone, but as luck would have it, the battery had died.

"One, two, three, four." I began to breathe.

I poured the contents of my purse on the floor. A lipstick, a bobby pin, a nail file, my license, and my mace. After staring at my only belongings for a minute or two, I picked up the bobby pin and crawled back to the lock. I'd seen a million movies and TV shows where someone escapes a locked room by using a bobby pin, so I decided there must be some truth to it. I inspected the lock. It was one of the old ones, and required a latchkey to secure it, but the large opening gave me an opportunity to glimpse the bolt's inner workings. I wondered if a bobby pin was strong enough to do the job as I stuck it inside and jiggled it about. After a few seconds of fiddling with no real strategy, I realized my plan was not working. I peered inside again. I thought I saw a sliver of space under which the pin might fit, thereby allowing me to lift the bolt high enough that the lock would give. I opened the bobby pin into a straight line to make it as thin as possible, and tried again. While I maneuvered the pin, I held the door handle and turned it every now and then in hopes of succeeding.

I really had no expectations of success, so I was completely shocked when, to my surprise, the lock gave way. My victory was short-lived, however, when I imagined what might be waiting for me beyond. Time was ticking. As frightened as I was, I could not leave those three candles sitting on my worktable without adding the fourth.

I pulled myself up, reclaimed my self-respect, and looked at the mess I'd left on the floor from Gina's purse. My can of mace had never looked so good. I picked it up, and wondered as I did how strong bra tape was. Returning to the door, I opened the package of tape and rubbed it against the side of the lock. I chalked it up to diva know-how that this was probably the strongest bra tape on the market. The lock stayed tucked in its bolt. With two successes under my belt, I decided I could get that candle. All I needed was the inn's passkey from behind Frank's desk.

I tiptoed to the lobby. The Melville was dead quiet. A couple of lights were on in case someone was awake and wanted to be somewhere other than their room. I looked about me and considered that it was about this time last night that someone had attacked Simon in the Game Room. The lights would have been dimmed, like now. There would have been no one else awake.

I wondered if Gina, whose perfume had infiltrated the Game Room, was the killer, or if someone else had crept about, too. I wondered, too, why Simon had stayed up so late after cards. I noticed that the doors to a library off of the lobby were closed. Someone could have easily hidden in the room before or after the murder.

Taking a deep breath, I headed to the reception desk where Frank stored the passkey in a small cubby. Suddenly, I heard a noise from Frank's room. For fear that he might have heard me and decide to investigate, I scurried across the floor and opened the door to the library. Without much thought, I entered the room and closed the door behind me. I say without much thought, because once the door was closed, I realized the room was pitch black. My three o'clock fears returned, and I stood with my head down for a moment, breathing carefully. It didn't take too long to recover myself, but in that time, my eyes had adjusted to the dark. When I looked up, I almost fainted.

A man was looking at me. I opened my mouth to scream but only the smallest noise left my body. Then I lifted my hand and sprayed the bottle of mace ahead of me.

I'm not proud of that moment. First, I learned that it doesn't take long to get through a bottle of mace. Second, when I finished, I realized I was looking at the painting of Captain Elijah Crawford, who was now dripping in liquid. Fortunately, the chemical had not damaged the paint, but I could not leave the fellow dripping in the smelly goo. I took off my apron and dabbed the canvas to keep the painting from getting damaged.

When I was close to finished, I heard a noise in the lobby. Frank. I stood still, afraid to make a single sound. I might be able to explain away my presence in the library, but I still wanted to steal his keys, so if I could avoid talking to him, all the better. Also, he might not be pleased with the smell in the library. It wasn't terrible, but there was a peppery scent in the room that probably would linger for an hour or so.

"Is anyone out here?" Frank said in a voice that was wavering between annoyed and terrified.

I did not answer.

After a moment, Frank went back to his room and closed the door.

I had barely made a peep when I'd been frightened by what I'd thought was Captain Elijah Crawford, in the flesh, standing before me. I wondered, now, how

Frank could have heard my whimper, but not the sound of Simon Sterling being killed.

I waited a few seconds, but heard nothing. It occurred to me, however, that Frank might call the policeman stationed outside to come in and check on things. After all, there had been a murder in his inn last night, and he'd already heard something tonight. I realized if I was going to do this, it was now or never.

I opened the door again and crossed to the front desk. Very carefully, I lifted the ring of keys from the cubby where I'd seen them kept yesterday. I thought about how much easier it would have been to kill Simon in his room instead of the Game Room. It was easy to steal the keys. Entering his room and killing him in private, versus the public space of the Game Room, would have been a smarter move. I decided the murder must not have been premeditated. Something had happened last night to anger someone enough to kill Simon Sterling. I agreed with Bellamy about one thing. Simon Sterling's murder had been a crime of passion.

I scurried to the staircase and began a silent climb to the second floor. When I opened the door, I found I could not move. I stared down the hallway, convinced someone would open their door. It wasn't until I noticed the scent of my candles that I relaxed. Honestly, I was comforted to know that many people had already opened their gift boxes and lit their candles. Finally, I began what was probably a short journey, but which felt like a mile-long walk down the hall.

At Simon's door, I stopped. I was happy to see that the yellow tape had been discreetly removed. Bravely, I lifted the key toward the lock, but then wondered if my mind was playing tricks on me. I was sure I heard something or someone inside the room. Perhaps a creak of the interior connecting door closing. I paused and listened. Only silence greeted me. I was really losing it.

"Snap out of it," I whispered. I reminded myself that I was part of the wedding staff and in need of a candle. I wasn't about to kill anyone. Someone had already done that, and it wasn't me. I just needed a candle for the bride and groom. Shaking off my fears, I plunked the key into the lock and opened the door.

Empty. But every shadow from the dancing trees and cloud-streaked moon outside was projected across the room's walls. I was in a full-on sweat as I closed the door behind me. The first thing I did, of course, was stub my toe on the edge of the bed. As everyone knows, this is a wildly painful thing, but given the circumstances, all I could do was bite my knuckle until the pain subsided. Once it did, I began to limp my way to the desk where I'd left the candle. As I grew closer, I detected the candle's faint aroma beneath the lingering scent of tobacco in the room.

"Joe?"

I froze at the sound of Joe's name in the empty room, my hand in midair as it was reaching for the candle. The voice was Jessica's.

"Joe," she said again.

I almost fainted with relief when I realized the voice was coming from the hallway, not the room.

"Are you in there?" she said.

I said nothing.

Jessica said nothing.

A moment later, I heard the footsteps retreat.

After standing still for what felt like a million more minutes, listening for more noises outside my door, I picked up the candle box, thereby adding another robbery to the list of crimes that had occurred at the Melville this weekend.

Now, I harbored a secret, too.

I crossed the room, let myself out, and flew down the stairs. Neither Frank nor the police were in the inn when I reached the lobby, but I stopped for nothing. I slipped the keys back into the cubby behind the concierge desk and raced back to the safety of my workroom to finish the candle. Without pause, I ripped open the box, placed the candle onto the lazy Susan, and delved into my work.

Two hours later, I had finished my last design, summer. In the decorative circle for this final season, I drew a rose of Sharon, a flower that blooms on the island. I took the other three candles and placed them on the plate, spinning them softly to admire the true unity of my design. It had been a long night, but a productive one. And I had to admit how much I loved my work.

My body ached with fatigue, and without bothering to wash my face or remove my chef pants, I grabbed a few more aprons to use as blankets, climbed right on top of the table that had been my work space all night, and fell asleep.

Chapter 18

"Well, this was not a sight I expected to see this morning," I heard Frank say. "What's going on?"

My shoulder felt stiff on the hard table that had seemed as soft as a pile of feathers when I climbed atop it. I realized that a ray of sunlight was hitting my right cheek, like an alarm clock I was sleeping through. I opened one eye to find Frank staring at me. Without saying a word, I pointed to the new unity candles I'd put on top of a shelf.

"Were you here all night?" he said. "I'd have at least given you a cot."

"It was sort of spur of the moment," I said, rising and rubbing my shoulder. I hopped off of the table and pulled my morning hair into a ponytail.

"It was worth it," said Frank. He approached the candles and gave the lazy Susan a spin. "They look fantastic." He turned to me and frowned. "Let me get you some coffee. It's already brewing. Emily and her team were over at the reception site this morning. They've already set up everything. It looks gorgeous. You, on the other hand, look like you're doing a walk of shame."

"As if," I said. "Aside from a few cheese and crackers on your lawn last night, I was working my fingers off."

"You still look guilty of something," he said, walking into the restaurant.

I followed Frank, and sat in front of the most delicious cup of coffee I'd ever seen or tasted. A couple of guys from Emily's crew walked past me to the staging room. They left a moment later with the unity candle, ready to drive it to the chapel where they told me that Emily was already at work. It was barely seven thirty.

"Have a minute?" I asked Frank.

"This is literally the only minute I will have all day," said Frank, joining me. "What a weekend. I've had some good news though. Maude came back. Tough lady."

"She is," I said, impressed that Maude was back on her feet already. "You don't believe that Bill killed Simon Sterling, do you?"

"It's hard to imagine," said Frank, ripping open a packet of sweetener for his coffee. "I mean, I've known the guy for a year now. He's hardworking, nice enough."

"I couldn't help notice how quiet the inn gets at night, when all of the guests go to bed," I said, wiping a phantom crumb off the table and getting to the question that had bothered me since last night. "Are you sure you didn't hear anything the night that Simon was murdered?"

"Nope," he said and stirred his coffee with energy. "I sleep like a log."

"Frank," I said. "A man was bashed on the head with a candlestick and died. There must have been some sort of stir. A crack, a fall, something. Even if Simon's death was quick and his attacker surprised him, that kind of violence makes noise. You were so close."

Frank looked into his mug.

"The thing is," he said. "Boy, I need to tell this to someone."

"What?" I said.

"I wasn't in my room that night."

I raised an eyebrow.

"I was with a friend," he said, and scratched the back of his neck. "The guest who broke his ankle."

"I didn't know you were friends," I said.

"More than friends," he said. "I can't have guests in my room, so I kept it low-key. I snuck him in for a two-night stay. The inn was basically empty this week, so I didn't feel bad. But of course, I ended up having to pay for the rooms once it became a police matter."

"So, you didn't tell Bellamy?"

Frank shook his head.

"I told him what I told you—I sleep like a log," he said. "I've been feeling so guilty though. Perhaps I could have saved the man."

"I don't think you could have," I said. "You might have been able to give the police a clue, but you wouldn't have saved him. He was hit hard."

It occurred to me that Frank could have ended up on the floor with Simon if he'd entered the Game Room at the wrong time.

"I guess you both have an alibi," I said.

"We do," he said. "Lance's foot is wrecked. I was taking care of him all night."

"What about the other guests?" I said. "It feels like Bellamy interviewed them quickly, and before anyone knew it, Bill was under arrest. Who were they?"

Frank shrugged.

"The Hopkinses seemed like a nice family trying to get in a little break at the end of the off-season. I felt bad for them. The kid got sick straight away."

"I noticed," I said. "What about the older couple? You said they were talking to Jessica and Joe."

"Ida and Al Heller," he said. "They seem kind of old to lay a deadly blow on someone."

"True," I said.

"And they were adorable. They fussed over Jessica Sterling's ring, and made Jessica glow. I think she liked showing it off to them. Even Mrs. Sterling chatted with them, before she said she didn't feel well and went to bed."

I thought about the ring. Jessica had been dismissive of it to her best friend, but eager to show it to the Hellers. She was certainly ambivalent about her mother's gift.

"You don't think the Hellers had anything to do with Simon Sterling's death, do you?" Frank said.

"No," I said.

"Me neither. Even Simon Sterling chatted with them," he said. "I mean, there weren't a lot of guests at the inn, so it's not strange for people to say a word or two to each other. Joe had a nice chat with them after he checked in."

"Why shouldn't Simon be nice to them?"

"Well, he should, but he wasn't nice to everyone. At least, it seems like he ripped off Joe and Tony at cards. And he and Mrs. Sterling really had it in for each other."

"What do you mean?" I said.

"Maybe she started it. I saw her knock on Simon's door before their family dinner, looking very cross. He opened the door and basically said, "Now what?" clearly not happy to see her. And he'd seemed happy enough a moment earlier when Joe left his room after a visit. Also, after dinner, she grumbled to Jessica that she shouldn't have invited Simon. In front of him. But Simon was about the only person who isn't afraid of that woman. He just laughed and told her she made more problems for herself than anyone he'd ever met and to put a sock in it."

Frank took a final sip of his coffee and rose.

"Duty calls," he said. "And, this look of yours today. If I were you, I'd get on the first launch out of here to wash up."

"I have to check out the reception tent first," I said.

Frank looked at me with sympathy, and then began his day.

I left the inn and walked across the street to where the tent had been erected for the evening's reception. The tent alone was something to see. Emily had out-done herself. Three flags in the pink, blue, and purple colors of the wedding pierced the pointed tops of the huge white tent and flew in the morning wind, to her-ald the coming nuptials. The clear sides of the tent were pulled down and secured to the earth, to keep nature out. As a result, the tables and chairs had been delivered and set, the flowers and candles arranged, and the lighting for the band was ready to go. Even the place cards had been set out on the entry table.

"Gorgeous," I said to myself.

"Stella!" Jessica called my name from across the room. I had been so dazzled by the space I had not no-ticed that she and her mother were also taking a sneak peek.

"Hi." I waved, sheepishly. "I finished the unity can-dles! They're already on their way to the chapel."

Jessica's face melted into a puddle of joy. Mrs. Ster-ling looked equally pleased. It was nice to see some of the tension in her face lighten. In spite of her misgivings about Joe, Mrs. Sterling had been absorbing a lot of the stress of the weekend, being strong for her daughter in order to move the wedding along.

After making sure that Jessica and her mother were happy with everything, I left for the launch that awaited me. Once onboard, I inhaled the clean morning air. The day was clear, not at all as chilly as it had been yesterday. It was as if the summer was starting along with the busy weekend. As the launch left, I looked back at the inn. There, I saw Maria Blane, maid of honor, with David on a small porch off of one of the rooms. I wondered what kind of candle I'd make for them one day. Lavender and lilac, I thought.

The breeze was a little stronger than I would have liked, so I curled up my legs as we headed across the harbor. It was only about eight in the morning and many tourist fishing excursions were returning about this time. Some larger boats were arriving for the weekend. The real yacht crowd, no offense to Peter's small dinghy.

As I looked at the sea, I noticed the familiar silhouette of a woman with a ponytail speeding across the water. I couldn't get a close look at her, but in the daylight, I noticed that her boat was not much larger than Peter's, with a single engine. She was flying.

As the Melville's launch pulled in to the pier in town a few moments later, I saw that Andy was waiting for me. He was holding a cup of coffee and a bag of donuts from the island's infamous diner, the Downyflake. Their donuts are the best on the island, and everyone who knows me knows I can't resist their chocolate glazed creations.

"Morning," he called out to the launch with a wave. "Busy night?"

He eyed my outfit as I disembarked in four-inch heels, Gina's couture top, and a pair of chef's pants. The look I returned dared him to ask me why I was still partially dressed up. He got my message and kept his mouth shut.

"Listen," he said. He handed me the bag of donuts. "Frank told me you were heading back. We need to talk."

"What's up?" I said, realizing the donuts were a bribe as I began to eat them. I didn't stop, however. "I've got to get home for a quick change before the store opens. The Candleers are having their last class today."

He handed me the coffee and we walked down the wharf toward some benches where we took a seat.

"I texted you last night, but you didn't respond," he said.

"My phone died," I said.

"Listen. I know you have some ideas about the murder, but I need you to back off on this sleuthing."

"That's ridiculous," I said. "You know as well as anybody that no one is giving this murder the attention it deserves and an innocent man is being accused. I can roll with a lot in life, but not that. We're talking about Bill Duffy. I thought you'd be outraged, too."

"I would be, except that things are looking worse and worse for Bill."

"Impossible," I said, my blood boiling.

"Bill put a down payment on a brooch at Jewel in the Sea on Friday afternoon," he said. "Looks like he and Simon made plans to scam Joe Handler and Tony Carlson as early as that afternoon."

"Bill and Maude are celebrating their twenty-fifth wedding anniversary. He wanted something nice to give Maude. He weakened and did the deal with Simon because the brooch was expensive, but that's where it ends. Well, it ends after the punch. By the way, there was five thousand dollars on the table that night, between the three men."

"That's where you're wrong," said Andy. "Bill took it all, and there was twenty-five hundred. There was no other money on Simon or in his room, only a couple of twenties in his wallet."

"Bill told me he only took his half of the money. That means there was another twenty-five hundred dollars," I said. "Why would he lie?"

"Why didn't you tell me this at the station yesterday?" said Andy.

Without saying another word, he took out his notebook, and looked at me.

"What?" I said.

"Let's do this," he said. "Who do you think did it?"

I knew he was humoring me, but I decided to take advantage of the situation.

"Where to start?" I said.

"How about Frank?" he said. "His room is closest to the Game Room and it's odd he didn't hear anything."

"I thought the same, but Frank was taking care of the guy with the broken foot. He has an alibi."

"OK, Detective Wright," he said. "I see you're a step ahead. How about Mrs. Sterling? She gave me a funny feeling when I interviewed her. I know you'll appreciate gut feelings better than Bellamy would. I had a feeling she was keeping something from me. And as much as I hate to admit it, that trip to the Nantucket Inn was definitely unusual if we're going to reopen our list of suspects."

"Suspicious, yes," I said. "But murderous, no. Especially if the murder is tied to that missing money on

Simon. She has no need for it. The trip to the motel was a whole other story. She went there to give a photo of the maid of honor to the concierge."

"And you know this because?"

"Because 'needing to go to the ladies'" is not always what it sounds like."

Andy rolled his eyes, but I held up my hand before he could interrupt.

"Maria used to be in love with Joe in high school," I said. "I think Mrs. Sterling is concerned that there's still some hanky-panky going on because Joe's been distracted this weekend. Frankly, I feel like Mrs. Sterling would love to stop the wedding. She's very attached to Jessica in a not so healthy way. But I don't think any of it ties back to Simon and his card game winnings."

"Fair enough," said Andy. "So where does that leave us?"

"I'm thinking that the money from the card game was not the only motive for murder," I said. "The man liked to toy with people. The card game supports his reputation. But maybe someone else in his past was there to get revenge. I asked Peter to look into the other guests."

"Peter?" said Andy.

I nodded.

"Listen, if you have any big ideas, please tell the police, not a reporter. We can handle things."

"I was reaching out to anyone willing to help," I said, a little more defensively than I wanted to sound.

"Out of curiosity," he said. "How do you think that an elderly couple could kill Simon Sterling? They were like eighty years old."

"OK," I said. I accepted his argument, but I'd also saved the best for last. "How about Gina Ginelli?"

At this Andy laughed, but I opened the purse I still carried.

"Look at this," I said. "It was in the purse that Gina lent for the rehearsal dinner. *To Tinkerbell.* Think about it. He had a tattoo of a bell. Don't ask, my cousin Kate told me. Plus, a cat named Tinker? I think they were having an affair. I think she was here to see Simon, not study for a role. And I'm sure she was in the Game Room at the Melville the night that Simon was murdered. I smelled her perfume last night." I held my wrist to Andy's nose to prove it. "I'd be willing to take an oath that this is the same scent I picked up in the Game Room."

Andy took the note and read it. Then he pulled from a pocket on the side of his pants a small plastic bag. I'd never seen an evidence bag before. It looked like your basic ziplock bag, but it was still very cool.

"Not that it would stand up in court, but you're sure about the perfume?"

"Yes," I said. "I should also tell you that I swear I heard someone in Simon's room last night. I got stuck in there for a moment and there was a knock on the door. It was Jessica asking for Joe. But why would she knock on Simon's door?"

"First, please don't tell me why you got stuck in his room," said Andy. "Second, Joe's room is next to Simon's. She could have made a mistake."

He had a point.

"I'm a little more interested in the Gina angle," he said.

"Do you have enough new information to spring Bill?"

"Spring?" said Andy with a smile. "You've become a real gumshoe."

"I know. I can't stop," I said. "But spring him any-way."

"We can't spring Bill," he said. "But I'm willing to quietly reexamine the facts. If things line up, I'll go to Bellamy. Meanwhile, don't go back to Simon's room. A yellow tape is a yellow tape. Even if there's a potted fern in front of it. Deal?"

"Deal," I said. I definitely was not going to tell him I'd taken the dead man's candle.

"Good," he said as we began to walk toward the end of the dock to town. He looked out at the moored boats. "Georgianna's found a new spot for her boat."

I followed his eyes to a cluster of small motorboats, bobbing in the harbor's water. One was the motorboat I'd seen last night, and this morning. I really wanted to like Andy's girlfriend, but I hoped she had not been the one to cut off Peter last night.

"Look," said Andy, pointing past the edge of the harbor to the first row of stores in town.

Tony was standing at the display window in front of Jewel in the Sea. The same jeweler where Bill had put in an order for Maude's anniversary gift. And the same jeweler where Jessica and her mother had had her engagement ring cleaned on Friday. He entered the store.

"That's odd," I said. "Last night, I heard him on the phone with his wife. He said he wasn't going to spend a penny, and then he told me he's pretty broke. If so, why's he there?"

"Bill said that he only took half the money?" said Andy.

I nodded.

Chapter 19

Andy and I crossed the street toward Jewel in the Sea. To the right of their entrance is a large display window filled with many of Nantucket's popular, high-end jeweled treasures. I'd also gotten my ears pierced here as a kid. It was the place to get your first gold studs. After that, it was a long time until you ever went back, but we could all say we had something from Jewel in the Sea.

I headed right for the door, but Andy stopped me.

We sidestepped to the window and pretended to look at the merchandise. It gave us a good view of Tony. The salesclerk was not in the showroom at the moment, so Tony was browsing the display cases. I found myself looking at the array of goodies in the window as well.

"Nice," I said about the engagement ring section. Nantucket is a place where spontaneous proposals do occur, so a healthy engagement ring display was a good idea.

"Expensive," said Andy.

"Is this thing with Georgianna serious?" I asked.

Andy looked at me funny and leaned against the side of the building. I turned away, not sure why I had asked.

"Look," I said.

I pointed through the window. Inside, the salesman had returned and Tony was handing a wad of cash to him.

"OK," said Andy. "I'll be right back. Stay here."

He opened the door. I followed right behind him.

"Hello, Mr. Carlson," said Andy.

Both Tony and the salesman looked at us from the counter. The moment Tony saw Andy in his uniform, he dropped the bag he was holding as if it was on fire.

"Hi," said Tony. "Can I help you?"

Andy took a plastic bag from his pocket.

"I'm going to have to take the money," he said to the bewildered salesclerk.

Andy pulled a tissue from a box on the counter and used it to put the money into another evidence bag, examining its value as he did.

"Twenty-five hundred dollars," he said to me.

I had a strong suspicion we'd found the other half of the money from Friday night's card game.

"Tony, give me the merchandise," said Andy.

"What's the meaning of this?" said Tony, indignantly, but he wasn't kidding anyone. He looked seriously guilty.

I followed Andy and Tony outside. People were looking at them, and the sidewalk was crowded.

"Cross the street," said Andy.

We crossed the cobblestoned street to a bricked sidewalk adjacent to the parking lot of the town's Stop & Shop, where it was quieter.

"I have some questions for you regarding the death of Simon Sterling," he said.

"I gave my statement yesterday," said Tony. "What's this about?"

"This is about how you got twenty-five hundred dollars when you told me you were broke and you told your wife you wouldn't spend a penny," I said.

"Can I do the questioning?" Andy said.

"Of course," I said. "Ask him where he got the money."

"Good idea," he said. I picked up the sarcasm, and shut up.

Andy looked at Tony.

"So?" he said. "If what Ms. Wright is saying is true, where did you get the cash?"

"From my bank account," said Tony, making a sort of duck face in his defense. It didn't suit him.

"Andy can check, you know," I said.

"Stella!" said Andy.

I pulled my fingers across my mouth. My lips were sealed.

"Is that the answer you want to go with?" said Andy. "Because Ms. Wright is correct. The police can check your account."

"On what grounds?" said Tony.

"On the grounds that we have new evidence to suggest there was more money that went missing from Simon Sterling the night of his murder. Money that Bill Duffy did not take."

"About the same amount you were just about to spend at Jewel in the Sea," I said.

Andy pointed to a bench about five feet away. I sat, but leaned forward so I could hear the rest of the conversation.

"Fine," said Tony. "But if I tell you anything, I want you to promise not to press charges against me. Actually, I think I need a lawyer."

"If you'd like a lawyer," said Andy, "I can take you down to the station, and we can wait until you get a lawyer. I can have you out of there by this evening."

"I'm the best man in a wedding today," said Tony.

"Suit yourself," said Andy.

Tony cursed a bit.

"After the card game, I went back to the Game Room," said Tony. "I was going to confront Simon about the card game. After I went up to my room, I thought about it and realized that he and Bill were probably in on some con together. The table was round, you know. It got me thinking."

"Excuse me," said a lady wearing a money belt and carrying a large tote and some shopping bags. Behind her were about seven people. All looked related, and each filled about the width of the sidewalk. I looked down the wharf and realized the latest ferry had arrived, filled with more day-trippers heading to see the boats cross the finish line this afternoon.

Andy pulled Tony aside as the high spirits of the FIGAWI crowd encroached upon our serious conversation. I noticed he held Tony's arm tightly.

"What happened when you went back to the Game Room?" Andy said when the crowd had passed.

Tony suddenly looked exhausted.

"Simon Sterling was dead," he said.

"You saw the body?" I said, rising from my bench. "Before anyone else? Why didn't you call the police?"

Tony stared at the sidewalk and said nothing. Andy studied him.

"Did you touch anything?" he said.

Tony nodded.

"What did you touch?" he asked.

"Simon Sterling," said Tony.

The best man closed his eyes as if he was trying to

wash away the image. I couldn't decide if it was because he felt tremendous remorse about having killed Simon, or tremendous guilt about having touched a murdered man. I now realized that when Tony had dropped his camera on Simon Sterling, he had done so on purpose. He was able to leave fingerprints on the body without arousing suspicion.

"Look," said Tony. He was sweating now. "I didn't kill the guy. I was just there to take what was mine."

He sounded an awful lot like Bill, and I gave Andy a look that said as much.

"He stole my money," said Tony, who was now on a roll. "I wanted it back."

I went right into Tony's face.

"You withheld information that probably put an innocent man in jail," I said. "You are worse than Simon Sterling on any day."

"No, I didn't," said Tony. "When I found the body, Simon was only carrying half the money. If anything, my theory lined up. I figured he had already given Bill his share, or that Bill had wrestled him for it. Not my fault if Bill's a maniac and killed him."

"Either way," said Andy, reaching for his cuffs, "you might want to think about that lawyer. You withheld evidence in a murder investigation."

"Wait a minute," said Tony, stepping back.

Another tourist with an overstuffed day bag cut between us.

"Sorry," the lady said.

In the moment it took for Andy to let her pass, Tony bolted. He outright bolted!

Poor Tony. He had no idea that Andy was on track in high school. He wouldn't stand a chance. Especially on these crooked sidewalks.

Andy dashed after him. Tony had on his side the

fact that the streets were packed for the town's sailing event and it was easy to fade into the crowd. I followed, but Emily is the only one I know who can rock heels and cobblestones. By the time I'd removed my shoes, Tony had already rounded the corner with Andy in pursuit, and I could no longer see either of them as I fought through the sidewalk and street traffic. I had a feeling, however, that they'd be heading right toward the movie theater, so I took a side road that cut through the streets. I picked up the most speed I could, but once again wished I'd been more devoted to the gym this winter.

At this point, the only thing I had going for me was my experience on the cobblestones. I basically know the layout and angle of every stone on these streets. As kids, we had a game to race each other along them. I came home with many a bruise and scrape, but my mom used to laugh and tell me it might come in handy one day. I was glad she'd been so understanding because now, ahead of me, I was reaching what I hoped was the intersection of Tony's escape.

"Ooooph," I said, colliding with our perp as I fell to the ground.

The victory was mine. Tony lay on the ground next to me. A couple of well-meaning pedestrians offered us a hand, but Tony brushed them off. I, on the other hand, accepted.

Andy reached us before Tony was even standing. He had Tony's arm and his handcuffs out.

"You OK?" he said to me.

I nodded, and put my shoes back on.

"Wait, wait," said Tony. "I'm sorry. I'm really not myself. What if I give you some information that might help you?"

"It would have to be darn good," said Andy. His

voice was pretty official and scary, I have to say, but I noticed he did not put the cuffs on Tony. "You just fled a cop and knocked Stella over."

"Look, I'm just a broke guy who needed some cash to buy an expensive wedding gift to make my friend look good. Jessica's friends are all fancy folk who give expensive gifts. Maria and I look like paupers next to them, and I wanted for once for Joe to have a friend in the same league. I love the guy. I took the cash because it's mine, by rights, and I wanted to buy something without my wife knowing. That's all I'm guilty of, I swear. I panicked when I saw the dead body, and I was not thinking straight when I took the money. Then, I was afraid to tell Bellamy," said Tony.

"So far, you're just whining," said Andy. "What's your information?"

Tony rubbed his neck. I got the feeling he really didn't want to say what he was about to say, but that he was desperate to have Andy let go of his arm.

"First, I knocked on Simon's door. He didn't answer, so I went back down to the Game Room," said Tony. "When I entered, I could swear someone was hovering outside the Sun Room doors."

"What time?" Andy said.

"A little after three?" said Tony.

"Did you see who it was?" said Andy.

Tony scratched his head and looked defeated.

"No," he said, "it was like a shadow, and light-footed, so I wasn't even sure of what I was seeing. If it helps, Simon was super dead. Like, he'd been dead for a while."

Andy looked at me, and I knew we were thinking the same thing. Gina Ginelli. My theory that she had been in the Game Room on Friday night was gaining strength.

"And here's another thing," said Tony, looking piti-fully desperate now. "Joe would never kill a guy, but he's been acting very strange all weekend. He's disappeared a few times and had me cover for him."

"Selling out your best friend?" I said.

Tony swallowed.

"I just mean he might know something," he said. "Yesterday, Joe asked me to tell Jessica he had a headache, but when I went to check on him, his room was empty. I mean, the night of the card game, Joe left in a huff. He told Simon that Mrs. Sterling had been right about him after all."

My mind flashed back to the creaking floor I'd heard last night.

"This is all so out of control," said Tony. "I mean, who'd really think a candle would kill someone?"

"Exactly," I said in defense of my beautiful, broken candle before I realized I was agreeing with a murder suspect.

"Listen," said Tony. "I'm buying a stupid wedding gift. That's not enough of a motive to kill a guy. I've been everywhere I'm supposed to be all weekend. Nothing I've done suggests I'm guilty of anything more than what I told you."

It was strange, I had to admit, that Joe was disappearing every now and then. I wondered if Mrs. Sterling was right, and maybe Joe really was cheating on Jessica with Maria. I tried out the idea that Simon found out about an affair between Joe and Maria, and then decided to blackmail Joe. That could give Joe a motive. Maria, however, didn't strike me as someone who was the homewrecking type. And from the smile she had this morning on David's porch, she wasn't pining over Joe.

I considered another angle. Perhaps, like Tony, Joe

needed the money from the card game for something he desperately needed to do without Jessica knowing. And maybe Simon found out what that was, and Joe had to stop him from telling her. If this was the case, I wondered what Joe might be hiding from his fiancée.

Or maybe the truth was as simple as what we'd accused Tony of. Joe was mad that he'd been swindled, he confronted Simon, one thing led to another, and next thing he knew, he had dealt Simon a deadly blow. That did not explain the sneaking around, however. No, if Joe was involved, there was something else going on.

"I'm going to ask you to stay on the island until we speak again," Andy said to Tony. "And I'm going to ask you to keep this conversation to yourself. You can go for now, but I may have further questions for you."

"What about my gift?" said Tony. "That was my money, fair and square. I mean, mostly my money. I guess some of it would have been Joe's. But I'm buying him a gift with it."

Andy held up his hands.

"You need to stop right there or I'm going to arrest you," he said.

"Fine," said Tony.

"Chin up," I said to Tony in a conciliatory tone. "I'll see you at the wedding this afternoon. No hard feelings about the crash. I'm fine."

Tony looked like he'd been hit by a truck at this point. I felt sorry for the guy as we watched him walk away from us.

"Assuming Gina was the shadowy figure, do you think she or Joe had anything to do with anything?" I said as his figure disappeared into a crowd of tourists that was growing by the minute.

Andy didn't answer, but I could tell his brain was working on the puzzle.

"I'm not sure," he said. "I'm also not sure Tony has said anything to change Bellamy's mind about Bill. After all, Bill was caught with Simon's money. He was the one in charge of the candle, and we know he punched Simon. Plus, he confessed he was looking for revenge against the dead man."

"That was just heat-of-the-moment talk," I said.

"It was heated talk that sounded a lot like a confession to Bellamy," said Andy. "But I'll look into a couple of things."

"I'm teaching a class now." I checked the time. With all the distractions, I wouldn't be making it home to change for my class with the Candleers. My heels, chiffon top, and chef pants would have to be my fashion statement until I got home. It was at least better than putting on Gina's couture skirt that was folded in my bag.

"Are you going to Chris and Suzie's cookout later?" he said.

I nodded.

"I could give you a lift to Gina's after," he said.

I smiled. He ignored me, but I knew he couldn't resist using me as cover to check into the case a little more, whatever his orders might be.

Andy's walkie-talkie crackled again.

He turned it off and sighed. "Someone found a stray buoy. They want to know if it has to do with the Buoy Bandit."

"See you later," I said.

"It's a date," he said.

"In your dreams," I said.

"In yours," he answered.

Men.

Chapter 20

I entered the Wick & Flame with a renewed sense of appreciation for my life's calling. In the quiet of my store, I inhaled the blend of the many scents I'd toiled over during the winter months. I straightened a few candles that were askew on their display stands. I didn't mind that they weren't perfectly aligned. The fact that they had been moved suggested that I still had some retail traffic coming in and out of the store, in spite of my candle's connection to a murder. And I loved tidying my store. If anyone saw my apartment, they wouldn't think I would. My place is a mess, but my store is perfection. I know what I'm doing here. I know scents. I know customers. I know how to match a color and an aroma to a person. And I had the satisfaction of running my own enterprise.

As I switched on the lights to the back room, I admitted that murder was a much trickier puzzle. I headed to a small sink in the back of the room to brush my teeth and hair. I'd learned years ago to leave an emergency kit under the sink, and I was happy to have it now. I brushed everything, thinking about how

Simon Sterling was a man I probably wouldn't have liked too much if I'd met him. Assuming I was right about his affair with Gina, I wondered what she saw in him. He must have been a smooth talker.

Returning my case back under the sink, I found myself heading to my collection of scented oils. I wondered what kind of candle scent I'd have chosen for Simon. Too easy. Tobacco and musk. I wondered, then, what I'd make for the killer. The idea made me queasy, but the truth was I didn't know. I started sniffing and combining oils in new combinations, my mind at work.

I hated to think that murder inspired me, but the adventure of the last couple of days was giving me new ideas. Moonlit picnics, fashion collaborations with celebrities, this morning's pursuit with Andy were an unexpected twist to my usually ordered life. I left my oils, and headed into the shop where I found the last postcard my mom had sent me. I'd tossed it under the register, but now I put it on the counter instead. *Love from Bhutan*, it said. My cheeks turned pink as I realized I wasn't even sure where Bhutan was. I caught myself wondering where Peter had traveled before arriving to Nantucket, and how he'd feel about the island once February arrived.

A knock on my door brought me back to the busy day I had ahead of me.

Cherry waved merrily, and I let her in.

"Hello, my dear," she said, immediately peeling off her long scarf. "The girls are behind me. They stopped to buy a ticket for the quilt raffle on the corner, but I never win those things, so I passed. The traffic is already starting to pick up. God help us today. Those youngsters get too rowdy during and after the race. And tonight, don't get me started. It's either the blare of the band at the charity ball, or they're lined up at the Chicken Box. Your poor cousins. I bet the place will be littered up by noon."

"Good morning to you," I said. I knew the old folks were a little wary of FIGAWI, but I liked our island's celebration of life and the sea. The revelry was all part of appreciating those bright sails as they flew freely across the ocean.

The ladies piled in behind Cherry, and started their own ritual of unwrapping themselves.

"Are you going to offer another class this summer?" Cherry said. "I'm thinking that a candle mold class would be fun. I'd love to make a candle that looks like a bunny for my granddaughter. She's coming to visit in July."

"I think we'll have time to work on something like that," I said.

Bunny candles. Cherry had great ideas.

I herded my gang into the workshop just as Lucy knocked on the door.

"Perfect timing," I said to her. "We have a busy day ahead. Are you ready?"

"Absolutely," Lucy answered. "By the way, you had a client call yesterday. Lauren Bing?"

"Ugh, don't tell me," I said. Lauren was one of my unity candle customers. I didn't need to hear of another cancellation.

"I convinced her to wait a couple of days to talk to you about her order," she said. "I told her you were busy with the Sterlings, who had asked you to develop an amazing new creation for them. She seemed intrigued."

"I could kiss you," I said. "No, I will kiss you!" I hugged her, too. "One day you might be running this place."

"Ha," she said. She looked skeptical, but once upon a time, I'd have looked skeptical, too.

"Is Lucy saving your unity candle business?" said Cherry from my workroom.

"Lucy is a businesswoman in the making," I said.

"You go girl!" said Cherry.

For the next hour, I worked with the ladies on their last projects, a challenge to everything we'd done: Ombre. The ladies loved it. One made a candle that matched her daughter's pink hair streaks. While the candles dried, we had a cup of tea.

"Who has news?" said Cherry.

"I have news," I said, trying to look as mysterious as I could.

"Tell," said Cherry.

"See this beautiful blouse?" I moved my apron aside to show off my top. The ladies all nodded. "Guess who gave it to me?"

Cherry leaned toward me, confidentially.

"We've been thinking you were doing the walk of shame thing," she said.

"No!" I said. What was it with everyone? "Ladies! Get your minds out of the gutter, please. This was a loaner from someone who will knock your socks off."

"Let me guess," said Cherry, raising her hands. "And no, we don't think you're a hussy. Get over yourself, my love."

"It really is a very interesting fashion thing you have going on today," said Flo. The ladies laughed as if they'd been holding in that comment all morning. I joined them. I looked ridiculous, and I loved that they had tried hard to let it go.

"The bride?" said Cherry. "What's her name?"

"Gina Ginelli!" I said.

"Gina Ginelli isn't getting married," said Flo.

"She means Gina Ginelli gave it to her," said Cherry, with just a little impatience in her voice.

"I got stuck over by the Melville last night without a dress, and she kindly offered it to me so I could look presentable at the rehearsal dinner. Can you believe it?"

"No!" said Flo, truly impressed.

"What a lovely lady," Cherry said, checking her candle.

I truly wondered if Gina was a lovely lady. I'd know by this afternoon.

I joined Cherry to inspect the candles. They were ready to pack up. The timing was perfect. I wanted to get home and change, as much as I loved this blouse.

"No way is Gina Ginelli ever going to marry someone else," said Flo, still confused. "That husband of hers is a dream. Can you imagine being married to Kevin Bunch?"

"I don't know," said Cherry. "There are rumors about him. I hear it's not the best marriage, but you know these celebrities. They have different rules."

"Poppycock," said Flo with conviction. "No one is going to tell me anything bad about Kevin Bunch."

"Flo," said Cherry, "I love your old-fashioned ways, but everything is more complicated than it seems these days."

"That's for sure," I said.

"Aside from being married to the most gorgeous man on earth, Gina Ginelli will be married forever because in her young and naïve days she signed a prenup," said Flo.

"I'm sure Gina Ginelli has made enough over the years that she doesn't need Kevin Bunch's money," said Cherry.

"Well, you don't know everything," said Flo. "It's not Gina who would get the money. It's Kevin. I read it in *Us* magazine about two years ago when I was getting my hair done. When they got married, Gina actually had more money. If she ditched him, he'd get a ton of dough. Anyway, they're Catholic and she's Italian. No divorce in their future. Period."

I practically dropped the candle I was wrapping.

"You OK, honey?" said Flo.

"Yes," I said. "So, if Gina were caught having an affair, then her husband could take all her money?"

"A whole bunch of it," said Flo. "And he could probably get a divorce, which would kill her as a Catholic."

Cherry laughed. "The affair part wouldn't bother her, but the divorce would?"

Any other day, I would have laughed along with Cherry. Today, however, I kept an open mind. Between the note I had found in Gina's purse and her perfume scent at the murder scene, I was pretty sure that Gina and Simon were romantically involved. Assuming Flo's hairdresser's magazine's information was legit, Gina definitely had a motive to keep her affair with Simon a secret. If Simon threatened to expose their affair, that could be motive for murder.

"Ladies," I said. "I need to change and get ready for a wedding today, so I'm going to say goodbye for now. Keep your eyes open for an email from me. Let's get Cherry's candle mold class going."

"Go. Do what you need to do," said Cherry. "We'll let ourselves out. I'm going to grab one of those pink candles in the window for a dinner party I'm going to next week."

"Lucy will give you the friends & family discount," I said with a kiss to each.

With a few words of business to Lucy, I was out the door and heading to my car, which I'd abandoned overnight.

"Really?" I said to my Beetle. More specifically, I said it to the parking ticket on my windshield. I shoved it in my purse and climbed inside.

Chapter 21

Pulling into my driveway a few minutes later, I felt like I'd been away from home for weeks. I climbed up the stairs to my apartment over Chris and Suzie's garage. I tossed all my clothes, except for Gina's top, into the hamper and stepped into the warm water of my shower, which steamed up the whole of my small apartment. As I enjoyed the luxury of running water, I decided to wear a dressy top, palazzo pants, and sneakers to the wedding ceremony that Emily expected me to attend. I wasn't going to let heels or hemlines slow me down today.

When I turned off the faucet and pulled the curtain aside, I almost slipped right out of the shower and onto my floor with surprise. Tinker, my friend, was perched on my toilet in his sentry pose. I noticed that Andy had not mentioned the fact that he'd dropped him off here when we'd met this morning. I was glad to see him, nonetheless. Without expecting to, I'd softened to the little guy.

"Good morning," I said to my furry friend. "Nice to see you."

Tinker let out a purr in answer, but he stayed poised as if he were waiting for some information.

"OK," I said as I rubbed my hair dry and began the protracted process of styling it. "What can I tell you since last we met?"

Tinker swished his tail.

I unloaded everything. I can't say for sure if Tinker followed all of it. At one point, my hair dryer certainly drowned out my monologue. The cat, however, seemed to be interested in everything, and I wondered if he'd have anything to add if he could speak. I would have welcomed anything to be honest.

"So?" I said, heading to the kitchen when I was finally dressed and ready to face the rest of my day. I folded Gina's belongings carefully and put them in one of the hundred shopping bags that I keep under the sink. I held up the shoes for Tinker to admire. "What do you think?"

Tinker tilted his head, but he looked more interested in the empty bowl on the floor. I was happy to see that Andy had at least picked up some food for Tinker. He must have noticed the cans in Simon's room because they were the same brand. Tinker lapped up his meal when I tossed it on a plate. When he was finished, he stared hard at me. I stared back. Then, if this is possible for a cat, he sighed, turned his back, and went to my room for a nap. I knew I was being a little silly, but I felt he was disappointed in me. I suspected he knew something about the death of his master. If I was right, I still had some work to do.

My thoughts about Tinker were interrupted by the aroma of Chris's amazing burgers wafting through my apartment. It reminded me that I'd needed my sustenance to get through the day. I opened my window and waved across our shared backyard. A sizable gang had already congregated. Emily was seated on a chair with her feet up, but I could tell she was still in full work mode as she stared at her phone and typed away.

"Howdy," I called out to Suzie, who was refilling a large bucket of soda and beer cans. "Do you guys need anything?"

"I'll take some extra ketchup if you have it," Chris said from his station at the barbecue.

"You're in luck. That's about all I have in my fridge," I said. "My ketchup is your ketchup."

"That should be our family motto," he said.

"Be right down," I said. "And throw on two patties for me if you don't mind. The aroma of your famous cheeseburgers is to die for."

I gave Tinker an extra snuggle, grabbed some ketchup and the bag of Gina's clothes, then ran down the stairs to join the party. When I opened the door, I practically fell right into Peter.

"Hello," he said.

"Hello," I said, remembering Suzie's invitation.

"You're about to like me a lot," he said.

I took his hand, and gave him a look that told him I already did.

"I looked into the guests," he said, giving my hand a squeeze.

"Tell me about the Hellers," I said. I didn't think any of the guests would be of interest, but now I knew the old couple had spoken with the wedding party. If any of them had anything to lend to the case, it would be them.

"I see you figured out their names," said Peter. "But I can add more. They live in New York. They're jewelers, specializing in costume jewelry."

"That explains why they wanted a glimpse of Jessica's ring," I said. I wondered if they had noticed something extraordinary about Jessica's ring, but I wasn't sure how to tie it to the murder. "What about the others?"

"Nothing," said Peter. "Typical suburban family."

"Sorry for the goose chase," I said.

"Don't apologize. It's always good to follow your nose," he said. "You never know where it will lead you."

I smiled in spite of myself. Somehow the Hound metaphor didn't seem so bad when Peter used it.

"And now for the good stuff," said Peter.

"There's more?" I said.

"The will. Not one of the Sterlings are beneficiaries. Simon recently made a new will. Everything goes to a woman named MaryJo LaMonte. She's probably a long-lost daughter or something."

"You're right," I said. "You are a good investigator. I have a feeling the wedding announcements and obituaries are about to get very interesting on Nantucket."

We headed toward the party lost in our own smiles.

"Hi," said Emily, waving at me.

"I've got to check in with the boss," I said to Peter.

"Go to it," he said, taking the ketchup from me and heading to Chris.

"What's up with you and the newspaper man?" said Emily when I reached her and took a seat beside her.

"Not sure," I said. "I stopped by the reception tent. It's out of this world. You must have been up for hours already."

She eyed my outfit. I raised my hand before she could lecture me about my lack of high style.

"Trust me," I said. "After the night I had last night, I'm going for freedom of motion today. I took your lead."

"I'm preggers, Stella," she said. "I have an excuse." At that, she winced.

"You OK?" I said.

"On top of fake contractions last night, I now have gas pains this morning," she said.

I put my arm around my friend, and she rested her head on my shoulder.

"If it's a girl, are you going to name her Stella?" I said.

"Neal likes Victoria."

"Not bad."

"I know," she said. "Tell me about the rehearsal dinner."

I gave her the download, and was happy to see that she looked pleased with my work, even how I handled the unexpected bird accident with Maria Blane. Once we got through business, we got down to fun. I started by showing her Gina's outfit. She almost died. In spite of the fact that Gina was still on my list of suspects, I felt bad that Emily had not met her, especially since I was about to visit her again, so I switched my gossip to the party. I was just sharing Joe's toast when Liz, my cousin who works at the real state office in town, joined us. She looked particularly interested about the new gyms that Joe and Jessica were planning to open.

"They must have a lot of cash on hand," Liz said when I finished.

"They're rich," said Chris, handing my two burgers to me, which I immediately began to devour, condiments be damned.

"Not that rich," I said. "Jessica's mom told me that Jessica and Joe won't have the really big bucks until she dies."

"She told you that?" said Chris. "Seems kind of personal."

"People share the most amazing stuff with their

wedding planners," said Emily. "The tell-all books we could write."

"I don't care what she told you," said Liz. "She was being dramatic. Or their idea of not having money is wildly different than ours. Chris, back me up. In order to buy land and then build a gym facility, you need a lot of cash, either on hand or borrowed. Unless she's borrowing on her mother's future death."

"Gross," I said.

"All power to them, however they got the money," said Chris, returning to his grill.

Liz waved to Kate, and left to say hello to her sister as she pulled up.

"God, I hate being pregnant," Emily said, rubbing her stomach. Neal stood behind her looking helpless and rubbing her shoulders. "Hold my plate, honey? I have to go to the bathroom again."

My friend pushed herself up with some effort and headed to the house with Neal by her side.

Left alone, I headed toward Peter, who was surrounded by my two cousins in the trash removal business.

"Dude," said Docker. "You should interview us. We've been collecting buoys for two days. I swear this is a good story."

"What is?" I asked.

"The Buoy Bandit," said Ted.

"I'll take what I can get," said Peter. "But my editor has someone else covering FIGAWI."

From behind me, Andy's girlfriend, Georgianna, materialized in one of her formfitting horizontal striped shirts, this one a nautical blue and white striped, coupled with formfitting white jeans. Emily was right, she did pull them off.

"Hi, Stella," she said.

Andy walked up beside her, and she put her arm around his waist.

"Hi, Georgianna," I said. "How've you been?"

"I'm exploring new chakras," she said, pulling her hair back and into a bun as she spoke. She gave off a conservative image, but one never knew what words would come out of Georgianna's mouth. I decided it was my favorite part about her. "Did you know there are seven spiritual powers in the human body?"

"I didn't," I said, but the businesswoman in me was wondering if anyone would be interested in candles that represented each power.

"Ready, Stella?" said Andy.

"For what?" said Peter.

"Yeah," said Georgianna. "For what?"

I felt oddly uncomfortable, which I knew I shouldn't. Once again, however, standing between both men seemed weird. I wasn't involved with either, but I felt I was cheating on both.

"I'm getting a lift," I said to Peter. "Andy's heading to the Melville and my car window's broken."

"I can tell you about chakras while they're gone," Georgianna said to Peter. "You'll be fascinated."

"Sounds great?" he said, looking less than excited to learn about chakras.

I squeezed Peter's hand and gave him a smile, then walked toward the pile of cars in front of Chris and Suzie's house. I must have kept my apartment door open a second too long when I'd left, because when we arrived at Andy's car, Tinker was on his hood.

I patted his head.

"Want a deputy?" I said to Andy as we opened the car doors. "He's good company."

"No can do," said Andy, but Tinker was already in the car and on the floor before he finished the sentence.

"It's no use," I said. "He'll find a way in either way."

We closed the doors.

"So, are you and Peter a real thing?" said Andy as he pulled out onto the road.

"We have much more important things to discuss than my love life," I said.

Chapter 22

Now that we were headed to Gina's, the idea of facing a murder suspect on her turf was all too real. I focused on the line of cars heading into town to see the regatta arrive as we headed out toward the inn. Traffic meant that people would be hitting the stores in town, so fingers crossed that would lead to business at the Wick & Flame.

I looked at Andy, who was studying the road. I could see he had a lot on his mind. He had put on his police cap, which he didn't often do. I was thinking he looked older in it, but then changed my mind when I saw a drawing in black ink behind his ear of a happy emoji with a mustache.

"Is that a tattoo behind your ear?" I said, tugging at his earlobe.

Andy pulled his head away.

"No," he said. "Georgianna thought it would be funny to draw it on me when I was asleep. I didn't notice it, of course, because who sees drawings behind their ear? She keeps doing things she thinks are funny jokes, but she's really, and I mean really, bad at pranks."

"It's kind of funny," I said.

I laughed. Andy looked at me and grabbed my nose between his knuckles. The gesture lasted only a second, but it was new for us, and we both got quiet for a moment.

"Georgianna's decided that if she is going to stay on Nantucket, she needs to get off the sea and get in touch with the land. And her chakras," said Andy. "She's given up sailing to become an artist."

"Good for her," I said, thinking that Voldemort could have learned something from Georgianna. As for the chakras, what was I going to say?

When we finally left town and hit the open road toward the inn, Andy glanced at me.

"Ready for this?" he said.

"Are you kidding?"

"This is not a game," he said. "This is a murder investigation. A violent murder, too."

"I know that," I said. "Need I remind you that while you've been chasing mischief makers on beaches, I've likely spent the weekend with a murderer?"

I immediately regretted what I had said. I had so much respect for Andy's work.

"Sorry," I said.

"Bah," he said. "I've been knee deep in lobster-trap buoys half the weekend."

A few minutes later, we pulled up to the cottage.

"Stella," he said before we got out.

"No speeches," I said. "I'll be careful. Anyway, who's going to think that the Candle Lady would pursue a murderer?"

"Someone who thinks like a murderer," he said. "Just know, I've got us covered."

"I appreciate the chivalry," I said.

"It's not chivalry. And by the way, as a police officer,

I don't like the idea that you might unwittingly tell something to your new boyfriend that might end up in the paper," he said.

"Are you accusing Peter of pursuing me for my pillow talk?" I didn't know whether to laugh or punch him.

"Pillow talk?" he said. "That's fast."

"Zip it," I said. "Peter will investigate what Peter investigates. He doesn't need me."

I opened the car door and marched straight to Gina's door with the bag containing her outfit. Any apprehension I had about talking to a potential murderer had dissolved. I was a woman with a mission.

I knocked. I noticed Tinker had not joined us. I wondered if his instincts were right.

There was no answer, but I was used to Gina's door-answering routine.

Andy was beside me. We waited a moment. Then, he put his hand on his gun as he raised the other to knock once more.

"Hold on there," I said, laying a hand on his forearm. "You brought me here for subtlety, right?"

I knocked again.

"I have to admit," said Andy as we waited. "If you were to change professions, this isn't a bad one for you."

The door opened, and Gina Ginelli stared at us.

"Thank God," she said. "I was afraid you'd be one of the gang of partiers that slept on the beach last night. We had a good laugh and a great swim, but in the light of day, I think it's better we all went our separate ways, if you know what I mean."

Gina looked very different from the woman I'd

seen weeping on the widow's walk last night. Her hair was tousled, she wore jeans and a man-tailored shirt, tied at the waist with the sleeves rolled up.

"I have your clothes," I said, raising my bag. "I hate to intrude, but I left my stuff in your car last night."

"Of course, come in, both of you," she said.

"Thanks," I said, happy that my ruse to get inside had worked. That done, I wasn't sure what to do next.

"How's your trip been?" said Andy to Gina. He eyed the cottage as he spoke. I looked around, too, casually of course. Everything was super tidy. Even the script that had been scattered on Gina's table yesterday was now in a neat pile.

"The trip's been very productive," she said. "I've gotten a lot of work done. Stella, I'll just trot upstairs and grab your bag."

"Ms. Ginelli," said Andy. "If it's not too intrusive, would you mind if Stella grabbed her things herself? I have a full plate today and I know I promised to tell you a little bit about small-town cops. I'd hate to let you down."

"You're not letting me down at all," she said. "I'll be right back."

"I've got it," I said and stepped ahead of her.

Gina smiled, graciously.

"Well, then, thank you for your offer," she said. "I always appreciate the opportunity to add a thing or two to my actors' tool bag."

I had no idea why Andy wanted me to do this errand alone. At the top of the stairs, I turned and waved to both of them. They both waved back. Andy was behind Gina. He pointed his fingers to his eyes and then made a circular motion with them. I took that to mean he wanted me to look around her room.

I saluted, then cringed at my response as I turned and walked into her room.

Gina was definitely in a housekeeping mood this morning. Her room was as tidy as the living space downstairs. I made a decision to clean my apartment.

My bag, as promised, was on her bed. Beside it was a shopping bag in which I found my clothes as well. I'd plumb forgotten them as I'd rushed out of Gina's car last night. The shopping bag was gorgeous. Thick and blue with a store name I did not recognize but which advertised that it was from Milan. I hoped it wouldn't turn out to be any sort of evidence because I really wanted to have it in my emergency collection stuck under my kitchen sink. I'd probably use it to hold all the other bags I shoved under there.

The room was ridiculously tidy, and nothing stood out, so I went into the bathroom. It was spic and span, too. Remarkably so. All the makeup that had been scattered around the vanity last night was put away. I glanced at the shower and towel racks that had been covered in all sorts of lingerie last night. This afternoon, there was no sign of them. I opened her bathroom drawers. They were empty. This was both exciting and terrifying to me, and in spite of my confidence only a few minutes ago, I admit I was glad Andy was in the house and carrying a gun.

I suddenly didn't want my disappearance upstairs to be too long for fear that Gina would catch on that I was snooping around. I decided, however, to do one more thing before I headed downstairs. I opened the closet door.

At least one mystery was solved. From the looks of it, pretty much everything Gina had brought with her on her trip to Nantucket was now shoved in the walk-in closet. On a luggage rack in the middle of the closet was a half-packed suitcase with most of the items I had seen last night. I surmised that the tidiness of the cottage was not due to a housekeeping bug, but because Ms. Gina Ginelli was no longer planning to spend the entirety of Memorial Day weekend on Nantucket. I confess the revelation did make me feel a little better about my own domestic habits.

"Do you see the bag?" Gina called up from below.

"Got it," I said, closing the closet door and quickly grabbing the bag.

On my way out, I glanced out the bedroom window and realized that it looked over the drive where Andy and I had parked. I realized that Gina could have easily seen us pull up and thrown her suitcase into the closet. A sneaky exit did not bode well for her.

I exited the room and held the bags up for both to see as I descended the stairs.

"I don't know what took me so long," I said, aware as the words came out of my mouth that I was not being too cool. "I just wanted to make sure everything was inside. It was."

"Good," said Gina. "Well, then, I guess this is good-bye. It was good to see you both. And thank you, Officer, for the description of how the police make arrests. I'll be sure to share it with my director."

"I'm so impressed with how tidy your room and bathroom are," I said, hoping that Andy would get what he needed from me by my hint. "I hope I didn't make a mess last night,"

Andy nodded to me. Message received.

"Not at all," said Gina, heading to the door.

"Ms. Ginelli," said Andy. He did not move to follow her to the door.

I had no idea what I was supposed to do. His formality was subtly crushing.

"Excuse me?" she said.

"Ms. Ginelli." Andy pulled out his notebook from his hip. "Were you having an affair with Simon Sterling?"

Chapter 23

I really wished Emily were here for this.
"How dare you come to my home and accuse me of having an affair with anyone?" Gina said without missing a beat. "What's this about, anyway? Is this some sort of island joke at my expense?"

Oh, she was good.

Andy still did not move.

"I will kindly ask you to leave," she said and opened the door.

"I'll ask the question again," Andy said. "Were you having an affair with Simon Sterling?"

I was sure Andy was about to show her the note from Gina's purse that I'd given him. If he was so worried about me being in danger, he was about to put me right into the thick of things. To my relief, however, he surprised me.

"We have copies of Simon Sterling's phone records," he said. "More than half the calls were made to a phone in your name."

I looked at him with an admiring glance, and he shifted his jaw in that wink-thing he does. As promised, he had done his homework, touched base with a couple of officers who'd been working on the case. In my book, he was one of the island's finest.

Gina closed the front door.

"*Dio mio*," she began muttering to herself in Italian. "*Sono stupida. Stupida. Stupida . . .*"

Gina left the door and sat on her sofa where she buried her face in her hands and burst into tears. I was not prepared at all for Italian or hysterics. I was prepared for running, threats, any sort of danger, but not tears. I looked at Andy. From the look on his face, I realized I probably had more experience with a woman in a love crisis than he did.

"Affairs, huh?" I said, sitting next to her. Andy could be the bad cop. I decided I would play the good cop. I looked at Andy with an expression that said as much. He nodded the tiniest bit, but enough to encourage me to continue.

Gina sort of laughed in the midst of her tears, which I took as a good sign. She pulled a tissue from a box conveniently placed beside the sofa and dabbed her eyes, taking a few deep breaths to compose herself as she did.

"The answer to your question, Officer Southerland, is yes," she said. "I was having an affair with Simon Sterling. I can't imagine how this matters to your investigation of that horrible man, Bill Duffy. I will ask you to please, *please*, do everything in your power to keep our affair out of the papers. It would be a terrible and unnecessary blow to my career and my personal life."

"When did you meet Simon?" I said, trying hard to ignore her disparaging description of Bill.

"Last summer," she said.

Andy sat down on a club chair across from the sofa.

I noticed he did not stop me from asking the questions this time.

"Where?" I said.

"Italy," Gina said. "I live in LA, but I summer in Italy. Kevin usually travels during the summer. Me? I like my cypress trees and the olives and the food and the people."

"Where is Mr. Bunch now?" said Andy.

Gina laughed a little bitterly.

"I see you don't read the social columns," she said. "He's yachting with a French model."

I looked at Andy, who was now scribbling down this information. I supposed he was wondering if Kevin Bunch had yachted his way to Nantucket to kill Simon Sterling for having an affair with his wife, but Gina flashed her phone at us.

We peered at the screen to find pictures of Kevin living it up on the Riviera. The lead picture was of an already legendary party on Friday night in which the model Gina had referred to was pouring champagne over Kevin Bunch. Unless he had a super-sonic speed boat, he was not Simon's killer.

"Do you and Simon have mutual friends? Is that how you met?" I asked, getting back to Simon. She had shared the when and where of their meeting, but not the how.

"We met outside of Naples, at a café," she said and grabbed another tissue. "We were seated at tables next to each other. I was impressed that a man of his sophistication was happy to spend an afternoon alone at a café in such a small town. I told him as much. One thing led to another, and we ended up spending all afternoon talking. By that night, I was a goner."

I had a feeling that the café near Naples was probably in the small town where the Sterling brothers had shared their land. Simon was likely enjoying his espresso and the southern Italian landscape after snooping out the land his brother wanted to sell. It occurred to me that perhaps Simon had changed his mind about selling the land because he wanted an excuse to stay near Gina. Why she wanted to be with him, however, was still beyond me.

"He called me Belle," Gina said.

"And what happened?" said Andy. "Was he threatening to go public? Was he blackmailing you? Did you track him down to the Melville and hit him with a candlestick?"

Gina laughed.

"Do you think this is some Hollywood B-movie?" she said. "Gina Ginelli does not go around killing people. Do you know how many people would be dead by now if I went around killing men who let me down? Give me some credit!" And with that, she tossed her crumpled tissue onto the side table.

"Do you have an alibi for the night of the murder?" he asked, holding steady.

"I was here. Working," she said, and shifted in her chair with a sudden shudder. "Why does it matter? Why are you asking me these questions? You have your man."

"We know you were in the Game Room," I said, cutting to the chase.

Gina sunk back into the sofa's cushions. She looked very small.

"How do you know that?" she said, without contradicting my accusation.

"Your perfume," I said.

She nodded. Defeated.

"How did you get into the Sun Room?" said Andy. "Did Simon let you in?"

"No," she said. She sunk her hands into her pocket and pulled out a room key to the Melville. Andy took it. "The key was on the kitchen counter when I arrived with a note from Simon to meet him in the Game Room from the side doors in the Sun Room."

"Why meet at the inn?" said Andy. "If you wanted privacy, the inn's not the best spot."

Gina buried her head in her hands. When she looked up, her face was older and sad.

"Did Mrs. Sterling tell you how Simon had once wanted to be an actor?" she said.

Andy shook his head and made a note.

"Go on," I said.

"He was the one who encouraged me to take this role. It's different for me," she said. "He loved to help me on it. I'm working on a scene where my character breaks into a hotel in the wee hours of the morning, to meet her lover. I told Simon about it, and he thought it would be fun for us to act it out. He had a wonderful imagination."

"And you brought the key with you to the Melville when you went to meet him?" I said.

She nodded. "He was going to open the door to the Sun Room himself to let me in, of course, but I brought the key with me anyway. When I got to the inn, I waited. Three o'clock came and went and he didn't open the door. It was getting cold, so I decided to go inside. That's when I saw the body. You don't think I killed him, do you? Because I would never do anything to harm that man. That's why I went to the hospital, to the inn. I've wanted to learn about his death. Not for my movie, but because I loved him. You don't understand, I thought you found the murderer. That's why I haven't said anything to the police."

"So, you went to the Game Room," said Andy. "What happened?"

Gina's eyes welled up again with tears.

"Nothing," she said. "He was dead. He was on the floor, splayed out with that hideous medieval candle broken in half beside him."

After that last comment, it took all of my will not to tell Andy to arrest her right there.

"What was your plan for that night?" he said, probably afraid I would do exactly that.

"He was very excited about the night. For the whole weekend actually."

"Was it why he told Jessica he'd walk her down the aisle?" I said. "So you two could secretly meet?"

Gina nodded.

"I made it clear we could never be properly married," said Gina, "but he didn't care. He said he wanted to prove his love to me. He said that he had a 'gift wrapped in a gift' for me that would symbolize our union and make us a family, even if no one else could ever know. He said he had branded himself for me, and that he had something for me to bind myself to him. It was such a riddle, and now I'll never know what he meant."

"Did you see anyone or hear anything when you went to the inn?" said Andy.

"No." She shook her head. "Except. Oh, I don't know."

"What?" I said.

"I thought I heard footsteps coming toward the room. That's why I fled."

If those footsteps were Tony's, he was off the hook.

"Did you see who it was?" said Andy.

"No," said Gina. "But I can prove to you I could not kill Simon."

"How?" said Andy. His question was open-ended, but his tone was skeptical.

"My shoulder," she said. "There was no way I could lift that candle and hit him over the head with enough force to kill him. Last year, when I was in a stage production of *Taming of the Shrew*, I hurt myself in rehearsal for a fight scene. I almost had to drop out of the play. I had surgery two months ago and I've been in physical therapy since. You can ask my doctors." She ran to the kitchen table, to her purse, and rifled through it until she produced a card that she handed to Andy. "Call Dr. Bilky. He'll confirm everything. You can even test me if you have to."

"If what you say is true, Gina," said Andy, "you need to think. Did you see Simon earlier that day? Was there anything unusual about him? Anything that would suggest that he was in danger?"

"I never saw him," she said. "Our first meeting was supposed to be that night."

A bottle of wine sat on the counter next to her purse. Gina opened a cabinet above her, took out a glass, and poured with a shaky hand.

"I was so angry about the injury," she said after a healthy sip. "Now, it turns out, the accident might save me from a life in prison. It's so unpredictable how life works, isn't it?"

It was a little melodramatic, but I got where she was coming from. Andy closed his notebook, but I was still thinking about Simon's riddle.

"I'll call your doctor," he said. "And in the meantime, please do not leave the island this weekend or we will put out an APB for your arrest."

She nodded, obediently.

"I'm sorry we've upset you, but I think I can answer a couple of the riddles for you," I said. "I think the brand that Simon was referring to was a tattoo of a bell that he had recently inked onto his shoulder."

Gina smiled and looked really, really sad.

"I'll always wonder what he meant by our own secret family," she said.

I nodded, sympathetically.

"And Tinker," I said.

Gina looked at me blankly.

"The cat you met yesterday," I said. "We found him in Simon's room. Could he have been a gift for you? His name is Tinker. Along with Simon's bell tattoo, the message is Tinkerbell. That might have been just the right kind of secret code for the two of you."

Gina's hand flew to her mouth.

"Poor Simon," she said.

"We have the cat in the car outside," I said. I felt an immediate loss over the idea of handing over Tinker, but he wasn't mine to keep. "I can get him for you."

Gina shook her head.

"Simon didn't know," she said. "Why should he? It's not the sort of thing that comes up much. The truth is, I'm allergic to cats."

"Ms. Ginelli," said Andy. His voice had softened significantly since our meeting had begun. "You said he had three secrets. His brand, a family, and something about a gift wrapped in a gift. Given the answers to the first two riddles, do you have any idea what he could have meant by the third?"

Gina shook her head. "No. I'm sorry I don't."

"OK," said Andy, opening the front door. I rose and followed him. "We'll keep in touch. I don't think you are in any danger, but I'll swing by later to check in on you."

"Please do," she said. "I was so scared last night. I

didn't really hang out with the revelers. I was packing."

My last image as we let ourselves out was of Gina pouring another glass of wine. Two steps down the path from her door, Andy stopped, his hand on my arm.

"Thanks, again, for your help," he said. "But promise me, no more sleuthing. This looks darker and darker. I don't want anyone else getting hurt."

"Here's the deal," I said. "You go to Bellamy and let him know what you've found so they can release Bill. Then I'll sit back and you can do whatever you need to do."

That was mostly the truth, but I was still reeling from Gina's description of my candle as a hideous medieval thing.

"I can't go to Bellamy yet," said Andy. "Think about it. She told us some interesting information about their love life, but nothing changes the facts about Bill. Something's missing."

We turned to head to Andy's car when the door to Gina's cottage flew open.

"Wait," she said. "I thought of something."

Chapter 24

"Last month," said Gina, running down the path toward us. "Simon asked me what my ring size is. Do you think that Simon was going to give me a ring? The tattoo was his sign of love, the cat was the family we could have. A ring could have been my symbol of our secret union. Not an engagement ring, but a sign nonetheless."

"Maybe," I said.

"Maybe not," said Andy.

Gina hugged her arms around her body. "You're right. Maybe, maybe not. It just felt like something Simon might do. He was a cool cat, you know. I fell hard, but I'm no dope. Simon clearly knew his way around women."

"Can I ask you an honest question?" I said. "It's not my place to judge, but you could have any man you want. And yet you chose Simon, who got himself killed because he cheated at cards and was cruel to his family."

"It was the card game that lead to his death?" said Gina, shaking.

I realized that she hadn't been out of the house much. For all the chatter going around the island, Gina probably had not gotten any details about the murder outside of what I'd told her on our walk to her house, which wasn't much. I hadn't even mentioned that the men were playing cards.

"Was it Simon's idea to play?" Gina said, carefully.

I nodded.

"Is there something we should know about the card game?" said Andy.

She touched a shaky hand to her neck. "Do you know if there was a stack of hundred-dollar bills by his side while he played?"

We nodded, surprised, and her shoulders sank.

"There's a scene in my movie where someone cons men in a card game and he has a stack of hundreds by him to psych them out," she said. "Simon wanted to try it, so I had some real-life data to go on. I told him not to, because he'd get in trouble, but he said he'd dole out all the money to the guys in the end, for no hard feelings. Everyone would be a winner, he said. He was doing it for me."

I didn't want to tell Gina, because she was already in so much pain, but I had a feeling that Joe, Tony, and Bill had interpreted Simon's laugh at the end of the game as purely malicious, not a cheerful one at the end of a good gag. After a late night, a few drinks, and other pressures bearing down on all of them, none of the men had taken his joke lightly. Joe and Tony had stormed out, while Bill had punched him. He'd never had a chance to tell them the truth, because not long after, he'd been killed.

"I'd also be careful about believing anything his sister-in-law said about him," Gina went on. "Consider the source."

She had a point. Perhaps there had been a very different side to Simon. One that supported the love of his life in her acting pursuits and who had decided to live beside her in spite of their limitations. His edginess around Mrs. Sterling might have boiled down to the fact that he simply didn't like her.

"We'll keep all of this in mind," said Andy.

"OK," she said. "And, thanks. For everything."

I felt really bad about thinking she was a murderer, and also for snooping through her house. She looked like a lonely woman who had a lot to handle as she walked back to her cottage and closed the door behind her. We headed to Andy's patrol car, both of us sobered.

"Hold on," I said at the car door.

I looked at Andy across the hood of his car.

"What's that brain of yours thinking?" he said.

"Gina's ring idea."

I hopped inside the car. Andy followed.

"Gina knew her man. If she thought of a ring, there might be something to it. What about the red ribbon in Simon's drawer?" I said, remembering the contents of the drawer.

"I'm not even going to ask how you know about the red ribbon," he said. "But why do you mention it?"

"Remember, Gina said he wanted to give her a gift wrapped in a gift. Maybe Simon meant to slip a ring through it and tie it around Tinker's neck," I said. "Two gifts, one wrapped in another. Maybe he never had a chance to put the ring around Tinker's neck."

"Why not? He liked the drama. He gave her a big speech and a riddle and then doesn't follow through?" Tinker, who had been laying low in the back seat, popped up and put a paw on the back of my seat, as if he were one of the gang.

"Don't forget. There's a very valuable ring at the Melville this weekend that's a family heirloom. Simon wanted Gina to be family. Maybe Simon had his eye on it. Maybe he had a plan to take it from Jessica? Maybe he got cold feet and decided not to tie such a pricey item around this maniac's neck. No offense, Tinker." I gave Tinker a pat to confirm there were no hard feelings.

My new theory got Andy's attention. He rested his hands on his steering wheel. His radio began to crackle with some information about rowdy surfers on Tom Never's beach and an overflow of tourists forming on Brant Point, which was the prime place to watch the regatta boats cross the finish line this afternoon. He lowered the volume, which I took as a personal victory of my sleuthing skills.

"Jessica's engagement ring?" he said.

"That ring is worth a lot more than a couple thousand dollars swindled in a card game. I saw a note in Joe's room for the value of the ring. It's worth $200,000." I raised a hand before he could ask about my visit to Joe's room. "I was in his room fair-and-square. Wedding business," I said, fudging the truth.

"Sure you were," said Andy. "But Jessica's been wearing her ring every time I've seen her. How'd he think he was going to get his hands on it?"

"Peter told me at the cookout that the elderly couple staying at the inn were in the jewelry business. Frank saw them talking to Simon in a friendly sort of way. Maybe Simon hired the couple to make a copy. One he somehow swapped for the real one," I said.

"And one of the Sterlings found out and killed him?"

"It might be worse," I said. The adrenaline was rushing through me by this point. Ideas were flying.

"What's worse than that?"

"Frank also said he saw the jewelers talking to Joe first. Think about it. Joe's planning to spend gobs of money on his new business. Chris and Liz said this afternoon how much it would cost. Where's Joe getting all this money from?"

"From the sale of a ring to Simon?" said Andy, starting his motor.

"From the sale of Jessica's ring," I said.

"Wow," he said. "That year you were consumed with conspiracy theories about UFOs is paying off."

"Darn right. Think about it. Jessica could unwittingly be wearing a fake ring that the elderly couple made for Joe, so that he could subsequently sell the real one to Simon—"

"—who had plans to give it to Gina."

"Perhaps he was going to blackmail Joe on top of buying the ring. That could be motive for murder."

"I can't decide if you're crazy or a genius, but too many things are lining up not to look into it. This doesn't look good for Joe."

"No, it doesn't." I knew I'd never liked that guy.

We were driving down the lane by this point, and close to the turn that would lead us either back to town or toward the inn.

"Stop the car," I said.

He stopped. I dialed Emily.

"Em," I said when she picked up. "Where are you?"

"At the inn," she said, "Hair and makeup have arrived. Bride and maid of honor are looking great." I could tell she said that last part for the women's benefit, not mine. "I saw the unity candles, up close and personal. You've outdone yourself. The chapel looks amazing. The purple hues for the other decorative candles are stunning."

"Thanks," I said. Normally, I would have loved to talk more about my work, but there was no time.

"Don't kill me, but I also brought your red dress," she said.

She really hated my outfit.

"How about Joe?" I asked.

I didn't want to outright tell her that Andy and I wanted to interrogate the wedding's groom an hour before the ceremony.

"He's doing great," she said, thankfully not catching on. "He's in his room, changing. Can't see the bride before the wedding, right?"

I motioned to Andy to take a right toward the Melville. He gunned it.

Chapter 25

"Let me know if there's anything I can do," I said to Emily as Andy sped down the road. "How are you?"

"Between indigestion and nerves? A mess," she confessed quietly into the phone so that the Sterlings could not hear. "It's been quite a weekend. Listen, gotta go, but see you at the chapel."

I put my phone away, worried about Emily. I really didn't want to add to her nerves. At the cookout, she'd really looked as if she could use a day with her feet up.

"Did you say you heard a sound coming from Simon's room last night?" said Andy as we pulled into the inn's driveway.

"Holy cow. I did," I said, remembering both the footsteps and Jessica's knock on the door. Was she onto her fiancé? Were his absences beginning to cause her to suspect something was up? If so, Jessica might be in danger, too.

"This is exactly why I'm afraid of you snooping

around on your own," said Andy. "You might have walked in on a murderer last night."

"I agree, that's not comforting," I said, grateful to Tinker, who put his head on my shoulder from his spot behind me. "On the other hand, maybe I stopped him from whatever he's up to. And maybe I kept Jessica out of harm's way, too. I had a good excuse for opening the door. I'm the help. Jessica would have walked in on something far more sinister."

"That level of loyalty falls outside of your job description," Andy said as he parked in front of the Melville.

Andy and I got out of the car. Tinker slipped out, too. As long as he didn't make his way into the inn, I decided he'd be fine on his own.

I followed Andy to the entrance of the inn. He passed right by Bellamy's man without a word.

"Wait," I said as we reached the front of the inn. "You'll stick out like a sore thumb in your uniform. How official do you want this visit to be? If we're wrong, Emily will have our heads."

"I'm supposed to be at Brant Point right now," said Andy. "I don't have time for any craziness."

"Exactly," I said. "Take off your jacket. Make this visit low-key until you know you don't have to. There are dozens of people in the lobby right now in wedding outfits."

Andy sighed and took off his jacket. He looked around for a place to put it, but settled on tying it around his waist. I stuck his hat into my bag.

When we opened the door, there was a level of excitement in the lobby that was at odds with our mission. Clusters of the Sterling-Handler guests were heading to a light lunch at Ahab's, courtesy of the

Sterlings. Some were in golf clothes, others were already dressed for the wedding. The compliments and cheerful chatter that accompany the happy occasion of a wedding abounded. It was sort of impossible to imagine that right above us, Joe might be in his room, guilty of murder.

Andy crossed the lobby straight away. He pressed the button for the elevator, but I pulled his sleeve to the stairs, which we took two at a time to the second floor. We headed to Joe's door.

Andy knocked.

"Tony, I'm OK, really," Joe said from inside. "You're the best, but I don't need a drink right now. I'll meet you down there in a few."

"This is Andy Southerland of the Nantucket police," said Andy. To make his point, he put his jacket back on.

"By the way," I whispered. "I did see a UFO that summer. How often do fourteen shooting stars explode one after another? Shooting stars my foot."

"Mr. Handler," said Andy. "Can I speak to you?"

The door opened.

"What's up?" said Joe. His hair was combed, his cologne was strong. I hadn't noticed cologne on him before. He was definitely stepping up his game for the big day. He wore a white, buttoned-down shirt and Nantucket Reds pants. If I had a nickel for every pair of Nantucket Reds I've seen at weddings on this island, I could retire. Nantucket red is more of a dusty, faded salmon color. They were made popular by Murray's Toggeries Shop in town, and at some point became part of the preppy uniform and much favored at Nantucket weddings.

"I need to talk to you," said Andy, entering and closing the door as I slipped in beside him.

"Dude, I'm getting married in, like, a couple of hours," said Joe, absently ruffling his perfect hair. "Can this wait?"

"Nah," said Andy. "Have a seat."

Joe sat on the edge of his bed. Andy stood. Very intimidating. For Joe, that is.

"Where were you the night that Simon Sterling was killed?"

"We've been through this," said Joe. "Listen, do I need a lawyer? I told you guys, I left the card game and went to bed."

"Can anyone support your alibi?" said Andy.

"Usually, Jess would be able to," he said. "But she made us take separate rooms. She can be old-fashioned that way."

"Joe's right," I said to Andy. "She is. It's really charming."

"Mr. Handler," said Andy, ignoring my digression. "We have reason to believe that your fiancée, Jessica, is wearing a copy of her engagement ring. We are on our way to take the ring from her, to have its authenticity confirmed."

Joe stood. Then he sat again.

"Please don't do that," he said, very calmly. Frighteningly calm.

I took a step backward, toward the door. I looked at Andy's gun and handcuffs, glad that he'd put his jacket back on.

"Is there anything you'd like to tell us?" said Andy.

"There's nothing I'd like to tell you," said Joe. "I'd like, frankly, to be getting married in two hours without you questioning me about Jessica's ring. But since that seems unlikely, let me answer any questions you have without you bothering Jessica. This weekend has been hard enough for her."

"OK," said Andy, opening his notebook. "Can you confirm that the ring that Jessica Sterling has right now is a fake?"

"Yes," he said.

I couldn't believe it. We were right.

On a table beside me, there was a platter with two drinking glasses and a water bucket. Lacking a gun, I picked up a water glass for protection.

"Do you have the original ring?" Andy said.

"No," said Joe. "I wish I did."

"Do you know who has the original ring?" Andy said.

"I'm not sure," said Joe.

"Has someone stolen it?" Andy said.

"I'm not sure," he said.

"Are you acquainted with Ida and Al Heller?" said Andy.

Joe exhaled. Along with Tony, Gina, and Frank, I realized he was the fourth person I had spoken to today to exhale like a person relieved to unload a secret. The Sterling-Handler wedding was just chock-full of them.

"Yes, I know them," he said, meekly. "Listen, this whole thing has gotten out of hand."

"Mr. Handler," said Andy. "I think we need to head over to the station. What you are about to say can be held against you in a court of law. If you would like to call an attorney, now would be a good time."

"Wait," said Joe. "I haven't broken any laws. There's no need for that. I'm not holding up my wedding."

"Joe," I said. "Andy's no fool. You were seen speaking to the Hellers. They specialize in fake jewels. You've already confessed that the family heirloom Jessica's wearing is a fake. The police think you commissioned the Hellers to make you a fake with a plan to sell the ring to Simon Sterling. With the money from the ring, you planned to buy the land for your new business."

"You've got this all wrong," he said. "That ring is worth a lot, but not enough to cover the land we're buying to build our gym."

"Either way, your fiancée has a fake and you can't find the real ring. Did Simon find out?" said Andy. "Did he try to blackmail you? Is that why you killed him?"

"Why *I-I-I-I* killed him?" said Joe, practically shouting now. "Are you insane?"

Andy said nothing. It spoke volumes.

"I think Jessica has to be part of this after all," said Joe.

I raised my eyebrows. I wished I had brought those tissues from Gina's cottage. It was going to be a mess in here in a few minutes.

Before Andy could argue, I dialed Jessica.

"Hello, my favorite candle artist," said Jessica when she answered the phone.

"Hello," I said. "I'm here with Joe and my friend Andy from the police force. Any chance you can pop down here for a minute? Joe wants to talk to you."

The line went dead. A moment later, there was a knock on the door. Andy opened it. Jessica was not yet in her dress, but she looked like a woman headed toward a big day. Her hair was lifted above her head in a stunning up-do. Her makeup beautifully highlighted every one of her features. And her diamond earrings were knockouts. Small drops, but as sparkly as sparkly can get.

"What's going on?" she said and walked over to Joe.

Joe took Jessica's hand in his, and twirled her ring around her finger.

"They've been asking me about your ring," he said to Jessica.

"Ms. Sterling," said Andy, "I regret to inform you that we have reason to believe your ring is a copy, and that your fiancé is behind the switch."

Jessica sat beside Joe on the edge of the bed.

"I'm so sorry, Jessica," I said.

"Don't be," she said. "I know the ring is a fake."

"You do?" I said.

"I do. It was my idea," she said.

I dropped into a side chair by the dresser.

Chapter 26

"You had it right, Officer Southerland," said Joe. "We needed the ring for money to invest in our business. But not how you imagined it."

"My father used to tell me to always take a good deal when one came along," said Jessica. "About a month ago, Uncle Simon called me out of the blue. He said he wanted to have the family ring. I almost hung up on him, but he asked me to hear him out. He offered to trade the land in Italy for the ring."

"Is that an even trade?" I said.

"Not even close," said Joe. "That was what was so shocking."

"He just really wanted that ring," said Jessica. "He wouldn't say why. I'm not sure why he couldn't buy one himself, but he seemed hell-bent on this one."

"It's a family jewel," I said, thinking how Simon wanted Gina to be family.

"The thing was," said Jessica, "I couldn't give it to him. My mother would have freaked out. It's meant so much to her for me to have this ring. It was hers, my grandmother's. It's something she holds dear because of my father."

"You don't think she'd understand?" said Andy.

Jessica gave a deep, long sigh.

"You don't know my mother, Officer," she said. "She's been very emotional about my wedding."

"Jessica's being polite," said Joe. "Bottom line, her mom doesn't want us to get married. Yesterday, she even tracked down Maria, who'd come early and stayed in town, and then tried to convince Jessica that I was cheating with her. She takes overprotective to a new level."

Andy made a note, which I assumed was related to getting an alibi from Maria.

"We had an idea that seemed harmless enough," said Joe.

"We had the Hellers make a copy of the ring," said Jessica. "The plan was that after we had the real ring cleaned in town with Mom on Friday afternoon, we'd swap it out for the fake and give the real one to Simon. Because the deal moved so quickly, the Hellers didn't have time to finish the copy until they delivered it to us in person this weekend. We had to make the swap here."

"I traded it with Simon, in his room, before dinner on Friday," said Joe. "And then everything went wrong."

"How?" said Andy, scribbling away.

"Simon had his altercation with the bartender and got himself killed," said Joe. "And now I can't find the ring. I've looked everywhere."

"That's why you've been MIA this weekend," I said. "And why you were sneaking around Simon's room last night. You've been looking for the ring."

Joe's jaw dropped to find out that I'd heard him.

"Here's a different theory," said Andy. "You signed

the deal, then gave Simon the fake instead of the original. He figured it out, you two fought, and you killed him."

"Why would we do that?" said Joe. He took Jessica's hand.

"It's a beautiful and valuable ring. That's why," said Andy.

"I don't care about the ring," said Jessica. "It's hideous."

"I'll give you the papers to prove we had no motive," said Joe. He rose and retrieved the agreement that I had seen in Jessica's room only a day before. "We signed an agreement, the ring for the land. Except, the estate needs an authenticated ring in order to release the land to us. Without it, no land. As you can see, there's no motive at all for us to have killed him. Quite the opposite. This has been a disaster for us."

He handed the agreement to Andy, who looked through it.

"May I keep this?" Andy said.

"Sure," said Joe. "Listen, I gave that ring to Simon, but it wasn't on him when he died. It isn't in his room either. Someone took that ring."

"Where have you looked?" I asked.

Joe ruffled his hair. Jessica smoothed it.

"I've looked everywhere," he said.

"I'll need specifics," said Andy.

"Simon's room, all the rooms off the lobby. The Game Room, of course, but only when we were in there with you. I looked in Tony's room, even my mother-in-law's room."

"Joe!" said Jessica.

"Sorry," he said. "I thought one of them might have found it on him. They both touched Simon's body in the Game Room."

"And?" said Andy.

"Nothing," said Joe. "It was a long shot."

"I think you've given us enough information to re-open this investigation," said Andy. "Bill might still be guilty, but so could many others. I'm going to talk to Bellamy."

I could have hugged him.

"I thought Simon was killed over that card game. I mean, you arrested the bartender. Bellamy assured us Bill confessed he took the money from the card game. That was the motive," said Jessica. Her shoulders sank. "Meanwhile, Joe's been looking for a ring that a murderer took?"

Jessica clasped her fiancé's hands. He looked at her with a brave and reassuring smile, but I gathered the reality of the situation was just dawning on him, too.

"My mother's going to kill me," said Jessica.

"After she guts me," said Joe. "You still want to go through with this?"

Jessica nodded. "But maybe after the wedding, we'll go pick out a new engagement ring. And Joe, don't be mad, but I'd like to find a different way to raise money for the business than that land. I don't want to start our life together this way."

"I agree," he said. "We can wait."

I'm a good judge of character, but I'd been wrong about Joe. I wasn't sure how Andy and I had even considered that these two could be murderers. The only thing they were guilty of was trying to trade that ugly ring for the opportunity to start a new life, without upsetting Mrs. Sterling. When news got out about the ring swap, Jessica and Joe would have their hands full with an angry Mrs. Sterling, but as far as I was concerned Mrs. Sterling was not thinking straight. She was lucky to have these two.

"We'll have to do a new search of the hotel," said Andy.

Jessica and Joe tore their eyes away from each other and looked pleadingly at Andy.

"It'll take at least an hour by the time Bellamy hears me out and decides to get a team out there," said Andy, reading their minds. "You'll be at the chapel by then. And I'll keep the wedding team abreast of the events as they unfold."

"Emily has had her hands full with us," said Jessica.

"Perhaps I can be your point person on the updates," I said, agreeing with Jessica. "I know a lot about the case at this point. Let's let Emily focus on the wedding."

Andy looked at me dubiously, but he nodded in agreement.

"I appreciate your help," said Joe. "But I've looked everywhere for this ring. I hope you have better luck."

"I hope we do, too, Mr. Handler," said Andy, closing his notebook to indicate the end of our meeting. He opened the hotel room's door. "And if you think of anything, call me. You have my card."

Jessica and Joe nodded. I followed Andy into the hallway and to the elevator.

"What can I do while you pitch this new information to Bellamy?" I asked as we stepped inside the elevator.

"Nothing," he said, and folded his arms. "You've done more than any person would do to keep this case alive and moving forward while all the players are on the island. If we're right about the ring, you're a hero, Stella. But Hound shmound. This is real stuff, and you aren't trained to pursue a murderer. I don't really need to explain that, right?"

"Seriously?" I said.

Andy put his hands on my shoulders. "Get a lift from Emily to the church. I promise I will give you texts on our progress. It will be just like you're here with us."

We locked eyes. It was like a game of chicken to see who would blink first, but I realized he wasn't going to back down.

"Fine," I said, but I couldn't believe he couldn't think of one more thing for me to do to keep things moving forward.

Thankfully, the elevator door opened. Andy adjusted his jacket and walked toward the door. At the exit, he looked back at me. I pulled out my phone and stared at the empty screen as if there was something important on it. When I looked back up, he still had his eyes on me. I gave him an innocent look and motioned for him to go.

The minute the door closed behind him, I approached Tony, who was sitting around a table by the lobby's fire with his buddies. They were all in Nantucket Reds and navy blazers. The groomsmen were evidently ready for the big day and having a couple of pregame drinks.

"Can I see the photos you took of the crime scene?" I asked.

Tony got up and ushered me across the room.

"I sent them to the police," he said, looking terrified of what I might say or do in front of his friends.

He opened his phone to his photos and handed it to me. I scrolled through and reviewed the images. One was of Mrs. Sterling, seated beside the body, her hand on Simon's arm, almost tenderly. She did not look like she could reach for a ring from her position without anyone else noticing. There were some of Jessica, seated beside her mother. She did not touch the body in any of them. There was a photo of Bill, his arms crossed and looking furious. It was followed by a couple of snaps of Bill and Maude hugging each other. Although I hated to admit it, I wondered if Joe had thought to search the Duffys' house. I swallowed hard as I realized that Maude had the keys to all of the rooms. If she had somehow learned that Simon had the ring, she might have broken into his room during the card game to steal it. The idea made me sick inside, but I had to consider it.

I continued to review the photos. Frank was in one, looking shocked and confused. In the background, I could see the old couple. They truly looked curious and dazed as they gaped into the room. If they were crooks, they were also good actors. There was one of me sitting at the card table, looking nauseous from the scene of death and the cigar smell. I really hadn't covered my emotions at all. When I finished looking at the photos, I had not found anything incriminating about anyone. I handed the phone back to Tony. He returned to his friends and took a big swig of his drink.

I, meanwhile, texted Emily to confirm that I needed a ride to the chapel. I also asked her if she needed any help. She responded that she was fine, and that I should meet her in the lobby in an hour.

I hated to do what I knew I needed to do. I left the inn and headed to Maude and Bill's cottage. I knew Maude was on duty this afternoon.

I would have the place to myself.

Chapter 27

As I walked down the dirt road toward the Duffys' cottage, I tried to imagine where Maude would hide a ring. I wondered if she would hide it in her jewelry box, or under the mattress, or in the sugar bowl. I decided to look in all of those places and more, including the garden for any freshly turned earth.

The Duffys' car was in the driveway, but I knew Maude walked to work. I wished I had an excuse to turn around, but I couldn't think of one. The cottage was quiet, and empty. Worse, a window was open on the first floor for me to climb through. It was as if I were being invited to enter. I crept softly toward the window.

The last time I'd climbed through a window was yesterday, when Emily and I had been locked in the staging room of the Melville. I'd already learned that it's not a graceful experience. At least now I knew a deep fall didn't wait for me on the other side of the sash. Unfortunately, however, when I bent forward to slip my body through the Duffys' window, I lost my balance and slipped onto the floor with a thud. I lay on the floor a moment to make sure nothing was broken. Realizing all my body parts were still working, I felt around me to make sure I had not damaged the Duffys' house. Thankfully, all I'd done was dislodge a small ottoman by a side chair.

I got up in the vacant room that was Maude and Bill's living room. It was an immaculate but well-worn space. The place looked as if it had been tended to with love. A real home. The furniture was familiar to me from my youth, but by now it had seen better days. Maude, however, had covered its more frayed areas with brightly colored quilts and pillows. There was a small fireplace with a simple wood mantle. On top of it, I noticed a photo of Bill and Maude in their early days of marriage. Bill had long hair and Maude was in a pink dress with a flower in her hair. Next to the photo was one of Jason, their son, when he was a little boy. He was holding up a comic book. I realized as I studied it that he was standing in front of my mother's store. Next to the photo was another of Jason, now a young man in his naval uniform. I almost turned and left the Duffys' house right then and there.

It wasn't until my eye followed the mantle décor and fell on a small trophy cup from a local golf tournament Bill had won in 1983 that I sobered up. I shook the cup and heard a clink. I looked inside. There was a ring in there, but I was happy to see that it was not shiny and jewel encrusted. Instead, it was a signet ring from the Naval Academy. Jason's ring, kept safely for him while he was away.

I was about to head into the kitchen when I noticed a knitting basket beside the sofa. It was overflowing with yarns and needles, a perfect place to stash a small item. I walked across the floor, which creaked as much as the one in my apartment. Old floorboards are gorgeous but noisy. Between the noise of the floor and the intermittent banging of the window blinds against the sash as the wind blew outside, every muscle in my legs felt stiffer and stiffer as I stepped forward.

I leaned toward the basket. The yarn overflowing from it was soft to the touch, as rich and luxurious as cashmere. It felt fancy compared to the rest of the room. My hand dug around in search of a small ring. At first, I was cautious, but after a minute, I was shoving around knitting needles and pulling out yarns. Something shiny caught my eye at the bottom of the basket, and I was thrusting my hand into it when a scream as loud as a banshee's tore through the house.

I turned in time to find the full force of Maude's body in flight across the room and heading toward me. She had a knitting needle in one hand. I could not help wonder how many needles Maude had around the house.

Fortunately for me, the rug upon which I stood gave way with Maude's leap so that as she flew toward me, I fell under her. In about two seconds, her torso lay flat across the couch while I was under her knees and thighs, on the Duffys' floor for the second time.

Maude moaned, but she was not ready to let the prowler in her home get away. She shuffled her legs to stand up, each time jabbing my jaw with her knees. I tried to push myself away, which she interpreted as an attack on her. By the time I extracted myself from under her body, I looked up to a knitting needle under my chin.

We both breathed heavily for a moment.

"Stella?" she asked.

I nodded.

Maude sat on the floor.

"What the hell are you doing here?" she said. "Why didn't you knock?"

She looked at the toppled knitting basket and raised her needle again.

"What're you up to?" she said.

I grabbed a needle from her basket.

"What're you up to?" I said, holding it up to her like a sword. As I did, I noticed that the shiny object that had caught my eye was nothing more than a pair of scissors. Given Maude's emotion, however, their proximity to her reach did not give me any comfort.

"I'm having my goddamn lunch," she said. "And now"—she rose, her needle still pointed toward me— "I'm calling the cops."

"Don't," I said. "I can explain."

"I don't care what you can explain," said Maude, picking up her phone. "There are murderers around, Bill's in jail, and now my house gets broken into. I'd have never pegged you as a thief, Stella."

"I'm not a thief. You know that. And the police will be here in about an hour anyway," I said.

She put down her phone.

"Why?" she said, her bottom lip trembling. "Has something happened to Bill?"

"No," I said. "Maude, I need to ask you something."

"*You* need to ask *me* something?" She looked around the mess in her living room, but she did not stab me.

"Were you home the night Simon Sterling was killed?" I asked.

"Where the hell would I be?" she asked.

"I don't know. You said to Andy that Bill was in bed with you, but Bill told me he slept on the couch," I said, gently. "He told me you never wake up at night, but that he had a blanket over him in the morning."

Maude raised her chin, proudly, but I could see she was fighting tears. After a moment, she looked straight at me.

"I was with Flo," she said. One of my very own Candleers. "She's been teaching me to knit. I'm a disaster. But I wanted to make Bill a cashmere scarf for our anniversary. I spent a fortune on wool and then I couldn't get anything to work."

She pulled from her basket a long and sad-looking scarf.

"It had been a long day at the inn, getting ready for the wedding," she said. "Flo poured a cordial for us while we worked, and before we knew it, both of us fell asleep. I didn't wake up until about five in the morning. I raced home to find Bill asleep and snoring on the sofa."

I hugged Maude. I could tell she was in no mood for a hug, but I was so happy to know that she was with someone who could give her an alibi.

"Now, why don't you tell me why you're here," she said.

"You'll want to sit down," I said.

I began to share our theory that Simon had the ring, that someone took it from him and killed him in the process. At first, I was afraid I'd made a mistake by telling her anything. She had a look that told me she'd call Bellamy before Andy could reach him. She pulled herself together, however. When I finished, she looked right at me.

"If you think that Bill or I killed a man to take a ring, we have nothing more to say to each other," said Maude. "But thank you. For all you've done. Now, which rooms did you say Joe searched?"

I gave her the list.

"What about Frank's suite?" she said. "He's a decent

boss, but he probably sees a lot of stuff. Maybe he caught on about the ring. The whole thing might have been too tempting."

"Can you come up with an excuse to poke around his room?" I asked.

"I'm the maid," she said, straightening her pale blue cardigan. "That's my job."

It was a short speech, but we were already out the front door by the time she'd finished. At the inn, I gave Maude my phone number and asked her to text me if she found anything. Once she went inside, I checked the time. I only had twenty minutes until Emily wanted to meet me in the lobby. I walked down to the edge of the lawn where it met the water and sat on one of the Adirondack chairs. Tinker was nowhere in sight.

I pulled out my phone and sent a text to Flo to confirm Maude's story. I believed Maude, I really did, but I had learned in a very short time that leads must be followed to their end.

I stared at my phone and waited for an answer. I thought of my short but lovely date there with Peter on the same spot last night. I was really, really, surprised, however, when Andy Southerland popped into my head. It was strange to even think it, but I felt a different kind of vibe with him these last two days. And I thought he might have noticed it, too. I was imagining things though. Andy had a girlfriend. He was off the market as far as I was concerned.

I called Peter.

"Any chance you're free later this afternoon?" I said.

"What're you thinking?" I thought I heard the sound of typing.

"I was thinking I'd enjoy a date after all," I said.

"Oh," he said with a laugh. "Why didn't you tell me? I can be free for a date."

"The Sterlings' wedding is at four o'clock."

"I dare you to catch the garter thing," he said.

"You're on," I said. "I'm getting a ride with Emily, so I'll meet you there? I should warn you, we'll be the help. This will be a stand in the back of the church and eat the kitchen leftovers kind of date."

"Perfect," he said. "We'll snag a plate of chicken from the vegetarians who forgot to fill out the cards and park ourselves someplace we can watch the action."

"That sounds pretty nice," I said.

"Funny," he said. "I thought you were going to give me a scoop."

"Why'd you think that?"

"Your voice?" he said. "I don't know. A hunch."

"Well, I don't have one," I said.

"OK. But if you get a hunch, go for it. Then give me an exclusive interview."

"See you in a couple of hours," I said.

I smiled at the phrase "go for it." They were the words I'd been wanting to hear all day. As I hung up, my phone pinged. Flo confirmed that she had been with Maude on Friday night. She confessed she had not mentioned it at class because she feared that Cherry might make a thing out of it. Cherry apparently fancied herself a pro at knitting with cashmere, but Maude was not a fan of her bossy ways. From what I knew of the two ladies, that made sense. I gazed across the harbor. The sun felt good on the top of my head. I decided I was glad that Emily had brought my red dress. I had about fifteen minutes until I left for the wedding. Just enough time for a wardrobe upgrade.

Chapter 28

Twenty minutes later, on the dot, I was standing outside of Emily's car as she looked me up and down appraisingly.

"Much better," she said. "I love that dress on you."

She was referring to my red dress and the strappy heels I'd quickly changed into. The look was not quite the diva aesthetic of Gina Ginelli's loaner, but it was a little more strategically cut, and a whole lot more comfortable. Emily pulled down the fabric on my shoulders. I pulled it back. Strategic was one thing, but I still think there's something to be said for allowing the imagination to work.

"Give me the keys," I said as she rubbed her tummy. "How're you feeling?"

Emily shrugged and got into the car.

"This is me these days," she said. "A kick here, a kick there. I just need to get through the weekend and this little guy can come any time he wants."

When we were about halfway to the chapel, I decided it was time to fill her in on a few things.

"I don't want you to freak out," I said.

Emily kept her eyes on the road.

"Talk to me," she said.

I filled her in about Andy and my conversation with Jessica and Joe. I explained that the death of Simon Sterling might have something to do with the ring. Then, I broke the news to her that the Melville would be searched while the guests were at the chapel and the reception.

"I'm sorry," I said. "I know you told me no drama, but one thing led to another. You know how these things go."

Emily said nothing, which was worse than yelling at me.

"What about Mrs. Sterling?" she finally said. "She loves her daughter, but there's been something a little off about her this weekend, don't you think?"

"I do, but I think it's because she's been concerned that Maria Blane still carries a torch for Joe. She found out that Maria arrived early and it freaked her out."

"Weddings," said Emily. "They're supposed to be the happiest day of a couple's life, but people lose it."

"Promise me, when I get married, you'll keep us all in line," I said.

We had a good laugh at the idea of Emily keeping all of the Wrights in line as we pulled up to the chapel.

A true professional, Emily rolled out of the car and headed into the chapel for her last look. I knew that as perfect as the chapel had been when she left it this morning, she'd find a flower to fix or a bow to retie or a program that was not perfectly centered on the pews. Her swollen belly might have slowed her down last night, but only under doctor's orders. Today was showtime and nothing was going to stop her from making sure the wedding went off without a hitch. As fast as she walked in her condition, however, her speed was an average gait, and we walked into the chapel together.

"You've outdone yourself," I said when we walked inside.

I was not exaggerating.

The Sciasconset Chapel is a simple space. The pews are white wooden benches. Two simple windows with gothic arches framed either side of the altar. A modest gold cross hangs between them. I've been to a lot of weddings here by now and I've seen all sorts of strategies to decorate the space. In the end, I always find that unpretentious décor to match the modest design of the space sets a warm and welcoming tone for the union of two people.

From my first meeting with Emily and Jessica, I knew I liked their vision for the chapel, but the execution was stunning. Down the aisles, at about every third row, Emily had worked with the florists to design small, but robust arrangements of purple, pale blue, and bright rose-colored flowers, all of which would match Emily's bouquet. The aisle's flowers were held in place in small Nantucket lightship baskets. If you go anywhere in town, you'll see these baskets. Here, the woven reeds added a warmth to the space.

When I undertook the candle theme, I knew I'd have a challenge with the chapel since sunlight would still be streaming in through the windows during the ceremony. It's easy to build dramatic effects at night, so the rehearsal dinner and the reception were not hard to envision. During the daylight, however, I went for a different approach. I designed hearty pillars in a lighter shade of the purples from the rehearsal dinner and placed them on five-foot-high stands so that there was a string of color around the white walls. To compete with the sunlight, I'd put three wicks in these candles. I was now really pleased with the effect. The candles cast a twinkle of light around the chapel. They brought an aura of peace to the room. Given what had happened all weekend, and the challenges Joe and Jessica had faced, I was thrilled that at the moment of their *I Do* they would be surrounded by this warm and loving energy.

I was most thrilled, however, with my unity candle wreath. I approached the altar, as pleased in the daylight with my work as I had been last night, in the half light of the storage room, spinning my lazy Susan to create these new candles. Emily had cleverly worked with the florist this morning to raise the four candles higher since they were shorter than the original unity candle. They now sat atop a wreath of flowers in the purple, blue, and rose-pink arrangements for everyone to see.

By the time I'd finished reviewing my contribution to the chapel, the guests had begun to arrive. The Sterlings had kindly arranged for buses to bring the guests, so their arrival was en masse. The first group included the ushers and bridesmaids. They were nervous, as members of a wedding party often are, but Emily calmed them immediately and reminded them about their duties. When the second bus arrived, everyone was ready. The crowd piled in and their *oohs* and *ahhs* warmed my heart.

I was standing in the back of the chapel, off to the side, near one of Emily's assistants, when I heard a voice behind me.

"Wow!"

I turned to find Peter in a navy blazer and a tie. In the breast pocket where he might have put a handkerchief, I noticed the spiral of a notepad. Behind his ear, there was a pencil. I appreciated that he had toned down the look by sticking a flower in his buttonhole, one which I knew he'd snagged from one of the decorative bouquets outside the chapel.

"Hi," I said. I pretended not to see the looks Emily was attempting to telegraph to me from across the room. I could tell she was putting all sorts of things together, including my sudden interest in changing into my red dress. I felt bad when I realized I'd forgotten to tell her about my impromptu date. Fortunately, the arrival of the bride outside competed for her attention, so I was off the hook.

"These two are starting life with a little drama, huh?" he said. "I wouldn't wish a murder on anyone, but I admire their spunk."

Before I could answer, the harpist Emily had set up by the altar began to play and the congregation quieted down. Joe Handler joined the groomsmen gathered at the altar and shook hands with Tony. Then he looked across the chapel as the congregation stood.

Jessica appeared at the doorway. The gown I had admired while hiding out in her room yesterday was even more beautiful than I remembered. Complementing the embellished flower beading, she wore a lace cap with a long, thin veil spilling from behind it. In her hands, she carried a bouquet of flowers with a radiant coral satin bow tied around it.

In all the commotion of the weekend, I had never asked who replaced Simon to walk Jessica down the aisle. I saw, now, that Jessica's decision was perfect. She stood with her mother, who looked prouder and more at peace than I had seen her look all weekend. Mrs. Sterling had been so sad that her daughter was leaving her. Now, I hoped she realized that her daughter was not leaving. Rather, she was expanding the dynamic of their tiny family to include the warmhearted Joe Handler.

The two women walked down the aisle. I noticed a few people both wipe their eyes and smile at their image. At the end of their walk, Jessica hugged her mother, then looked down at Joe. He looked back up at her as if he could conquer the world and pass out at the same time. I couldn't help but feel giddy.

The reverend greeted the couple and smiled at the guests.

"Dearly beloved," he began.

As he spoke, I sank into the moment, enjoying it all. For the first time since I had found Simon Sterling dead in the Game Room, I was happy to let Andy and Bellamy do their jobs. Here at the Sciasconset Chapel, we were all drunk with love. Maria smiled from the altar at David, who waved and gave her a thumbs-up. Even Tony, standing by his old friend, looked like he had forgotten the tough aspects of marriage. He laughed along with the reverend's stories about Jessica and Joe. When it came time for him to recite his reading from Ecclesiastes, the inspiration for my new unity candle, he cleared his voice emotionally before he could begin. His deep voice filled the room, and I was so thrilled at how the reading would segue to lighting the unity candle.

"How's Emily doing?" Peter whispered into my ear.

I shifted my glance to Emily, who was standing on the side of the chapel, about midway down the aisle.

"You mean because of the lopsided basket in the fourth row?" I asked, referring to one of the pews. "She'll be fine about it. Emily's attitude is that once the event begins, whatever happens happens."

"No," he said. "I mean she looks a little wobblier since Chris's BBQ."

I looked at Emily, who was wincing again. The reverend asked the congregation to stand and state its intention to support the couple throughout their marriage, which they did, followed by a few cheers. Emily was lost to me behind the standing crowd, so I made my way toward her to be sure she was OK. There was no way we were going to have her pass out, while this wedding was taking place.

"Hey," I said as I reached her. "Everything OK?"

"I think the little one has the hiccups now." She pointed to the altar. "Vows."

"I, Joseph—"

In less than a second, her attention turned back to the altar.

Jessica and Joe finished their vows. Before they exchanged rings, they headed to the unity candle. As Jessica took her position on one side of the wreath of candles, she looked out at the chapel and caught my eye. I smiled. She winked. I had to admit it, but Andy was right. I was the Candle Lady.

There was an endearing moment when the match Joe tried to light would not catch fire. Then, Jessica and Joe held hands around the long match and lit each candle. After they were done, the reverend joined them and the couple began their ring exchange. Tony handed the rings to Joe, who in turn handed one to Jessica. The reverend lay his hand on Joe's shoulder.

In the midst of the ritual, my phone vibrated. I know it's terrible etiquette to check a phone during someone's wedding, but I had to look. I needed to know if Andy had succeeded in getting Bellamy to send a team to the inn to start the search for the ring.

A text from Maude greeted me instead.

Can't find ring. It said. *Even checked toilet tanks and between mattresses. But I found an old picture of Mr. & Mrs. Sterling with Simon in her room.*

Send it to me, I responded.

A moment later, I received another text with an attachment. I opened it to find a photo of a young Mrs. Sterling between Simon and her husband, Henry. From the date that used to be stamped on old photos, I realized the picture was taken before Mrs. Sterling had married Henry. The reason the picture struck me as interesting was Mrs. Sterling's expression. She was looking up at Simon as if he were a God, while barely turning her shoulder toward Henry. Simon, however, seemed not to notice her, while Henry had his arm thrown over her.

Then another photo came from Maude. This time it was the back of the photo. Across it was one handwritten note: *Simon, my love will last forever. Beatrice.* I'd been wondering what Mrs. Sterling's first name was. From this picture, I formed a new impression of Mrs. Sterling's feelings for her late brother-in-law.

Mrs. Sterling had liked Simon, who, in turn, must have known how much Henry loved her. To distance himself from her, he never paid attention to the young woman. When that didn't work, he probably went the extra mile and was cold to her. Spurned, she told Henry she never wanted to see him again. The legend of Simon's cruelty was born. In Mrs. Sterling's story, Simon loved her and his jealousy led to his cruelty.

I felt that I was closing in on something. I was missing one final clue. One more secret.

I put the phone in my pocket and stared straight ahead.

Jessica placed a wedding band on Joe's finger.

Then, the strangest thing happened. Something that sent a chill into the bones of everyone who had spent any time with Simon Sterling, alive or dead. The scent of Simon Sterling's cigar wafted through the chapel.

Chapter 29

Jessica stopped speaking.
Joe squeezed her hands.
Tony looked at Joe, visibly alarmed.
Mrs. Sterling sat upright and scanned the chapel.
I, too, looked for Simon Sterling.
"You may kiss the bride," said the reverend.
Jessica and Joe smiled, but they still looked a little confused by Simon's cigar. They kissed as the organ music picked up, then headed down the aisle, now as Mr. & Mrs. Handler. Cheering guests followed behind them to reboard the buses and head to the reception.
Peter walked with Emily outside. I, on the other hand, stayed behind.
Once I was sure that the chapel was empty, I followed the scent of Simon's pipe tobacco. It lured me to the altar. I approached my unity candle wreath where I inhaled the scents of the burning wax. As I suspected, the one I had taken from Simon Sterling's room last night held the hint of his pipe's tobacco. The candle for summer. The one with the rose of Sharon on the side. I blew out the flames, took a deep

breath, and lifted his candle, turning it over to look at its bottom.

"Holy—" I stopped, remembering I was in a house of worship.

I had been so focused on designing a new candle last night that I had barely examined it before setting it upon the lazy Susan. Now, however, I had the answer to the puzzle of the missing ring. It was buried in my candle. The softer wax of the votive candle was easy to melt, and had clearly been tampered with. There were circular marks in a darkened shade, which can happen when wax is melted and recast. Another thing that can happen during such an operation is the infusion of other scents. In this case, the new scent had been some tobacco from Simon's pipe that had fallen into the candle. When Jessica and Joe had lit the candles, that scent had been released along with their own.

Looking very carefully, I thought I saw the shadow of green emerald. I also noticed a fingerprint, and suspected it was Simon Sterling's.

He had had the ring all along.

Something or someone had scared him, and he had hidden the ring in the candle while he had smoked his trademark pipe. That is why it had never made it around Tinker's neck.

I lit a match, ready to melt the bottom of the candle and free the ring. My concentration was broken, however, by the sound of the chapel door opening. Quickly, I blew out the match, took the candles, and retreated to the side of the altar, to a small nook between the chapel and a side exit. It gave me cover while I figured out what to do. I peeked around the corner and saw Jessica enter and walk down the aisle, holding her bouquet.

Alone, she knelt at the altar and lowered her head in prayer. I suddenly felt very awkward, hiding in the shadows while she prayed. She took her time, too. After a minute, I was itching to do something. I noticed that the box for the unity candles was beside me in the small enclave where I was hiding. I thought about wrapping up the wreath, but decided I'd make too much noise. Instead, I looked at my phone. The police were on their way to the Melville to search for a ring I had in my hand. I began to text Andy about my discovery. When I hit send, I silently tossed up my hands. My phone told me that the message failed to deliver.

I was toying with the idea of revealing myself to Jessica, when the door opened once again to the chapel.

"Jessica, dear," I heard Mrs. Sterling say. "Everyone is waiting for you. We need to get to the tent for photos."

"Mom?" said Jessica. She looked up, and I saw a tear on her cheek from my hiding place.

"What is it, my love?" said Mrs. Sterling. She walked down the aisle to her daughter to a spot where I could see them both.

"Did you," Jessica said, then faltered. "I think I might be crazy, but I thought I felt the aura of Uncle Simon during the ceremony. Did you?"

"We've been through a great trauma, Jessica," said Mrs. Sterling, soothingly. She stood above her daughter, who was still kneeling.

"But I thought I smelled his pipe," she said. "Like his ghost was here."

"Wedding day jitters," she said. I had seen Mrs. Sterling during the ceremony, and she had looked just as disturbed as Jessica had when the aroma of Simon's pipe made its way across the chapel. Now, all she wanted to do was protect her daughter from further stress.

"It's not jitters," said Jessica. "Mom, I have to tell you something."

The bride took a deep breath, and told her mother the story about Simon and the ring, just as she had told it to me and Andy. At the end of the story, Mrs. Sterling sank into a pew before the altar.

"Why didn't you tell me you wanted to sell your ring?" said Mrs. Sterling.

"I couldn't," said Jessica. "I know you don't like Joe, and I know how much you love that ring. I knew you wouldn't approve, but I also knew we'd never have such a great opportunity again. That land is worth so much more than the ring."

"What have I done?" said Mrs. Sterling. She rose and hugged her daughter. "I'm so sorry. From now on, no more secrets between us."

"Joe and I told the police this morning," said Jessica, looking relieved and reconciled with her mother. "They think that whoever took the ring from Simon is the murderer."

"I'm sure that bartender must have it," said Mrs. Sterling.

"They're on their way to the Melville to search the hotel during the reception," she said.

At that moment, my phone made a buzzing noise to let me know that my text still had not gone through. In the intimate mother-daughter moment, it sounded as loud as a fog horn. Jessica and her mother turned toward me.

"Hi," I said, revealing myself with an innocent smile and hoping they thought I had just entered from outside.

Jessica touched her mother's wrist.

"Stella knows the whole story," she said. "In fact, she's the one who figured most of it out."

Mrs. Sterling stared me down coolly and quietly.

"Stella," Jessica said. "Did you happen to notice a certain, um, scent during the ceremony?"

"I did," I said, wondering how much information to share.

I decided to at least drop a hint about the ring's location. If they were innocent, I would put them at ease. If one of them, perhaps Mrs. Sterling, was guilty, I might be able to learn something from her reaction.

"This probably won't make you happy," I said, "but the scent came from one of the unity candles. I was short a candle last night, so I took Simon's votive from his room."

"You stole his candle?" said Jessica.

"Why would the tobacco scent be in the candle?" said Mrs. Sterling, looking genuinely confused.

If Mrs. Sterling had been searching for the missing ring this weekend, my hint had not registered. Even Jessica looked at me blankly. I realized that all I had probably done was confess that I had behaved unprofessionally. I could tell them that I had discovered the ring, but right now I wanted it in the safe hands of the police. "I'll pack up the unity candles and bring them to the inn," I said, to both appease my clients and keep the candle in my possession.

"Perfect," said Mrs. Sterling, thankfully moving on. "Put them in my room for safekeeping. See, Jessica? Mystery solved. And as for the ring, I'm sure the police will find it stowed at the bartender's house. Shall we?"

Mrs. Sterling helped Jessica to her feet, and the three of us headed outside. I opened the chapel doors to bright sunlight, a cheerful crowd, and a beaming groom who was shaking hands with everyone with his best man beside him.

"Stella," said Peter, coming to my side. "Where'd you go? Emily's back at the inn, waiting for the police with Frank. She said we should head over to the reception tent and keep an eye on things until she arrives."

Gentleman that he was, he reached for the box I was holding with the candles, but I held it tightly and made a beeline for his car.

"OK," he said. "You hold that. I'll get the door."

Ahead of us, Jessica, Joe, and Mrs. Sterling were taking off in a horse and buggy carriage.

"Get behind them," I said.

We followed in slow procession as the buses behind us began to board as well.

"What's up?" said Peter. "You have a funny look."

I didn't think I was making a funny look.

"Do you have the Hellers' phone number handy?" I asked.

Peter gave me a funny look.

My text went through to Andy.

Chapter 30

"What's your password?" I said to Peter, lifting his phone.

"That's a relationship kind of thing. Are you sure you want to know?" he said.

"I love that you can flirt in the middle of a car chase," I said.

Peter looked at the road, and the horse drawn carriage ahead of us. I realized he had not known this was a chase. There was no way we were letting the three people in the carriage ahead of us out of our sight.

"Seven, seven, seven, seven," he said.

I opened his phone and went to his contacts where I easily found the Hellers' information. Hitting their number, I waited.

"You going to tell me what this is about?" he said.

"I think the Hellers'," I said, then held up my finger.

"I told you, we have nothing more to say," said an old but feisty woman's voice. "If you call again, Al will call our lawyer. Al, it's that reporter again."

"Tell him we'll call our lawyer," said a voice in the background, equally old. Equally spunky.

"I told him," said the woman, who I'd gathered was Ida.

"Excuse me," I said. "This is Stella Wright. Calling from the Wick & Flame in Nantucket. I'm borrowing Mr. Bailey's phone."

"The candle store?" said the woman. "I liked the coconut-scented sample you have on the counter."

"Thank you," I said. "I'm so glad you stopped by."

"Did we win something?"

"No," I said. "Mrs. Heller, I'm helping the police force here in Nantucket and we have a couple of questions to follow up on."

"What a small town," Ida called to her husband. "The candle lady is also with the police."

I let it go. At least she called me Candle *Lady*.

"Can you tell me what Mrs. Sterling said to you the night before Simon Sterling's murder?" I said, trying to focus the conversation.

There was unexpected silence on the other end of the line.

"Oh, yeah," said Peter, with a mischievous grin. "Stella's onto something."

I shushed him, afraid if Ida heard his voice she'd hang up.

"Which time?"

"How many times did you speak to Mrs. Sterling?" I asked.

"Let's see. The whole thing started because she saw me deliver the ring we made for Mr. Joe to him when he checked in. We were discreet, like he wanted, but that lady always has her eyes on him. I smiled nicely, but she was not so polite as that. I guess she went on the Internet because she came up to me later and told me she knew we were jewelers. Then, she wants to get the dirt on Mr. Joe. What did we give him? Why did he know us? But Mr. Joe had been very clear. If we want the job, we had to say nothing to nobody. So I told her to mind her own business, in the nicest way I could, mind you."

"Of course," I said. "And you spoke to her again?"

"Let's see," said Ida. "Al, what did the mother say the second time she came up to us?"

"The money, Ida!" said Al, sounding as if his wife were crazy.

"She came up to us on her way to dinner with her family that night. She was wearing a dress that was tan, and she had a shawl over it with bright colors that I thought were very flattering. So, I'm standing at the elevator, waiting to go up to my room because Al and I had been to town, that's when we saw your store, and we ate an early bite and we decided to go to bed early. So, she gets off the elevator, in this beautiful outfit. She was alone, I guess the others had already gone inside the restaurant. Anyway, she looks very happy to see me all of a sudden. And she says, why don't you come over here for a minute so we can talk? So, I'm a nice person and I say fine. And we walk over to the fireplace, and she pulls out a stack of money. So tacky for such a respectable lady. And I say what's this about? And she says she wants me to tell her more about the business we did with Mr. Joe. A bribe! Can you believe it?"

"I can't believe it," I said, matching her indignance.

"Don't say anything more," said Al. I heard a TV go on in the background.

"More about what?" I said.

"About nothing," said Ida.

"Ida, did you take the money?"

Ahead of us, I saw the Melville come into view.

"What if we did," said Ida.

"Ida!" said Al.

"What's the big deal, Al? All this secrecy. The police are asking," she yelled. "Why are you asking anyway?"

"Just tying up loose strings, Ma'am," I said, trying to sound official.

"Loose strings," she shouted to Al.

I heard him sigh, and could almost see him throw up his hands in defeat.

"Many people make copies of valuable jewelry, and I told Mrs. Sterling exactly that. Rich people with valuable items put the originals in the vault and wear the fakes. Half the time, you're admiring a fake, you should know."

"I didn't know," I said. I really never had heard about this practice.

"I told the mother that I thought Mr. Joe had a good head on his shoulders, but she didn't look convinced. And that was that. She went to dinner. Except there was the third time, too."

"She spoke to you a third time?"

"She crossed the line that time," said Ida. "She went up to Al and asked him if Jessica was wearing the fake when they left the dining room after dinner. We came back downstairs to sit by the fire because Al was feeling antsy."

"Could Al tell it was a fake?" I said.

"Of course, Al can tell his own work, but I didn't like the implication that she thought our work could be detected, and I told her as much. I pointed out that even the unusual setting of one of the rubies had been copied perfectly. What does she do? She gives me an unfriendly look and goes upstairs. One minute nice, one minute not nice. She's too much. I only saw her the one other time. When they found the dead body. I didn't like her much, but I wouldn't wish that on her."

"What's she saying?" whispered Peter.

"She talked to Mrs. Sterling three times," I said.

"Is that important? Is Mrs. Sterling in on it?" he said.

I wasn't ready to commit, but it wasn't looking too good for Mrs. Sterling.

"She knew that Jessica was wearing the copy of the ring after dinner on Friday," I said. "She's known about the fake the whole time."

"Could she kill Simon about that?" he said.

"There's a missing link," I said. "But it's suspicious."

Peter nodded in agreement, and drummed his fingers on the steering wheel, impatient with our chase.

"Dear, I have to check on my pot roast," said Ida. "Do you want to talk to Al? You have to speak up though. He's hard of hearing."

"You've answered all my questions, Mrs. Heller," I said. "Enjoy your meal."

"You're a very nice lady," she said and then the line went dead. Ida was on to her cooking.

I looked at Peter.

"Well?" he said.

"I don't know."

My phone pinged another text from Maude.

Found this in pieces in Mrs. S cosmetics bag, put it back together. Useful?

It was.

I looked at a photo of a ripped up check for $200,000 made out to Simon Sterling.

"Jackpot," I said.

"What do you mean?"

Peter pulled the car in front of the Melville as Jessica, Joe, and Mrs. Sterling disembarked from the carriage, a photographer taking photos of their every move.

My phone pinged again. This time there was a text from Andy that said he was on his way to the chapel to pick up the ring.

Come to the Melville, I responded.

Hang tight and don't do anything foolish, he said.

Suddenly, there was a knock on my window. I looked up nervously and let out a shriek when I saw Mrs. Sterling's smiling face up close to my window.

Peter locked the doors.

"What are you doing?" I said.

"I don't know," he said. "You screamed."

I turned to Mrs. Sterling, smiled calmly, and opened the window.

"Hi, Mrs. Sterling," I said.

"Stella," she said. "We need you in the tent. Emily's not here. Chop, chop."

She turned and headed into the tent. I looked at Peter.

"Chop, chop," he said.

Chapter 31

"I'll park and meet you back here in a minute," he said. "Make a quick appearance so no one is suspicious, and then let's bring that box over to the inn for safety. The police should be here soon."

"Good plan," I said.

I got out of the car, my knuckles gripped around the box of candles. Beside the tent, a photographer was taking photos of Joe and Jessica, while Mrs. Sterling was giving orders to an eager-to-please server to add ice to a pitcher of cocktails at the bar. She did not glance at the box in my hands. She seemed focused on the evening ahead as she joined the photographer. In fact, since her conversation with Jessica at the chapel, she was now showering her daughter with affection. It was a bit of a role reversal, and even Jessica seemed surprised, if not delighted. Behind me, I heard the bus arrive and the photographer call out to the wedding party to join them for photos. In another few minutes, the rest of the guests would soon descend on the reception.

In spite of the circumstances, my eye was drawn to

the tables inside the reception tent, to one, in particular, in the back of the room. The largest taper candle was crooked. Peter had not yet joined me, so I walked across the room. With each step toward my candle creations, I felt a growing confidence. No one was in the back of the tent, so I took a chance and put the box on the table, then leaned forward to straighten the long taper, a bright pink that was a wonderful pop of color against the blue sky beyond the tent. I approached a couple more tables, bringing the box with me, and I straightened another candle or two, more to enjoy the familiarity of my creations than because they needed it. I was wondering where Peter had gotten to when a server approached me in a crisp white jacket. I knew her. She was Lucy's older sister.

"Hi," she said. "Emily, the party planner, said I should bring the candles to her and that you should stay here so no one gets nervous. She said you'd understand."

"Really?" I said.

I typed a message to Emily, but once again my text did not send. I realized Peter must be with her since she knew about the candles. I still wasn't wild about letting a $200,000 ring out of my sight.

"Stella," said Jessica from the other end of the long tent. "Can you help? The wind is blowing and I need someone off-camera to hold my train."

The hotel was not far, and I knew Lucy's sister was trustworthy. I took a chance and handed the box to her.

"Go," I said as the two of us walked the length of the tent. "Be quick."

Jessica was standing with her bridesmaids, waiting for my help. Her mother was in the crowd, holding her daughter's bouquet and watching Jessica with a bittersweet smile. The photographer handed me a string that was attached to a weighted clothespin. I stood to the side, holding the string that was attached to the veil. Very clever. After a few snaps, I was done, but when I looked back at the crowd, I noticed that Lucy's sister was now holding Jessica's bouquet.

"Where's Mrs. Sterling?" I said to her.

"She took the box over for you," she said. "She's the one who gave me Emily's message."

I looked across the field to the path leading to the Melville. Mrs. Sterling was walking toward the inn with the box in her hands. I immediately took off after her. As I gained speed, I watched as she veered past the inn's entrance and toward Maude and Bill's house. I realized she was on her way to plant evidence at the Duffys'. What a piece of work. She would probably dig out the ring, leave it in the sugar bowl, then put the candles in her suitcase to head out of town with them. Her move erased any lingering doubt I had about the identity of the murderer. Mrs. Sterling had killed her brother-in-law, Simon.

"Stop," I called out to her when I was close enough.

Mrs. Sterling looked back at me. She smiled lightly, then turned her path toward the inn, picking up speed as she did. In a moment, we were both running. She slipped through a side gate that led to Ahab's. I followed, with no thought about how I would stop her, but blind confidence that I could.

As the gate banged shut behind me, Peter, Emily, and Frank stepped out onto the restaurant's patio.

"Hey," Peter said to me. "Why'd you tell Lucy's sister you'd meet me here? I thought we had a plan."

"Mrs. Sterling," I said, somewhat out of breath and waving my hands in her direction without stopping. At the end of the rolling lawn, Mrs. Sterling was untying what looked like Peter's boat.

"Hey!" said Peter as he immediately joined my race.

"What's your boat doing here?" I said as we flew down the lawn.

"Frank let me bring it over earlier," he said. "I wanted to take you home in it later tonight."

"I know our date's not turning out like you planned," I said, a cramp starting in my stomach from the running, "but that was a very sweet idea."

"Thanks," he said. "Hey!" he shouted again to Mrs. Sterling. "Come back here!"

Mrs. Sterling, however, was receding into the distance on Peter's motorboat.

I called Andy. The call went straight to voice mail.

"What are we going to do?" said Peter.

I looked at the inn's launch. Across the landing dock was a chain and a sign.

Launch closed today due to FIGAWI

Without breaking stride, I hopped over the chain and jumped onto the inn's boat. As I hoped, the keys were in the ignition.

I'd already started the motor and Peter was untying the lines, when Emily wobbled down the last few steps of the lawn to us.

"Wait up," she said.

"Call Andy," I said to her. "Tell him we're going after Mrs. Sterling."

Emily turned and screamed up to the lawn to Frank to call Andy. Then she stepped onto the boat.

"Don't even try to stop me," she said. "I've missed seeing Gina Ginelli. I've been kicked from my insides for the last twenty-four hours. I still don't understand why the box of candles is important, and I'm not going to become one of those mothers who is out of the loop on everything."

By this point she was seated firmly on the benches along the boat and pulling on two ends of a seat belt to fit across her tummy.

"You're a nut," I said as I pushed the throttle ahead and began our pursuit of Mrs. Sterling.

Emily laughed for the first time in two days, so maybe it was worth it.

"Oh my God," she said. "Is that Tinker?"

Sure enough, Tinker had fallen asleep under the helm of the boat. He looked up in alarm as some sea spray hit his face, and then curled in a tight ball under the protection of the seats. It seemed that cats did, indeed, hate water.

"What are we going to do once we reach her?" said Peter. "Crash into her boat?"

"No," said Emily. A look of panic spread across her face, and I could see she was rethinking her spontaneous decision.

"No," I said in agreement.

Our eyes were peeled on the seas. We watched as our boat gained on Mrs. Sterling. I should have been cold in my strategically cut red evening dress, but I wasn't. We were quiet, hanging on to keep our balance, and focused with great intensity on the boat ahead of us. After a few minutes, we had driven far enough that the steeples of town were in view.

It was time for a plan. I looked around the boat for inspiration. My eyes fell on Peter's anchor. I wondered if any of us had the skill to throw an anchor with the aim required to hit Mrs. Sterling in her moving boat. I doubted it.

Next, my eyes fell on a blow horn stashed behind the wheel of the boat. It was kept for emergencies, and

I knew this was one. Unfortunately, it was now about three o'clock, the time that the sailboats competing in FIGAWI rounded Brant Point to finish the race. Their colorful sails made for a stunning nautical parade, and in the spirit of victory, many spectators were ringing cowbells and blowing horns from shore. I was not convinced that anyone would distinguish our call as an SOS.

Finally, I saw the answer. Under the last row of seating on the boat, the inn had stored a couple of its water skis, a guest amenity that would become available when the weather warmed a teensy bit more. I dashed across the deck and began to pull out the skis.

"Are you crazy? You're in a cocktail dress," said Emily. "The Slosh?"

I nodded. Having spent most of my life on an island, I was confident in my water-sport skills and ranked water-skiing at the top of the list. As teens, we kids had enjoyed a questionable period one summer where we liked to ski as close to each other's boats as possible to splash our friends. The Slosh. We had developed nerves of steel sidling up to each other.

"Peter, stop the boat," I said.

"Why?" he said. "We're gaining."

"And then what?" I said. "We need to stop her."

As the boat came to a halt, I threw the skis into the water and slipped off my shoes. Emily was already threading a rope to the stern. The inn's launch was not designed for water skiing, but she made it work. I threw a leg over the railing, swung the other beside it, took a deep breath, and plunged in.

The agony!

I wondered for a moment if I might die of hypothermia before I rose to the surface, but finally I broke through the water to see two skis bobbing beside me. Shivering already, I grabbed one ski, then another, and found the rope.

"Go," I shouted to Emily.

"Go," she shouted to Peter.

Quickly, I rose to the surface as the boat resumed our chase. The water had been so cold that the May breeze against my skin actually warmed me. If Emily had wanted my outfit to be a tad more formfitting tonight, her wish had come true. The drenched bodice of my red dress clung to my skin, while the skirt was now hiked to my waist as I jumped from wake to wake. Although I was sure my mascara was dripping down my face, I felt very wise to have shaved my legs.

As Peter regained the distance between us and Mrs. Sterling, we passed a familiar motorboat and I noticed the driver struggling with string tangled in her motor. The string itself was attached to what looked like a shark kite. Flying by, I caught one glimpse of the driver. She was wearing horizontal stripes in blue and white. I also noticed her boat's contents. Buoys. And lots of them. I wondered how chakras and buoys worked together. At the moment, they seemed like a terrible combination, however strong Georgianna's commitment to art was.

Boy, could Andy pick them.

Our boat had closed in on Mrs. Sterling. I took as wide a berth as possible in the opposite direction of her boat, then made my way across the waves toward her. It had been a long time since I'd tried to pull off the Slosh, and today I was going for more than a spray of water. I adjusted my hold around the rope that pulled me across the harbor, psyching myself up for the next few seconds. I could now see the chiffon layers of Mrs. Sterling's blue dress that flew behind her. My skis pulled up starboard. When I could almost touch the boat, I let go of my rope. For a moment, I coasted along the top of the water, and then I leaned to the left and fell into her boat.

It wasn't the smoothest landing. I fell hard. I felt something sharp hit my head. I jumped to my feet, however, without pain. Honestly, I felt invincible. I knew I'd be bruised in the morning, but I was thrilled and shocked by my feat. As Mrs. Sterling turned around to register my unexpected arrival, I heard Peter slow the launch and begin to circle us.

"It's over," I said, feeling a trickle of blood down my forehead.

Mrs. Sterling stopped the boat. I didn't think the woman could surprise me anymore, but she did. Without skipping a beat, she lunged at me. I braced myself for the impact of her leap and felt my hands automatically clench into fists. Before she reached me, however, I heard her scream and saw her clutch her head.

"Get off," she shouted. "Get off! Get this thing off of me!"

I dropped my hands and watched as Tinker clawed at Mrs. Sterling. In spite of his fear of water, he'd made a several-yard leap across the seas to help me. I took one step forward to join the fight, but Mrs. Sterling tripped over Peter's anchor and landed in a thud, knocked out cold.

The box of candles was safely tucked into a basket of wine and glasses. I smiled at Peter to acknowledge his thoughtful evening preparations, then grabbed a rope from his tackle and began to bind Mrs. Sterling's feet.

"Guys?" said Emily. "I'm in labor."

Chapter 32

Peter pulled the launch up beside the boat. Quickly tying the two boats together, he took off his jacket and reached his hand to me. I took it and climbed back to him and Emily, where he engulfed me in his jacket, warm from his body. Under its cover, I rolled down the bodice of my dress and let a wave of heat nourish me.

"Take Emily to the beach at Monomoy," said Peter, switching boats with me. "It's two minutes that way. I'll call an ambulance and Andy. I've got Mrs. Sterling."

Tinker, who had been sitting victoriously on Mrs. Sterling's body, jumped back onto the launch with me.

Emily moaned.

"Got it," I said, and took off.

"Tell me how Mrs. Sterling killed Simon," Emily said as I drove the boat as quickly as I could without bouncing her around.

"Let's think lovely thoughts?" I said.

"I'm having a baby! In a boat," said Emily. "Keep my mind off of things."

"OK," I said, stroking her hair as I drove. "Where to begin? The murder was a combination of love and greed. I realized from a picture that Mrs. Sterling loved Simon and had spent a lifetime repressing her feelings. When Simon arrived this weekend, all of her feelings came back."

"But he's so icky," said Emily.

"As it turns out, he was a good guy," I said.

"Keep talking," said Emily. "What happened next?"

"The afternoon that Mrs. Sterling arrived," I said, "she saw Joe in conversation with the Hellers. She asked them what they'd said, but they wouldn't tell her. Later, she saw Joe leave Simon's room after he'd given the real ring to Simon in a ring-for-land swap. I don't think Mrs. Sterling knew what was up between them, but she'd been wanting to bust Joe for something. Frank saw her knock on Simon's door immediately after Joe left. I'm sure she confronted Simon ferociously as she tried to find out what was going on, so much so that after she left he hid the ring, just in case. I should have noticed the candle had been tampered with, but I was so worried about getting the new unity candle done. I only figured it out when the tobacco smell hit the chapel."

"Easy mistake," said Emily, breathing loudly.

"Rookie mistake, and you know it," I said.

"Happens," she said. "Keep talking. I think I might be having a contraction."

She squeezed my hand hard, so I kept talking.

"When Simon was heading out for his walk an hour or so later," I said, "Mrs. Sterling was reading the paper in the lobby and heard him talking to the Hellers. She probably heard him compliment their good work, so she Googled them. Once she figured out they were jewelers, she got more suspicious about Joe's chat with them. The sad thing is that she didn't know she was the source of their secrecy."

I started to make those pregnancy breathing noises that I've seen people do on TV. Tinker curled up at Emily's feet for support.

"Mrs. Sterling went to town and took out cash, which she used to bribe the Hellers. They told her that Joe commissioned a copy of the ring, no more. Later, she ascertained from them that Jessica was wearing the fake. She jumped to the conclusion that Joe had sold her daughter's ring to Simon and had given her the fake one to unwittingly wear. She never, ever, imagined that Jessica was in on the deal. That night, after tossing and turning, she went downstairs to confront the men at the card game. The game was over, however. Joe and Tony had left. Bill had punched Simon, and he was waiting for Gina to arrive. They were alone in the Card Room."

"Wait. Simon was having an affair with Gina?" said Emily.

"I know, can you believe it? He wanted the ring for her."

"This is all about Gina Ginelli!" said Emily. "To think I was considering asking Neal this morning if he liked the name Gina."

At this point she squeezed my hand again, so I kept talking.

"Mrs. Sterling told Simon in the Game Room that she knew Joe commissioned the ring and that he was in on it. She demanded he tell her everything, which he refused to do. Then she offered to pay him for the ring. He refused."

I breathed some more. Emily joined me. To my relief, as we neared closer and closer to the shore, I heard sirens. Peter had gotten through to the hospital.

"Why did Mrs. Sterling kill Simon?" Emily said.

"As Bellamy said, a crime of passion. I think she lost it," I said, finishing my story as we pulled to the shore. "She picked up the candle and hit him with the anger of all the years of feeling scorned by him, and all her fears about her daughter marrying the wrong man. The problem was, however, that she killed him without finding out where the ring was."

"So, along with Jessica and Joe," said Emily, "Mrs. Sterling was looking for the ring all weekend?"

"Yup," I said.

"I'm having a baby!" Emily cried, and smiled as two EMTs ran to the water's edge with a stretcher.

"I know! And you're so cool!" I said.

Another EMT arrived with a stretcher as Emily was whooshed away. I realized that one was meant for me, and that the blood from my forehead was flowing freely. As the ambulance door shut on me a minute or so later, my last view was of the colors of the sails in Nantucket's harbor. I decided that next year I'd kick off the season with a FIGAWI line to celebrate the colors of all of the sails. We pulled away with me in one ambulance and Emily in another. Tinker warmed me with a sweet purr. I checked him for bumps and bruises, but, luckily, he had nine lives and had escaped without injury.

Moments later, the doors opened again. My cousin Kate was standing before the emergency entrance looking worried. Peter came running toward us from the parking lot.

"The police have Mrs. Sterling," said Peter. "Andy was on the scene, along with Bellamy."

"What happened to your head?" Kate said.

Peter followed us into the hospital, explaining the events of our chase to my cousin as she cleaned my wound and checked me for any broken bones of which I thankfully had none. Once I had a ridiculous bandage on my forehead, Emily's doctor poked her head into my room and said that Emily wanted to see me. My headache—in fact, any ache from the tension of the day—melted at her invitation. Peter could barely keep up with me as I headed to the maternity ward.

A pink balloon was wrapped around the doorknob of her room.

"It's a girl," she said when I opened the door.

Neal was beside her. He kissed his wife and baby, who cooed at him. She was a beautiful bundle.

"Neal's furious with you," said Emily.

"Furious," said Neal.

"I'm so sorry," I said.

"My wife takes her job too seriously," said Neal. "I depend on you to keep her from getting into more trouble than she already does. I know that's impossible because I know the both of you, but you two really crossed the line. My daughter was out there on the seas."

"Your daughter," said Emily, looking the proud parent.

Neal smiled back at her.

We all peeked over the pink blanket in Emily's arms to gush over the rosy-cheeked bundle she held.

"You want to tell her?" Neal said.

Emily looked at me.

"We named her," she said. "Victoria."

"Well done, Neal," I said.

"Victoria Stella," said Emily.

I cried. Emily cried. We hugged until the nurse came in and told me and Peter we had to leave. There were loads of Wrights who would be happy to pick us up, but we walked out of the hospital, where Tinker was waiting for us on a bench, and called a cab.

"Feeling better?" he said.

"I think I'm going to skip the Sterlings' reception," I said. "Sorry this wasn't a better date."

"This was an awesome date," said Peter. "This is like the best date I've ever had. Don't you think?"

I laughed. "I guess it was," I said.

"You guess?" he said, putting his arm around me.

"No, I know," I said. "It was pretty darn good."

"If you want a more traditional first date, however, we can do that," he said, kissing my bandaged forehead. "How about we go to FIGAWI's closing party tomorrow night?"

"It's a deal," I said.

Chapter 33

I had to give the police a lot of credit. Their job is a lot more than I bargained for. Maybe I was suffering from a mild concussion, but the moment I arrived back at my apartment, the adrenaline slowed and the fatigue kicked in. My appetite did, too. I was so hungry and my fridge was so bare that I was almost tempted to boil the macaroni off my *Leftover* sign. Fortunately, Chris and Suzie met me with a plate of homemade spaghetti and meatballs and an ice-cold beer. We sat at my kitchen counter with Tinker purring at my feet while I told them all of the details of Mrs. Sterling's arrest, Emily's new baby, and the discovery of Simon Sterling's hidden ring.

The last thing I learned before my head hit the pillow was that Andy had been the one to break the news to Jessica and Joe about Mrs. Sterling's arrest. From what I gathered, the newlyweds, who had been so careful about protecting Mrs. Sterling's delicate emotions for many months, decided the news was the last straw. After a short, angry call between Jessica and her mother, the Handlers packed their bags and left in their Just Married carriage before the party ended. Maria and Tony turned out to be the best attendants anyone could have ever wanted. They took over as host and hostess of the party, which went on into the wee hours. None of the guests even knew what had happened to Mrs. Sterling until the next morning, and by that time Jessica and Joe were in Southern Italy. I wondered if they would ever come home to open their gyms. Jessica and Joe would have a lot ahead of them, but I figured they'd make it. They'd already shown a lot of fortitude.

When I awoke, it was late Sunday afternoon. Tinker was at the bottom of my bed, keeping my feet warm. As I lay in bed, reviewing the past forty-eight hours, there was a knock on my front door. I figured it was Suzie, and that if I didn't answer, she'd think I was still asleep and come back in a couple of hours. A few seconds later, however, the knock came again.

"I'm sleeping," I called out, knowing my voice would travel down the stairs.

"Sorry," a voice said. It was not Suzie's.

I sat up and threw off my covers.

"Wait!" I said. "Hang on!"

I shuffled around my room for some clothes, but could only find my jeans on the chair by my window. I was wearing my super fluffy leopard print pajama top, but it would have to do. I threw on the matching slippers and ran down the stairs.

Gina Ginelli was at my door. Tinker ran down beside me and purred at her feet.

"Hi," she said.

This morning, my Hollywood idol was wearing a heavy cable-knit sweater with a quilted vest over it. She wore no makeup and her hair was pulled back into a bun. The only giveaway that there might be a superstar at my front door was the large pair of black sunglasses she wore.

"Hi," I said.

"I'm heading out, but I wanted to say goodbye to you," she said, and then looked down at Tinker. "And you."

"Come in," I said, wishing I'd tidied up a bit more before falling asleep last night. The unwashed bowl of spaghetti was still in my kitchen sink and the empty can of beer was on the counter. Added to that was my bloodstained red dress that was crumpled in a ball outside my bathroom door. I picked it up and shoved it in my hamper, but otherwise it was too late for any other improvements.

To her credit, Gina did not seem to notice anything. She waltzed into my small apartment and took a seat on my sofa.

"Tea?" I said.

"That would be lovely," she answered as Tinker jumped on my coffee table and looked at her steadily.

He purred, and put out a paw.

"Aren't you the gentleman," she said with a catch in her voice. "I wish I could shake your hand, but I'd be sneezing all day."

Tinker dropped his paw.

"But I wanted to see you, and if you don't mind, take your picture," she said to the cat. She pulled out her phone and took a picture. "You will always be family in my heart, but if our friend, Stella, doesn't mind, I think you'll have a nice life on Nantucket with her."

I stopped pouring the boiling water for a moment to nod my head in agreement.

"It would be my honor," I said. I took two cups of chamomile tea and joined Gina. "And I'll send you photos any time."

"That would be nice," she said.

Sitting so close to Gina, I was reminded again of the unique scent she wore. I realized I might never have such a perfect opportunity to talk to her about it. I gathered my nerve and shared my idea of the Ginelli candle. As I spoke, I noticed she avoided my eyes.

"It's a lovely idea," she said when I'd finished. "And I'd do anything I can for you, but I'm about to have my life raked across the coals. People might not be wanting a Ginelli candle."

I looked at her questioningly.

"Because of Simon?" I said.

"And more," she said. "I've decided to leave Kevin. He's broken every vow. I think I can get an annulment."

"I'm sure that was a hard decision," I said. "I'm sorry I know this, but I heard there was a big prenup."

"There is," she said, "but I have enough for two lifetimes. I recently came into a large fortune, unexpectedly. From Simon. Or I should say, the real Gina Ginelli has come into money. My given name is MaryJo LaMonte."

And here, I'd always thought that Gina was an Italian diva. She'd done quite a good job of creating a character the world could enjoy in Gina Ginelli, but I had a feeling MaryJo and I would have been good friends.

"I'm sorry," I said. "But also, congratulations."

"I hope you can understand that there are a few things in life I'd like to keep as my own. My scent is one of them."

"I think I understand better than most anyone about that," I said.

"I might have something better for you anyway." She opened her purse and pulled out a card. "This is the name of the perfumer who created the scent for me. He works in a little shop in Southern Italy. I'll tell him to expect your call and I'm sure he would love to work with you."

"This would be amazing," I said. "In fact, my mother is the one who would most love to meet him."

"At her own risk," she said with a wink. "He's a very charming man."

"May I ask another favor of you?" I said.

"Anything," she said.

"My friend, Emily, just had a baby. She's a huge fan. I'm wondering if we can send her a picture of you?"

"The woman from the motorboat?" said Gina with a smile. "She's a local celebrity. We divas have to stick together. Forget a selfie, I'll stop by the hospital."

We chatted for a while longer. After we said goodbye, I looked at the perfumer's card, then pulled out my laptop. I emailed a note to my mom, and told her I would love to see her sometime soon. I'm not sure when I had last said that.

I hit send. It might be days or weeks or months before I heard back, but I was glad I had written her. My inbox had a couple of good offers for Memorial Day sales, so I surfed around a little, hoping to find something good. I'd just hit a link to J.Crew when my inbox refilled with a note from my mom. It was a record for her. It was even more amazing when I opened her email to find that she would work on a trip home to Nantucket for some time soon.

Tinker jumped on my lap and we took a snooze. By the time I woke up, my head had mostly cleared and I was looking forward to my date at the FIGAWI party. The Sunday night FIGAWI party closes the event. It's a festive, but not fancy, affair. I threw on cream-colored leggings, a cheerful red top, which tied at the side in a bow, and added some red sandals that I had owned for about three years now, but still adored. I'll probably be buried in these sandals. I was putting on a poncho that Cherry had made for me when I heard a knock at my door.

At eight o'clock, with Peter by my side, we entered the FIGAWI tent to a great cheer from the locals who knew what had happened this weekend. It was a funny sight. Most of the room was dancing, intoxicated, and having the time of their lives, while my group was celebrating the release of Bill and the ocean adventure that had led to Mrs. Sterling's arrest. To my sheer delight, Bill was at the party, holding Maude's hand. They came up to me and gave me the biggest hug of my life. I noticed that Maude was wearing the spectacular lightship basket pin with a small diamond in it that Bill had bought for her from Jewel in the Sea. When I complimented it, she touched it and smiled at Bill.

"The boys at the precinct helped me out so that Maude would have her special gift by our anniversary today," he said. "They knew I'd missed out on overtime at the inn this weekend, so they passed the hat." He leaned toward me and lowered his voice. "And I've already made a call to Gambler's Anonymous. I haven't forgotten our deal."

I nodded confidentially, but I knew I was beaming.

"They're good boys at the precinct," said Maude. "It was that Andy of yours who had the idea."

"Well, not mine, of course," I said. I turned to Peter. "He has a girlfriend. We're just friends. You know."

"I don't mind a little competition," he said with a wink.

"No, really," I said, but I was interrupted by a drunken arm tossed around my shoulder.

"Stella Wright," said the first of my clients to have canceled a unity candle order this weekend. "You are a star. Forget my message. We're going to have loads of candles. Whatever you think is good. You have my vote of confidence."

"Thanks," I said with a smile, and thought I might get a new license plate for my car, *CNDLDY*, along with a new window. "I'm glad you reconsidered. I promise we'll do something unique and unforgettable."

"Woohoo!" she yelled and jumped back onto the dance floor.

"Look," said Peter, "there's Bellamy."

Sure enough, Bellamy walked into the party. We caught eyes. To my surprise, he made his way toward me. I suppose I should have been happy that he was acknowledging me after such a rocky weekend, but instead, I felt my temper begin to rise. If Bellamy had had his way, Bill would still be in prison, Mrs. Sterling would never have been suspected for murder, and I might have lost my new, rent-friendly wedding candle income. On the other hand, if it weren't for Bellamy, I would not have discovered how much adventure existed right outside my doorstep.

"Captain," I said. I opened my purse and pulled out my parking ticket. "Given the circumstances of this weekend, I'm wondering if you can void this ticket for me?"

"That's not really my domain," he said, but he took the ticket and crumpled it in his hands.

I smiled, and wondered if I'd be getting a new copy in the mail next week.

"I have a good story for you if you want it," Bellamy said to Peter. "We picked up a truck filled with stolen bicycles about an hour ago. A kid whose bike was stolen followed the crook on his scooter, of all things, and called in the license plate. Kid's over there now if you want an interview. One of my infamously speedy arrests."

"Thanks," said Peter. "But I'm on a date. I'll have to pass on this story."

"Suit yourself," said Bellamy. "But it's a good one."

Bellamy put his empty glass on a table beside us. Without so much as another word, he waved to the event's chairman across the room and moved on. I looked at Peter, my eyes rolling with frustration. Peter smiled and clinked my glass. I drank, then I took his glass from him.

"Can I make a confession?" I said.

"More confessions?" Peter said. "I think we're covered with Mrs. Sterling's for at least a week. Or at least until the next issue of the paper comes out on Thursday."

"Seriously," I said. "My head's still a little fuzzy and the music isn't helping. Maybe I'll go home and you can interview that kid in the police station."

"Are you OK?" he said, looking concerned.

"Nothing a good night's sleep won't fix. How about a picnic, tomorrow, Tupancy Links?" I said. "Nice and quiet."

"Perfect," he said.

With an unexpected but thoroughly impressive kiss on my lips as he dropped me off at my apartment a few minutes later, Peter was off to his next story. That kiss haunted my lips all night, and all the following morning. As the revelers from the sailing event of the season still slept on Monday morning, I made my way to Upper Main Street where a crowd gathered around the Civil War monument for Memorial Day.

As I approached, I noticed Andy among the crowd. A few of the younger kids from town were surround-

ing him to touch his uniform and ask him questions.
As he knelt down to speak with them, one kid climbed
onto his shoulders. He laughed and handed the small
girl his hat to wear. I waved and he waved back.

I carried with me a basket filled with my simple
white unscented candles. I passed them out to anyone
who asked for one as we quietly assembled to remember our heroes. Maude and Bill stood side by side,
thinking about their son, who was far away from them
on their anniversary weekend.

"Any left?" said Andy, coming to my side.

I handed my last candle to him.

"How's Georgianna?" I asked.

He looked back to the monument. "She'll survive.
Turns out she and I have a very different idea of adventure. And art."

I nodded, my eyes not leaving the monument either.

One of the little kids waved him over, and he oblig-
ingly left to see what was up.

"I like that young man," said Cherry, who I had not
noticed was standing not far from me. "I'll always remember when you were teenagers, and he set off
those fireworks for your birthday because he knew you
were at the observatory."

"He did?" I said, remembering my close encounter.

"Who did what?" said Peter, coming up beside me.
He planted a kiss on my cheek which made my knees
weak.

"Hi," I said.

Peter raised his basket, one filled with cheeses,
wine, and, to my delight, a new kite.

"Ready?" he said.

STELLA'S "CANDLES 101" WORKSHOP NOTES

WHY MAKE CANDLES?

Candles are a source of light, a symbol at celebrations, the start of a romantic night, a balm for the senses, the heart of ceremonies, and a wonderful way to make a house into a home.

THE ABC'S OF A WICK & FLAME

- A **wick** draws oil from a candle's wax and holds the flame. It is usually made of soft spun threads that absorb the liquid wax while the candle is burning.
- The **wax** holds the wick in place and fuels the flame. The coolest thing about candles? Wax has a memory! Tip: The first time you use a candle, let the wax melt to its edges, otherwise it might refuse, yes, *refuse!* to melt beyond a limited surface area when you light it again.

COMMON SENSE WITH CANDLES

- A burning candle should not be used as a nightlight. If you're feeling sleepy, blow it out!
- Keep your candle 2–3 feet from your stuff and put it on a flat, sturdy surface . . . especially if your furry friends like to stare at flames with uncanny devotion.

HOMEWORK: Spend a night by candlelight! Maybe you have a good book you want to read?

ACKNOWLEDGMENTS

Many thanks to everyone who helped bring the Nantucket Candle Maker series to the bookshelves. I am most grateful to my agent, Christina Hogrebe, and my editor, Norma Perez-Hernandez, who have both been such strong advocates for the series. These heart-felt sentiments extend to the entire team at Kensington Publishing, a family-run company that immediately made me feel at home.

Thanks to Jonathan Putnam and Michael Bergmann for their fantastic assistance on this book. It was my lucky day when I met you and the talented writers at the New York Society Library's Writers Group. Additional thanks go to the Gray Lady herself, Nantucket Island, where Lieutenant Angus C. MacVicar kindly answered my law-enforcement questions, and the staff at the Whaling Museum educated me about Nantucket's fascinating history in candles.

The list is long and the page is short, but I am so grateful to all of my friends for their encouragement. Valerie Steiker and Peggy Boulos Smith guided me into the publishing world. Jill Furman and Alicia Cleary cheered at every step. Above all, my love and endless thanks for their help go to my parents, Rini & Tom Shanahan; my talented brother, Mark; my niece, Cate; and, so deeply, to Steve, Tommy, and Carly Brecher, who have mastered the mantra "You can do it!" when I'm staring at my screen and wondering where Stella will find herself next.

Keep reading for a sneak peek at

MURDER MAKES SCENTS

The next Nantucket Candle Maker Mystery

Available March 2020

From Kensington Publishing Corp.

Chapter 1

It was my last day in Paris, and I was in heaven among candles of every size, color, and scent at Cire Trudon, the city's finest candle store. I reverently admired a display of tapers, piled in tidy rows by color against the back wall. Then I marveled over an elegant circle of bell jars that encased sophisticated scents on a round table in the middle of the room. I lifted one jar from a candle called Byron, melting into its peppery scent, and thought how wonderful the aroma would be during a winter's day on Nantucket. Thirty miles off the coast of Massachusetts, my hometown is a chilly place in February, and a warm scent does wonders for body and soul. My nose sated, I crossed the store with the quiet reverence one saves for museums, to admire their *piece de resistance*. On a credenza at the far side of the store was a remarkable group of wax busts featuring characters in French history, tempting customers to light the wicks atop their heads. Marie Antoinette stared at me, daring me to try. As if I would. Her molded hair was too fabulous to mess with.

Most visitors to Paris look forward to the cheeses

and breads, the art, the bridges linking the Left and Right Banks, the sparkle of the Eiffel Tower at night. As the proprietor of the Wick & Flame, my candle store on Nantucket, I arrived for a long weekend with my own sacred list of Parisian enchantments. This beautiful autumn morning, I had already made a pilgrimage to Diptyque, the internationally renowned French candle company. My senses alit, I'd followed my visit with a stroll through the Tuilleries Gardens and over the Pont Royal, where the Bateaux Mouches floated below me on the Seine. Once across the river, I'd visited Quinetessence Paris, a one-of-a-kind establishment that leads customers from room to room of a grand home to enjoy candles designed for each living space. I particularly wanted to visit this store because, like me, it is run by a woman from a perfume family. I'm the daughter of one of the finest perfumers I've ever come across. In fact, I was in Paris for a long weekend because of my mother, Millie Wright. The World Perfumery Conference was taking place this week, and they had invited her to speak on a panel entitled *The Art of Scent Extractions.*

When Millie had called me three weeks ago to propose I meet her in Paris, I knew that the invitation was an unspoken apology. This summer, she'd had plans to come home, a rare event, but then she'd canceled at the last minute. An opportunity to visit scientists in the rain forest to learn about indigenous scents had come up. Something about absorption traps. All very scientific. The trip had ultimately led to her invitation to speak at the conference, and I think she wanted me to see that her detour had been worthwhile.

I had one caveat, which was that she had to return with me to Nantucket for a visit as well, but the truth is she and I both knew I would accept her goodwill gesture. A *sorry* is nice, but Paris is Paris, and this was one case where our sense of adventure aligned. Millie is happiest roaming the world, seeking unique and exotic scents to create perfumes. In contrast, I find my buzz on Nantucket, running my store, the Wick & Flame, and tackling my candle creations. I also solved a murder a few months ago, so I argue that you can discover the mysteries of the world right outside your front door.

The sales associate at Cire Trudon politely indulged me while I took a few snaps of the candle busts on display. As I zoomed in on a stern-faced Napoleon, my phone pinged a photo from my boyfriend, Peter, who was back home. His lopsided grin and the wisp of blond hair over his forehead reminded me of his boyish charm, while the look in his eye made me miss his warm embrace. I smiled at the image of him holding up four fingers, and I sent a thumbs-up selfie back to him. We'd recently hit the four-month mark in our relationship, and we were feeling pretty smug about ourselves. I hated to jinx myself, but life was good. In addition to the magic of new love coursing through my veins, my business had been strong enough over the summer that I'd felt confident to leave for a long weekend abroad. Even the timing of the trip was perfect since everyone back home had begun to remind me that my birthday was coming up. The Big 3-O. I might have been imagining it, but the reminder was often followed with a look that made me feel like I had spinach in my teeth.

"May I help you?" the sales associate asked. From her subtle pout, I realized that I'd crossed a line when my attention had shifted from her candles to Peter's text.

"*Non, merci,*" I said, practicing my accent. I checked

the time. It was later than I'd realized. With one last tour of the establishment and a friendly *"au revoir,"* I picked up a healthy pace to meet Millie for a snack at a café across the street from the conference center on the Left Bank.

Today was the end of the conference and tonight we'd be heading back to Nantucket, but Millie and I had likely patronized a years-worth of cafés over the last few days. We'd had a ball sitting at small round tables, unlit Gauloises cigarettes dangling from our lips for a cinema-noire effect as we drank our café cremes and people-watched. The parade of high style, fabulous couples walking hand in hand, even the dogs enjoying croissant crumbs from the pavement beside the cafés, was captivating.

It took a few minutes longer than I anticipated to reach what had become our favorite haunt, Café Bonne Chance, because I had to wait by the Odeon as a caravan of black cars with a motorcade on each side passed. The much talked about Peace Jubilee was being held the following week in Paris. Already, the city was filling up with important foreign leaders for strategic meetings and with citizens from all walks who had opinions to voice. It was an exciting moment to be in the city. Unlike other peace summits, leaders from small kingdoms, in some cases from remote areas, were invited to share insights into how they promoted peace. Including these new voices at the table had created excitement around the globe. I couldn't help think what good sports the Parisians were. The closed-off streets, demonstrations, and obligations that came with such an undertaking made me appreciate the simplicity of my small-town life.

When I finally arrived, Millie was already seated at an outdoor table with the coat check lady from the

World Perfumery Conference, Olive Tidings. The two women both loved the spot for breakfast, and had become fast friends over the last few days while enjoying their morning's pastries.

"*Bonjour*, Stella," my mom said with outstretched arms as I pulled up a chair.

We kissed on each cheek as if we were French. We both knew how silly we'd look with such formality back home, but we could not resist. In honor of the panel, Millie's fabulous red hair, a Wright trait that contrasts starkly with my dark, wild mane, was pulled into a soft up-do. She wore a thick navy sweater, secured with big black buttons, high black boots, and bright red lipstick. Her storytelling skills are even more striking than her looks. Her audience was in for a treat.

"Maybe it's because we're leaving," said my mother, "but the croissants are particularly delicious today. I ordered one for you."

"I couldn't agree more," said Olive, wholeheartedly, over a bite of her own pastry. She waved at two men in business suits, who returned a friendly greeting as they passed us. Through her job at the coat check room, Olive had seemingly met everyone.

"I think this week was a sign you need to travel more, Olive," said Millie with a speech I knew she liked to make to anyone she thought she might convert to her nomadic lifestyle. "I can see you like people and places too much to be cloistered in that school all the time. And people love you."

Millie and I found it endlessly fascinating that the conference's coat checker was actually a literature teacher from an all-girls boarding school in England. Olive was on sabbatical and had always dreamed of visiting Paris. After three days of rich, French foods, however, she'd realized she wasn't a lady of leisure. Noticing an ad in *Le Monde* about the conference, she'd applied for a job and landed one working at the coat check.

"I always say, greet people with a smile, or your day will be rubbish," she said.

"To smiles," said Millie.

The ladies clinked their cups. I ordered an espresso, and shared my morning's excursions as they peppered me with questions and looked at my photos. Finally, Olive looked at her watch.

"I'll say my goodbyes," she said. "And head off to make some others. I had a lovely time meeting you this week."

"I never say goodbye," said Millie. True, but after six months without coming home, I knew there were some folks back on Nantucket who felt they'd seen the last of her. "And remember what I said about travel. *Mi casa es su casa.*"

"Thank you," said Olive. "And be careful what you say. I have a lot of time on my hands."

We hugged and said our goodbyes, and Olive Tidings took off ahead of us in thick-soled shoes. A stocky woman, she wore skirted tweed suits every day. She was warm enough on even the chilliest occasions with no more than a matching tweed fedora.

"We should head over, too," said Millie, after enjoying one more croissant at Café Bonne Chance.

Picking up her large black purse, which also held perfume samples she planned to share during her presentation, Millie linked arms with me, and we headed to the last day of the World Perfumery Conference. Three blocks away, the sliding doors of the conference hotel opened automatically. The lobby was a vast expanse of people with rolly bags, name tags, and all carrying folders of some sort or other. Posters lined the walls with advertisements for new perfumes. Some of the brands were familiar, mass-market products, and others were for the kinds of companies that catered to the industry—mixers, distributors, packagers. The heart of the conference was taking place down a long, wide corridor covered in a deep red carpet off of which there were meeting rooms, large and small.

I pulled out my phone and flipped it to video. I'd been making short, documentary-style clips of the trip all weekend, and this was the highlight I couldn't miss.

"How does it feel to be a scent extractions expert?" I said to my mom. "Look at the camera."

"Hi." She waved.

I was about to ask her another question, but the lobby was crowded and noisy with people bumping into each other as they headed to their panels or meetings without so much as a *pardon*. I decided I'd try again later at a better location.

My mom and I entered the conference's main area where people registered or met for impromptu meetings in one of several lounge areas. We headed to a map displayed against one wall that outlined the day's events, so that we could confirm how to get to her panel. While I located where the meeting was to take place, and where we could find a rest stop along the way, Millie opened her bag on a bench beside me and looked through her inventory one last time. She took out her vials, examined them carefully, opened one or two. She is a perfectionist when it comes to her work, and her black bag is like an on-the-go lab. She'd had her prized accessory custom designed around the time I was born by a leather-maker at the San Lorenzo market in Florence, Italy. That bag had been around so long, I sometimes wondered if it held some deeper meaning for her. Between my first name, my wild mane of hair, and my Mediterranean complexion, I sometimes fancied as a child that I could be Italian. Millie, however, had always been quiet about my father's identity.

When I'd figured out the lay of the land, I turned on my phone again.

"Let me get a video of you in front of the map," I said.

Millie gathered her belongings, and struck a pose like Vanna White on *Wheel of Fortune*.

"Welcome to the World Perfumery Conference," she said to the camera, her arms gracefully directed to the map. "Here you will see—"

Her speech was interrupted by a collective cry from the lobby. A woman screamed, a man yelled something in French, another person cried out in Japanese.

I searched the hallway where we were standing, up and down, as panic grew like a wave among the crowd. My mind went immediately to the worst. Shootings. Terrorism. I heard others around me express the same fear, which made my blood run cold. My beautiful morning, and our excitement about the afternoon's panel, had suddenly been hijacked by chaos.

"What's going on?" my mom said.

"I'm not sure."

I looked for a familiar face, anyone we'd met this week, in hopes we could find out. Suddenly, I saw a group of people forming by the Grand Ballroom. They were yelling and calling for help. Their circular formation suggested that a single person lay in its midst. In moments, the fear that had grown across the crowded lobby shifted to the sort of curiosity that accompanies drivers on a highway who want a glimpse of an accident. We were grateful it wasn't us, hopeful help would come quickly, and slightly morbid in our desire to see the scene unfold. My mom and I took a few steps forward.

"Probably a heart attack," she said.

"I hope the French paramedics are fast," I said.

"*Meurtre*," someone cried from the middle of the crowd.

My French is rudimentary at best, but there are certain words which, when said a certain way, and given the right context, can be universally understood. This was one of them.

"Did he say murder?" I said, but I did not need to wait for an answer.

From the cluster of people in front of the Grand Ballroom, I saw the hand of a man reach out, followed by a head. The crowd parted, and we watched a young man, about my age, crawl forward. He was neither handsome nor ugly, neither flashy nor shabby. He was average on every level. He was the sort of person who might walk by you without catching your eye. The sort of person who could fade into a crowd and even into a small gathering, except for one thing.

There was a knife sticking out of his back.

Connect with

U(s)

Visit us online at
KensingtonBooks.com
to read more from your favorite authors, see books
by series, view reading group guides, and more.

Join us on social media

for sneak peeks, chances to win books and prize packs,
and to share your thoughts with other readers.

facebook.com/kensingtonpublishing
twitter.com/kensingtonbooks

Tell us what you think!

To share your thoughts, submit a review,
or sign up for our eNewsletters, please visit:
KensingtonBooks.com/TellUs.